For my husband, Larry,
because I would marry you all over again.

And for Murphy, Roxie, and Friday,
who have a zest for life and a nose for trouble!

NEARLYWEDS

1

STELLA

"Yum." I stretched my arms over my head and curled my toes into the zillion-thread-count sheets of the Cartwell House Inn's luxurious honeymoon cottage. "Honey, that was fantastic."

Mark grinned. "You enjoyed your wedding day, Mrs. Porter?"

"And how." I let my head drop back against the pillow, closing my eyes to relive the ceremony, the dancing, and Mark's champagne toast, which had brought tears to my eyes. "Total dream come true. *Modern Bride* and Vera Wang and Cinderella all rolled into one ginormous lacy orgasm." Well. Except for the white-hot glares my new stepdaughters kept shooting my way.

"And the wedding night?" He waggled his eyebrows at the

blue garter, Richard Tyler gown, and ivory satin sandals scattered across the hotel room floor.

"Also a dream come true," I assured him.

"Are you sure? Because you know I can get my hands on some Viagra samples."

"I'm satisfied, I'm satisfied. Thank God I met you after your sexual peak or I probably wouldn't be able to walk."

"Just checking. Men of a certain age have to make sure our nubile young trophy wives are happy."

I reached over and swatted his arm. "That's all I am to you? A fluffball trophy wife with a sick body?"

"A sweet, kind, smart trophy wife whom I will cherish for the rest of my days," he corrected. "Who also happens to be drop-dead gorgeous."

"Too late. Don't try to butter me up," I huffed, turning over on my side so he wouldn't see me smile. "I'm unbutterable."

He wrapped his arms around me, pulling me back against his chest. "You trophy wives are so temperamental."

"High maintenance, but worth it." I yawned, tucking my head under his chin.

He stroked my stomach through the sheet. "Can I ever make it up to you?"

"Nope."

"Are you sure? No way to weasel my way back into your good graces?"

"Hmm. Maybe. But it's gonna cost you."

"Name your price. Jewelry? Handbag? Insanely overpriced shoes?"

I turned my head back far enough to give him a flirty wink. "Well, I'm going to need a new winter wardrobe. I can't tromp around the Berkshires in a fur coat like I did in Manhattan. It's ostentatious. But I don't want to stock up on size fours if we're going to get pregnant, so it'll have to be shoes or jewelry. Or both. We trophy wives are crazy materialistic, y'know."

Long pause. Then a forced chuckle. "Heh. I don't think we need to worry about you getting pregnant anytime soon."

"Why not?" I flipped over to face him. "I know I've only been off the pill for a month, but it could happen. Wouldn't it be romantic to have a honeymoon baby? My gynecologist said most women are very fertile right after they . . ." I trailed off as his expression changed. "What?"

"The pill?" He scratched the stubble on his chin. "Sweet-heart, I can't believe you kept taking the pill after our conversation in Bermuda."

I pushed back from his chest. "What conversation in Bermuda?"

"About my vasectomy."

The warm, dreamy afterglow evaporated in the first icy twinges of shock. "Mark. Quit it. Is that supposed to be funny?"

"We talked about this. At the French restaurant on the sea

cliff, remember? I told you I'd had a vasectomy after I divorced Brenda, and you said you were fine with it."

I rocketed into a sitting position, because I was suddenly, horribly afraid that he wasn't kidding.

"What the hell are you talking about?" I yanked the blankets up to cover my chest. "How much did you have to drink tonight?"

"I'm not drunk." He reached over, covering my hand with his. "But we discussed this, Stella. Right before I asked you to marry me."

He had surprised me in Bermuda with a diamond ring and a proposal on the pink sands under the huge, white moon. I had cried when I'd said yes, so stunned and grateful that I had found such a wonderful man, that I would get the chance to start a family with my soul mate. "We did *not* talk about this. I definitely would have remembered you mentioning a vasectomy."

"I told you," he insisted. "I did. The night we went dancing, remember? We had dinner in that restaurant with the amazing wine list and then—"

And suddenly I knew exactly which night he was talking about. The third night of our vacation, when I had decided to overindulge in frosty, pastel-colored drinks topped with paper umbrellas. "Oh my God. You mean the night I got so drunk I threw up in the bushes behind the hotel?"

He nodded, looking relieved. "Yeah. That night."

"That's when you told me about your vasectomy?"

He nodded again. "You said you were fine with it. You said as long as we were together, nothing else mattered."

"Because I'd had a bottle of rum instead of dinner! Mark! You could have said you wanted to have a threesome with me and Brenda and I would've been fine with that, too! You know how I get when I drink on an empty stomach. And you know I hate French food but you insisted on—" I clapped my hands over my mouth. "You *knew*. You planned this whole thing!"

"Sweetheart." He looked alarmed. "Don't be ridiculous. Hand to God, I thought you—"

"You picked that French restaurant on purpose so I'd have all wine and no food and then mix it with rum and then . . ." I scooted way over to the edge of the bed. "You lied to me!"

"Stella, listen." His voice took on an edge of desperation. "I would never lie to you. Ever. I love you more than words can say and—"

"Don't you even! You know how I feel about this." I glanced down at my belly, which, according to my new husband of twelve hours, would not be swelling up with a honeymoon baby anytime soon. "When we met, I was a nanny, for God's sake!"

"Well." He paused. "As of this morning, you're a stepmother to my lovely daughters."

"Your lovely daughters want me dead. And one of them's older than I am!" I leapt out of bed, stomped over to the rustic, wood-paneled bathroom, and wrapped myself up in the plush white bathrobe hanging next to the Jacuzzi. "How is that anywhere in the same ballpark as a baby?"

"They don't want you dead," he soothed.

"Ha. Taylor held onto her steak knife for the whole reception. She was just waiting to get me alone."

"Try not to take it personally, sweetheart. She's never liked any of the women I dated after the divorce, but she'll come around in time. Marissa likes you. Or she will, anyway, once she gets to know you. Tell you what: we'll have both girls over to the new house for Thanksgiving and—"

"I want a baby!" I exploded.

We both froze, assessing each other like a lion and an antelope on one of those Discovery Channel shows.

"Well." He shrugged. "I can't give you a baby."

I crossed my arms. "Can't you get the vasectomy reversed?"

"I had the procedure over ten years ago. And even if the reversal went flawlessly, you have to remember that my age is going to affect our chances of conceiving. Best-case scenario, we're looking at a twenty, twenty-five percent chance of success."

"Don't give me that." I yanked the robe belt around me so tight that I could hardly breathe. "You're a surgeon. You've played golf with the best doctors in New York. We can do in vitro if we have to. We can go to a specialist, take fertility drugs, whatever, but you have to at least—"

"No." He shook his head slowly.

I took a giant step back, nearly tripping as my foot got tangled up in the rumpled wedding gown. *"No?"*

"No. Even if we could reverse the vasectomy, I don't want to."

I reminded myself to breathe. "Then we'll adopt."

"No." He dropped his head. "I've raised a family, Stella. Two wonderful, exhilarating, exhausting daughters. But I was a lot younger then, with my whole life still ahead of me."

I leaned back against the doorjamb and looked at him. After our whirlwind ten-month courtship, I still couldn't believe Mark was fifty-three. He was, as some of my snippy friends from prep school felt obligated to point out, old enough to be my father. But he didn't act fifty-three. And with his full head of thick dark hair (graying at the temples, but in a distinguished way) and a tall, lean body kept fit by a disciplined ritual of predawn jogging, he certainly didn't look fifty-three.

"Well, you're going to live another fifty years, at least." I slapped on my sweetest smile. "And a new baby will keep you young. And I can . . . we can . . . I'm certified in infant CPR," I finished lamely.

"Can we talk about this later, please? Let's not ruin our wedding day."

I checked the clock. 12:27 a.m. "Our wedding day was over at midnight. We're talking about this now."

"Well, I don't know what else to say."

"How about, 'I'm sorry I tricked you in Bermuda and I'll make an appointment tomorrow morning to get my vasectomy reversed'?" I suggested.

He stared down at the snowy white sheets on which we'd had wild, passionate sex just minutes ago.

"Mark." I took a step toward the bed. "I have to have children. That is my calling in life. I cannot *not* have kids."

He nodded.

"And you have known that since our first date."

Another nod.

"So this is nuts. We're having a baby. I already know you'll be a great father—that's part of why I said yes in Bermuda."

I waited for the next nod. And waited. And waited.

"You'll change your mind," I said with a confidence I didn't feel. "You're just nervous. Everybody says if you wait until you feel ready to have kids, you'll never have them."

"I've already *had* kids." He finally met my gaze. "Why can't you be happy with just us, Stell? You, me, in love, carefree. We're so happy. Why can't that be enough for you?"

I marched over to the door and yanked it open, letting the chilly September breeze into the cabin. "Get out."

"You're not serious."

I grabbed his huge leather suitcase and heaved it out onto the cabin's front porch. *"Get out."*

"Have you lost your mind? It's the middle of the night! And there's a frost advisory!"

I marched into the bathroom, bundled up his toiletries, and flung his shaving kit out into the night.

"The innkeeper said they're booked solid for the weekend," Mark protested. "There are no other rooms for me to move to."

I ripped the blankets off him, marched him out the door, and hurled his boxer shorts out after him. When the door slammed shut between us, I turned the dead bolt.

Then I wadded my beautiful, bias-cut wedding gown into a ball and sobbed for hours, blowing my nose on the delicate imported silk.

2

ERIN

The extra wedding cake at the reception (because "not everyone likes chocolate, dear, and you should give your guests a choice") should have been a clue.

The illicit extra order of invitations (because "I know they said the reception hall only holds two hundred people, but the girls in my bridge club would never speak to me again if I didn't invite them")? Those should have been a clue, too.

But really, if we're talking clues, the peanut brittle was the opening salvo that should have sent me running for cover.

"I'm so happy for you two!" Renée exclaimed when David and I announced our engagement over his family's annual Christmas Eve dinner at her house in the Berkshires. She hugged me so hard my ribs practically snapped, then blotted the tears from her eyes with a holly-embroidered linen napkin. "Of course, I always assumed that David would *be* a doctor instead of marrying one, but I suppose times have changed. Girl power and all that, right?"

I glanced over at David, who was accepting a hearty handshake from his cousin Sarah's husband while pretending not to have heard his mom's little barb.

So I followed his lead and smiled determinedly.

"Here, dear." Renée released her death grip on my torso long enough to shove a platter of Christmas cookies into my face. "Have some peanut brittle."

"Oh, thank you, but I can't."

"Don't be ridiculous; you're wasting away! All those long days at the hospital . . . if you don't take better care of yourself, you'll never be able to carry my grandchildren! Here." She attempted to force a jagged shard of peanut brittle between my clamped lips.

I sidestepped the issue of her grandchildren (David could break the news that we weren't planning on procreating anytime soon) and jerked my head back. "No, honestly, Renée, I can't. I'm allergic to peanuts, remember?"

"You are?" She furrowed her brow and whisked the jaunty red Santa cap off her sleek brunette bob. "Are you sure?"

"Very sure." We'd been over all this before, but maybe she'd forgotten.

"Oh. Well, all right, then, if you say so. But please do eat something." She moved on to interrogating David about which date would be best for a wedding at her country club. I waited for him to tell her that we'd decided to have a small, casual ceremony in Boston, but he just changed the subject.

The next morning, Renée served me oatmeal for breakfast. With peanuts chopped up in the brown sugar instead of walnuts. The traditional Christmas turkey dinner was followed up with peanut butter cookies and a caramel peanut butter cake.

"I can't have peanuts," I kept repeating. "Truly. I could die."

"Of course!" She'd smite herself on the forehead. "How silly of me. I'm turning into a senile old biddy, I tell you."

Yet the peanuts kept showing up in increasingly inventive disguises. Soups, sauces, salads. I finally borrowed David's car, fishtailed to the grocery store through a blustery nor'easter, and bought five boxes of granola bars to get me through the rest of the weekend.

Before David slipped that diamond ring on my finger, I thought that women who bitched about their mothers-in-law were petty little drama queens. With no respect for the sanctity of family. Who weren't trying hard enough.

I was such an idiot.

David and I were scheduled to return to Boston the day after Christmas—as a pediatric resident, it was a miracle I'd been able to get Christmas off at all—and Renée spent the entire morning slaving away in the kitchen.

"A culinary send-off for my only child," she explained, waving the spatula at me. "I know he doesn't eat well in the city . . . all those crazy hours you have to work."

"Don't worry too much about him," I said. "He's an excellent cook."

Her eyebrows shot up. "Oh, is he?"

"Absolutely." I grinned at David across the kitchen table. "As long as he follows the directions on the back of the box."

"Orange macaroni and cheese." He smiled back. "It's what's for dinner. And breakfast. And lunch."

Renée pursed her lips. "And when you have children? I hope you're not going to feed them out of a box, too. I'll send some leftovers back with you, David. You can freeze it and have a few decent meals."

My brand-new fiancé shrugged, emanating vitality and good cheer in his cabled wool sweater and mussed, pre-shower hair. "Great. What're you making?"

"Roast duck." Renée rinsed her hands under the faucet. "And stuffing." She shot me a look. "*Not* from a box."

I pushed back my chair. "Let me help you, Renée. What can I do?"

"Don't be ridiculous, darling," she cooed. "I'm almost finished. You just run upstairs and fix yourself up."

I glanced down at my khakis and crisp white shirt. "I'm fixed. Please let me help—we're family now."

"Not quite." She raised one index finger into the air, as if testing the wind. "We're not family till you walk down that aisle at the country club."

I looked pointedly at David, who mumbled something about needing to shave and escaped upstairs. Traitor. I took a deep breath and tried to be gentle. "Well, actually we thought we might get married in Boston. It'll be so much easier to plan, and with most of my family flying in from California—"

Her smile never wavered. "The country club is tradition in our family. David's father and I were married by Pastor Rick and had our reception at the club, and we always knew David would do the same. Rick's a wonderful pastor, but his health is getting worse all the time—you two better hurry up. What about Labor Day weekend? The weather will be lovely, the leaves will be turning."

"Yes, but . . ." I studied the gleaming black and white tiles on the kitchen floor. "With my work schedule, I won't be able to come all the way out here to pick out a caterer or a florist, and—"

"Don't worry about the details, dear. You career girls don't have time to fuss about centerpieces and whatnot. Just leave all that to me." She turned her back on me and shoved her hands into bulky red and green oven mitts. "I'll take care of everything."

"Renée, you've really outdone yourself," I said as we sat down to lunch. "This is fantastic."

"Oh, thank you, dear." Renée winked. "After the wedding, I'll give you the recipe. It's a family secret."

"Duck is Aunt Renée's specialty," David's cousin Sarah informed me. "And her stuffing is legendary. Although . . . today it tastes a little different."

"That's because I added juniper berries," Renée said. "For extra oomph. Do you like it?"

Sarah frowned. "I guess. It doesn't taste like berries, though, it kind of tastes like—"

"Oh God," I wheezed. My fork clattered onto my plate as I clutched at my throat.

"Erin?" Renée watched me intently. "Are you all right? Do you need a glass of water?"

"My EpiPen," I squeaked at David, pointing frantically at my purse, which was perched atop my suitcase by the front door. "In the—"

"What's wrong with her?" Sarah clapped her hands over her mouth. "David, what's—"

"Anaphylactic shock," he yelled, toppling his chair as he raced across the room. "She needs epinephrine *now.*"

I tried to tell him that my EpiPen was in my purse's inside zippered pocket, but all that came out was a faint hiss. My tongue had swollen, my throat was closing up, I couldn't speak, couldn't breathe, couldn't—

"Mother," David bellowed as he rooted through my suitcase, scattering clothes and shoes and frilly lingerie all over the dining room floor. "What the hell is in that stuffing?"

Her eyes widened. "Well, I . . . oh dear."

"What did you do?"

"One of the secret ingredients; I can't believe I forgot . . ."

I stood up to get my own damn EpiPen, took two faltering steps on the blue-and-green patterned rug, and crashed to the floor.

"Peanuts," Renée confirmed. "But only a few."

"Blrrrgh," I gargled, flailing toward the suitcase.

"Got it!" David held up the small yellow tube triumphantly. "Hang on, sweetie!"

But I couldn't hang on. The sparkling crystals on the chandelier started spinning, then receded into black as I gasped for air.

"Oops," I heard Renée trill as I lost consciousness. "Is she going to die? What a shame."

3

CASEY

"Why isn't he here yet?" my cousin Danni asked as she zipped up her chocolate brown bridesmaid dress. "Do you think he changed his mind?"

"For the last time. He didn't change his mind." I turned back to the makeup artist, who held out a tissue for me to blot my lipstick. "He did *not* change his mind."

"Of course he didn't," the makeup artist soothed. Her voice was the auditory equivalent of Valium—she dealt with frazzled brides every single weekend. "Maybe his car broke down."

"Nope." Danni smirked. "He hired a limo."

"Well, maybe the limo broke down," the guardian angel wielding the lip gloss suggested. "Maybe he's stuck in traffic."

"In Alden, Massachusetts? On a Sunday morning? On Labor Day weekend?" Danni tossed her red curls. "Doubtful."

I bit my lower lip. The makeup artist applied more gloss and said, "Try to relax. He'll be here."

"Then why hasn't he called?" Danni crowed.

The makeup artist lowered her voice and squeezed my hand. "He'll be here."

I nodded, desperate to believe her. And I did, for about ten seconds. Then I lunged across the dressing room, grabbed my cell phone, and redialed Nick's number.

It rang and rang, then went to voice mail. Again.

"No answer?" Danni *tsk-tsk*ed when I hung up. "I hope he hasn't gotten cold feet. After the way you pressured him for that ring . . ."

I ground my molars together, careful not to smudge my lipstick. "I didn't pressure him."

"Oh, come on, you don't have to pretend with me! I was rooting for you two all along. My mom said he'd never propose—girls like you don't marry guys like him, blah blah blah—but *I* said he'd cave in eventually, and sure enough, he bought you that cute little diamond—"

"*He'll be here!*" I turned to the makeup artist for backup, but she was packing up her brushes and mascara tubes as fast as she could.

A soft knock at the door. "See?" I couldn't keep the triumph out of my voice. "There he is!"

But it was just Melody, the wedding coordinator, giving us a fifteen-minute warning. "You should be in your dress by now," she admonished when she saw me still wrapped in my blue robe.

"Sir, yes, sir." I helped her lift my ivory tulle ball gown out of the garment bag hanging on the back of the door.

"Your hair looks gorgeous," she assured me as she climbed up onto a metal folding chair. "Hold your arms up like you're about to dive into a swimming pool . . . there, like that . . . okay, keep your face down . . ."

She slipped the dress down over me. The cool silk (okay, poly-silk blend) lining whispered against my skin. This gown was by far the most expensive piece of clothing I'd ever owned. It felt rich and regal, a promise of things to come.

"Now, listen, there have been a few last-minute snags, but that's normal, that's to be expected."

"Like what?" I demanded, suddenly terrified that my sister Tanya's bratty sons had ripped down all the pew decorations. Or my mother's new husband had started hitting the champagne a little too early. Or, oh God, what if my mother's *last* husband had shown up? It would be a bloodbath down there . . .

"Well, Pastor Rick is all ready to go, but we have an officiant from Lenox waiting in the wings." She held up a hand before I could panic. "Rick was complaining of chest pains after the rehearsal dinner last night, but he refuses to go to the doctor until after the ceremony. His wife is spitting nails. I lined up a replacement, just in case. So that'll be one extra plate at the reception . . ."

But the wild look in my eyes wasn't about reception costs. "What about Nick?"

She blinked. "What about him?"

"He's not here yet," Danni sing-songed. "She's afraid he's gonna leave her at the altar."

"Danni." I closed my eyes and clenched my hand into tight fists. "It would be a real shame if I got blood on this wedding dress. Capeesh?"

Melody tried to maintain her placid, maternal façade, but I could tell she was worried. "Nick's not here? But I just saw his brother handing out programs. I gave him the boutonnieres and he never said a word."

"Of course he didn't." I sat back down. "I'm sure his family will be thrilled if he leaves me at the altar. Then they won't have to pollute the family tree with a girl who grew up in a trailer park." Even as I said this, I knew it wasn't fair—Nick's parents had never been anything but sweet to me. They had me over for brunch every weekend. His mother had thrown me a shower straight out of *Martha Stewart Living* and loaned me a pair of sapphire earrings that had belonged to her grandmother for my something borrowed and blue. The problem wasn't Nick's family. The problem was Nick.

"Well." Melody squared her shoulders and prepared to marshal the troops. "We'll just have to send out a search party. Maybe something's happened. Things happen, you know, incredible things." She patted my shoulder.

"Nothing's happened," I murmured. "He's . . . if he's not down there, then—"

"Casey?" Nick's voice drifted through the door.

"Nick! Thank God! I love you!" My knees almost buckled with relief.

"I have to talk to you." He eased the door open and popped his head into the dressing room. When I saw the expression on his face, my anxiety made a big comeback.

"No! No! You're not allowed to see her before the cere . . ." Melody trailed off as we got a load of his wedding-day attire: jeans, sneakers, and a raggedy Amherst T-shirt he'd had since college. "What happened to your tux, hon? It's go time in fifteen minutes and counting!"

"I need to talk to Casey." He coughed nervously. "Alone."

Melody's eyes widened, but she swept out the door without another word. Danni dawdled, shooting me knowing looks until I jabbed her in the solar plexus with my elbow.

"When did you get so violent?" she huffed as she flounced into the hall. "I'm just trying to be supportive."

"Support me from the hall. And no eavesdropping."

The moment the door slammed behind her, I turned to my fiancé, arranged my face in what I hoped was a neutral expression, and braced myself for the letdown that part of me had always known was coming. No matter how many years had passed since high school, the star basketball player-slash-prom-king just didn't marry the frumpy girl with glasses from the wrong side of the tracks. It went against every law of God and man. "Where's your tux?"

He shoved his hands into his pockets. "At home."

My neutral expression faltered. "And that means . . ."

"I need more time, Casey." He stepped toward me and tried to hug me. I backed up against the wall, shaking my head.

"More time? More than fifteen minutes?"

He ducked his head and shrugged.

"You said you wanted to get married!" My voice ratcheted up into a shrill, tinny wail. "You promised me that—"

"I know." He looked miserable. "I know."

"So?"

He scuffed one sneaker against the floor.

"Why didn't you bring this up at the rehearsal dinner yesterday?"

"Because I was fine yesterday! When I got up this morning, everything felt great, but then as soon as I went to put on my tux, I freaked. It was like a panic attack or something. I couldn't even breathe."

I slapped my palms against the wall. "Nick, everyone we know is out there! The whole town! Your family, my family— what there is of it—all our friends. I have spent months, along with all my savings, prepping for this day." I threw out my arms. "Hello? I'm wearing the big white dress?"

"I know." He finally looked up. "You're beautiful."

"And I can't . . ." I stared up at the ceiling, blinking back tears. Heaven forbid I should ruin my makeup job. "You need to decide what you want. Right here, right now."

"That's not fair. I just need a little more time."

"You've had three years—that's plenty of time. So make up your mind. You either love me or you don't."

"Of course I love you."

"You're ashamed of me, aren't you? Everyone out there thinks you could do a lot better."

"No one thinks that," he swore, but we both knew that was a lie. His high school buddies thought he should have stuck with Anna Delano, the sultry, sassy cheerleader he'd dated in high school. And his parents, no matter how sweet they'd been to me, had hoped he'd settle down with Julia, his girlfriend from law school.

"Well, if you don't want to marry me, then don't," I spat. "I'm not your charity case."

"Casey, stop it." He set his jaw. "This isn't about you."

"Isn't about? . . ." My eyes felt like they were going to fall out of my head. "I'm standing here in church on our wedding day and you're calling the whole thing off and you have the nerve to say *this isn't about me?*"

He held up his palms. "Okay, yes, it sounds bad, but if you'll just hear me out—"

"No. The only thing I want to hear is the answer to this question: are we getting married or breaking up?"

"It's not that simple."

"It is for me. I can't keep my life on hold anymore. I want a future. A house. A partner."

"I want that, too." But he wouldn't make eye contact. "I do. I just . . ."

I pressed my lips together and shook my head. "You have fifteen minutes to decide."

He turned and left without another word. Deep in my heart, I knew that he'd leave me.

But that was the thing about Nick—he always managed to surprise me. Five minutes later, Melody bustled into the dressing room, handed me a tissue, and chirped, "You ready to walk down that aisle?"

I wiped my eyes and stopped sniffling. "Nick?"

"All dressed up and waiting at the altar."

So I got in line behind Danni and the flower girls in the church vestibule. The huge double doors swung open, and everyone stood up to watch me walk myself down the aisle. (My father hadn't been available for paternal escort duty since I was seven.) I'd always hated being the center of attention, but now I barely noticed the stares. I kept my back straight and my eyes focused on Nick, who was shifting from foot to foot at the end of the altar. He had apparently borrowed his best man's tux, which was a little too big for him. The pants bagged down, hiding his sneakers. The sleeves enveloped his fingers.

Nick Keating, the golden boy I'd yearned for from afar all those years, was finally going to be mine. We were going to have a good life, and I'd never have to introduce myself as Casey Nestor again.

I never paused in my low-heeled white pumps, but as I watched him fidgeting in the oversized suit, I couldn't shake the feeling that I was about to say my vows to a boy instead of a man.

4

ERIN

I found out my marriage was a sham two weeks before Thanksgiving. From my mother-in-law. Who could not have been happier to deliver the news.

I'd spent the day at a pediatrics conference in Florida, and after hours of sitting through lectures and making stilted small talk, all I wanted to do was call David, mumble "I love you," and collapse into my hotel room's king-sized bed. So I stripped down to my black cotton underwear, dialed my cell phone, and sank down into the sumptuous down comforter.

After three rings, I heard, "Hel-*looo?*"

Either David was embroiled in a clandestine affair and had carelessly allowed the other woman to answer his phone at eleven o'clock at night, or Renée had barged into our new house the minute I'd left for the airport.

I closed my eyes and prayed that he was having an affair.

"Hello? Erin, is that you?"

I whimpered softly. "Renée?"

"Call me Mom, dear." Her tinkling, girlish laugh grated on my last nerve. "And of course it's me. Who else would be answering your phone this time of night?"

"David might," I ventured.

"Oh, he's been asleep since ten. He works so hard at the hospital—their research is shockingly underfunded, I told him they should go on strike—and since you're always too busy to make a hot meal or do his laundry, well, he was simply tuckered out."

Through near-Godlike force of will, I managed not to take the bait. I stayed on topic and tried to match her saccharine tone. "Well, I'm just calling to say goodnight. Would you knock on the bedroom door and tell him to pick up the phone?"

"Oh, I just couldn't." She clicked her tongue. "He needs his rest, dear. But I'll tell him you called when he wakes up tomorrow morning. How's that?"

"Renée . . ."

"Call me Mom."

"When did you move into our house?"

"Oh, I haven't moved in, I've just come by for a few days to keep David company while you're gone. He's so lonely in this big house all by himself."

Ah, yes. Our new house. Our new house located a scant

three miles away from Renée's. Halfway through our engagement, David had pitched a whole spiel about how his mother was a frail, lonely widow and we should move to his hometown after I finished residency. In a moment of weakness—and despite grave misgivings—I'd agreed to leave Boston behind and join a primary care practice in the Berkshires. Family came first. Everyone else was moving out of the city; it seemed the grown-up thing to do. So why did I wake up every morning with a single question running through my mind: *What have I done?*

"Erin?" Renée chirped. "Are you there?"

"I'm . . . yeah."

"Good. Don't worry about a thing. We're having a wonderful time. Absolutely wonderful. I packed him a lunch to bring to work, and I made a chicken pot pie tonight. From scratch, not that frozen junk full of preservatives. That's his favorite, you know. Then we sat in the family room after dinner and chatted and watched TV. It was just like old times, just the two of us."

"Sounds peachy." I sighed. Maybe it was me. I didn't want to be one of those screechy, possessive wives who exploded into a jealous rage every time her husband called his mother. How degrading, not to mention clichéd. Maybe I should just take a step back and—

"You stay in Miami as long as you like, dear. Take a few days extra to shop, get your hair done. I know how you love to shop.

Even though the two of you both have some hefty student loans to pay off. And now you've got the mortgage, too . . ."

This was my cue to heap praise upon her (again) for gifting us with the twenty-thousand-dollar down payment for our house, but I was fresh out of gratitude. I heaved myself off the bed and hunkered down to rummage through the minibar. "May I please speak to my husband? *Please?*"

She sighed, sounding truly regretful. "Oh, it would just break my heart to wake him."

I twisted the top off a miniature bottle of Absolut with my teeth and spat it out. "Please?"

"Don't be selfish, darling. Just because you're on vacation doesn't mean David gets a vacation."

I snatched up a three-pack of chocolate truffles to go with the vodka. "I am not on vacation. I am at a medical conference."

She seemed to sense she had pushed me too far. "Well, don't worry, the house will be spotless when you get back. And I bought some new drapes for the den. The ones you put up really didn't go with the carpet and the davenport."

"Thanks." I crammed a truffle into my mouth. "And, um, when will you be leaving?"

The tinkly laugh returned. "Can't wait to be rid of me?"

Yes. "No, of course not! I just don't want you to put yourself out."

"It's no trouble, Erin. We're family now, not to mention neighbors."

I threw back my head and guzzled the mini-bottle of vodka.

"Oh, and you got a letter today from the county clerk."

"Okay, well, put it aside and—"

"I already opened it. And guess what?" Her voice soared in sudden triumph.

"What?"

"You and David aren't legally married."

5

STELLA

"Surprise, sweetheart!" Mark puffed up his chest as he strode into the kitchen. "I got you something."

I reached into a cardboard box marked "pots/pans/misc," grabbed a mystery item swathed in paper, and unwrapped what turned out to be a blender. "A vasectomy reversal?"

His smile disappeared. "Stella. We've been over that and over that."

We sure had. For the past ten weeks, while we'd written our thank-you notes to wedding guests and moved into the new house and had dinners with all of Mark's married friends and pretended everything was blissful, the tension had been steadily mounting. But I couldn't seem to force a direct confrontation with Mark, and to be honest, I didn't want to; we hadn't even been married three months. I knew what people had said behind my back as I'd planned the wedding: *She's too young. He's too old. Gold digger meets midlife crisis—I give it a year.* No way would I give them the satisfaction of being right. We were going to be happy, damnit, even if it killed me.

I reached into the box and pulled out another wad of paper. "We've been over it, but that doesn't mean we've solved anything."

He sighed. "Sweetheart, I understand that you want to have a baby, but you're going to have to accept that vasectomy reversal's not a realistic option." He leaned back against the gigantic Viking stove he'd insisted on installing, even though he knew I survived on takeout and Lean Cuisine. "Can't we please table the topic until next week? Let's not ruin our first Thanksgiving in the new house. I want us to have good memories to look back on at our silver anniversary."

Silver anniversary, my ass. He just didn't want his daughters to see us bickering and report back to his ex-wife that Daddy and his new bimbo trophy wife weren't getting along.

Hmm. Now that I thought about it, I didn't want that, either. No sense loading Taylor and Marissa up with more ammunition.

So I tried to remember that we should still be in the honeymoon mood and asked, "Okay. I'll try. Now what's the surprise?"

"Ta-da!" He whipped out a tiny pink leather dog collar, glittering with jeweled studs and a heart-shaped silver tag.

I took a step back. "If this is your way of trying to talk me into some freak show, S&M bondage fantasy—"

"I'm getting you a dog!"

"A dog." I gave him the dead eye.

"A puppy. Specifically, a maltipoo."

I frowned down at the bedazzled collar. "A whatie what?"

"A maltipoo. I found a breeder in New York and put our name on a waiting list as soon as we got back from our honeymoon. The litter's due right before Christmas. You said you wanted one. Remember?"

"Like a maltese-poodle mix?"

"Right! White, fluffy, nonshedding. Like that singer has? You said it was the cutest dog you'd ever seen."

I squinted at him, trying to remember any of this.

"You did," he insisted. "Back when we first started dating. You said you used to love that show with that blonde singer and her husband, and you said he gave her a puppy onstage at a concert and it was a grand romantic gesture because he'd wanted to get a big dog instead."

"A husky," I murmured, a blush creeping into my cheeks. It was all coming back to me now: my youthful obsession with the reality show *Newlyweds*. Before Nick and Jessica's scandal-soaked tabloid divorce. Before I'd married a man who'd pulled a vasectomy bait and switch on me.

Just a few short years ago, I'd been stupid and sappy enough to believe that my future marriage would turn out like the expertly edited fairy tale I'd seen on TV.

"What's wrong?" He looked disappointed. "You don't want a dog?"

I squared my shoulders. "A puppy is not the same thing as a baby."

Guilt seeped into his voice. "I know."

"This isn't going to change my mind," I warned. "About anything. Not now, not after Thanksgiving."

He didn't say anything else.

"Call the breeder," I snapped. "Tell her to sell that guiltipoo puppy to someone else."

Then I ran out into the frosty November chill, crossed the brick-paved circular driveway, and fired up the blue BMW convertible—Mark's wedding gift to me—that had no room for a car seat in the back.

As I gunned the coupe down our deserted suburban street, I called my mother and told her everything.

"A dog the size of a toaster, Mom. He thinks that's going to make me forget about having a baby."

I waited through the usual pause as my mother dragged on her customary morning cigarette. "Cutting back to one a day is almost the same as quitting," she'd said defensively. "And with what's happened with your father, I need all the stress relief I can get, so don't you dare judge me." I imagined her sitting at the sunny breakfast bar in the airy, lakeside house I'd grown up in (that was about to be foreclosed), sipping tea from a bone china cup so thin it was almost translucent.

"Well, no one ever said marriage was perfect. Why don't you wait and see what happens? Maybe you'll end up adoring this dog."

I tapped the brake as the car approached an intersection. "The dog is not the point, Mother. The point is, he lied to my face about having children. That's fraud. That's grounds for annulment."

She gasped. "Stella Rose, I don't ever want to hear that word come out of your mouth again! Mark may not be perfect, but he loves you. He stuck with you through all that messiness with your father's company—"

By "messiness" she meant embezzlement and insider trading and an ongoing stint at a white collar prison, but I wasn't allowed to let any of those words come out of my mouth, either.

"—and he can provide for you." I heard a clatter as she replaced the teacup in its saucer. "Let's face it, darling, even if your father's attorneys win the appeal, we just can't take care of you the way we used to."

"I can take care of myself," I insisted.

Her laugh was brittle. "Oh, please. As an au pair?"

"I was a nanny, Mom; don't be pretentious. And for your information, I liked being a nanny. I loved the kids, and I made decent money."

"Stella." She had put on her best *Steel Magnolia* voice. "The Goddards hired you as their au pair so you would have room and board while you went to college. They employed you as a favor because your father and Mr. Goddard go back to Princeton. But you are meant for better things than child care, darling."

"I'm meant to be a mom," I said flatly. "AKA, full-time child care with no paycheck."

"You won't need a paycheck; you've got Mark. And you'd be well advised to hold on to him. A good man is hard to find."

"You mean a rich man is hard to find."

"All I'm saying is, marriage takes compromise. Perhaps if you had taken my advice and majored in business or finance, we wouldn't be having this discussion, but you insisted on studying, what was it? Early childhood development? And then you didn't even finish your degree. You've put yourself in a very untenable position, and now you have to make the best of it."

I gripped the steering wheel even harder. "But he had a vasectomy, Mom! And he didn't tell me until after the wedding. I mean, who does that in real life?"

"Stella, what did I always tell you?"

I sighed and repeated her worn-out old catchphrase: "You never know a man until you marry him."

"That's right. Now, enough with the temper tantrums. Take the puppy and make the best of it."

"But he's my husband!"

"Exactly. And now you're finding out what he's really like. He's a good man, but he's still a man. You can't expect too much."

Part of me wanted to reach right through the phone and strangle her. The other part was horribly afraid she was right. Maybe I should stop worrying about my needs and start focusing on his. How could I call him selfish when he gave me every single thing I asked for except a baby?

I hung up and considered turning the car around and apologizing to Mark. For about two seconds. Then I stomped on the gas pedal and took a right on County Road 56. Mark had shown me who he really was; now it was my turn to show him.

6

CASEY

I had just finished ringing up Mrs. Adelman's purchase—fifty-five cans of cat food for her ever-growing band of ferals and strays—when Dr. Porter's new wife walked in. We hadn't actually been introduced, but the whole town had been buzzing about her ever since Dr. Porter had proposed with the gigantic diamond that Taylor and Marissa swore cost them their future inheritance.

Dr. Porter had gotten married over Labor Day weekend—the same weekend as Nick and I—and rumor had it his new wife was a ruthless, gold-digging, material girl whose CEO father was embroiled in the biggest corporate scandal since Enron. Since he'd split with his first wife, Brenda, ten years ago, Dr. Porter had dated steadily, but all of his previous girlfriends had been a little less flashy . . . and a little more age appropriate. So when he'd finally popped the question to a poor little rich girl half his age, everyone in town practically got whiplash rubbernecking at the impending scandal. There were at least two active betting pools going at the Blue Hills Tavern—one on how long the marriage would last (the current over-under was eighteen months) and one as to how long the citified Ms. Porter could hack it out here in the sticks (the smart money said she'd force a move to Manhattan by Memorial Day.)

But with her long, shiny black hair, milky skin and huge blue eyes, Stella Porter didn't look ruthless. She looked like a younger version of Jennifer Connelly. You couldn't help staring—girls like her just didn't *live* in Alden, Massachusetts.

She stood stock-still in the store's doorway for a moment, her face frozen in a tentative half smile. I wasn't sure if she was confused or just "making an entrance" in her red wool coat and spotless black boots before she deigned to come in and let me serve her.

Then those clear blue eyes locked on mine.

"Excuse me," she said in a small, shy voice. "Is it all right if I bring a dog in with me?"

"Sure." I jerked my head toward the sign in the corner of the front window reading Pets Welcome.

She glanced back over her shoulder. "A big dog?"

"Sure," I repeated, losing patience as the arctic November wind blasted in. "But do me a favor and shut the door, okay?"

"Oh. Right." She hurried inside, dragging a dog behind her on a filthy, fraying leash.

I'd pegged her for a Havanese owner. Maybe a bichon frise or a poodle. But the dog on the other end of this leash was no pedigreed, pampered puppy. It was, well, a behemoth.

"The lady at the shelter said he's a Great Dane mix," she explained when she saw my reaction.

"Mixed with what?" Mrs. Adelman demanded. "A Clydesdale?"

I watched the burly black blur of matted fur scrambling wildly to escape the confines of his collar and leash. "Newfoundland, probably. Maybe some Rottweiler?"

She dropped the leash as her hands flew to her mouth. "Rottweiler? Really? Do you think he's vicious?"

The dog saw his opening and took off. His nails clicked against the tile floor as he raced toward the bags of kibble at the back of the store.

"He doesn't seem very aggressive," I pointed out as the dog stopped running to sniff a 30-pound bag of holistic food. "Forget what you hear about Rotties on TV—most of them are big babies."

But Mrs. Adelman wasn't taking any chances—she collected her bags of cat food and held her spine ramrod straight as she stalked out the door. As the cowbell hanging on the door jingled behind her, I turned back to Stella. "You got this dog from the pound?"

She nodded, her cheeks pink. "Twenty minutes ago. But, I have to tell you, I'm having second thoughts. He doesn't even fit in my car—I had to put the top down and it's freezing out there—and I have no idea what he likes to eat and he probably has a zillion kinds of worms and fleas . . ."

Her voice trailed off and her eyes widened as she contemplated the ramifications of what she'd just done.

"What's his name?" I asked gently.

"He doesn't have one. He just had a kennel number. Like a prisoner."

"No, I mean, what are *you* going to name him?"

She watched with dismay as the dog grabbed a bag of dry food between his teeth and shook his head back and forth.

"I don't know. 'Bad Dog'?" Grimacing, she wiped at the dirt the makeshift leash had left on her fingers. "Do you happen to have a tissue I could use?"

I managed not to roll my eyes at her princess routine. She was going to be the kind of pet owner who bathed her dog in noxious floral-scented toxins every weekend and screamed bloody murder if he dared place a single paw on the couch. Forget Great Danes—this chick should've gotten a stuffed animal.

"Thanks," she said as I handed over a paper towel. "I've really screwed up this time. I guess it goes to show, you should never go to the pound when you have a fight with your husband."

"I guess," I said neutrally. "'Cause when the fight ends, you'll still have the dog."

She nodded. "How long do Great Danes live, anyway?"

"Not that long, by dog standards. Eight, maybe ten years."

"Ten years? Seriously?"

"Sure, if you keep them healthy. But Great Danes and Newfoundlands are tricky breeds. You really have to stay on top of all the medical and nutrition stuff. Big dogs have a lot of joint problems. They're prone to hip dysplasia and arthritis, not to mention bone cancer, bloat . . ."

"Bloat?" She wrinkled her nose. "That sounds gruesome."

My reply was drowned out by a sharp ripping sound as the dog tore open the bag. Dry kibble pinged across the floor like BBs.

"Oh God. Sorry." She knelt down and started scooping handfuls of food back into the bag while the dog commenced gorging himself. "I don't . . . this dog . . . I didn't really think this through."

"Yeah, you mentioned that." I grabbed a red nylon Martingale collar from the display rack, along with a thick leather leash, and headed toward the dog.

Stella rocked back on her heels and looked up at me as I looped the collar around the dog's neck. "This was a huge mistake."

"What? Getting a Great Dane?"

"Everything. Just . . . everything. Hey, do you want him?"

she offered hopefully as I scratched the dog behind the ears. He closed his eyes, leaned back into my hand, and luxuriated in the affection.

"Nope. My apartment doesn't allow dogs. Besides, I have two cats, and they wouldn't exactly be thrilled to have a canine roommate."

"Then I guess he'll have to go back in the shelter." She resumed scooping up dog food.

"Back to the shelter?" My eyebrows shot up to my hairline.

"Yeah. I can't possibly . . . I don't know the first thing about taking care of dogs. Especially giant ones."

I glared at her. "Tell me you're kidding."

She wouldn't meet my gaze. "Well. It wouldn't be fair to the dog to—"

I jerked my hand up and launched into one of what Nick referred to as my "spirally eyed animal-rights rants." "Listen. Stella—"

"How did you know my name?"

"Everyone knows who you are. You're the nanny who married Dr. Porter."

She looked stricken. "Oh no. You're friends with Taylor and Marissa, aren't you?"

"Not really, but this is a small town. Word gets around. So listen, Stella. Perhaps this little detail has escaped your notice, but dogs? They're living creatures. They're not like shoes or handbags. You can't just get buyer's remorse and return them. And I have news for you: no one else is going to adopt this dog."

"But . . ." She blinked back what appeared to be tears. Give me a break. "But *I* did. Maybe somebody else will see him and—"

"You take him back to the pound, he dies," I said bluntly. "And it'll be your fault. Simple as that. He's a big, black, male dog. Three strikes against him. This time of year, people are looking for fuzzy little puppies to stick under the Christmas tree. They want ten-pound yorkie mixes that won't shed too much or eat them out of house and home. Not a shaggy, un-trained oaf who'll knock over their toddlers."

Tears spilled down onto her cheeks. She was one of those freaks of nature who managed to look beautiful even while cry-ing. No red, puffy eyes. No runny nose.

"I don't have a toddler," she whispered, all tortured.

"Well, then, you're perfect for this dog," I snapped.

"I'll never have a toddler."

"Great. You'll have plenty of time to take him to obedience classes."

Her slender body shook as her crying intensified, and just when I was about to weaken my resolve to hate her and offer the poor kid another paper towel, the cowbell on the door jin-gled again.

"Casey Nestor, tell me you're not making your customers cry again."

I waved as Erin Maye, the new pediatrician in Dr. Lowell's office, strolled past the chew toy display, still wearing her white doctor's coat under her puffy green parka.

"What was this poor girl's crime?" Erin lifted an eyebrow toward the quivering waif surrounded by kibble. "Did she feed her dog the wrong kind of food? Forget to add daily digestive enzymes?"

"She's dumping her dog at the pound. And it's Casey Keating now," I corrected. Like Stella, Erin was a recent transplant from the big city (Boston), but unlike Stella, she was no-frills and down-to-earth.

"This dog?" Erin held out her hand for the Great Dane to sniff, which proved to be an unnecessary formality—the dog tackled her like a linebacker and licked her ear.

"I am not dumping him at the pound!" Stella insisted, her blue eyes flashing.

I just rolled my eyes at Erin and mouthed the words "drama queen."

"Erin, this is Stella Porter."

"Oh really?" Erin eyed Stella with renewed interest. "I know your husband—I've seen him around the hospital."

"Erin's a doctor," I explained.

Stella crossed her arms. "Why are you guys looking at me like that?"

"Like what?" I scoffed.

"No one's looking at you." Erin dismissed her with a wave

of her hand and reached into her leather briefcase. "Did you get a letter last week?"

"A letter? What kind of—" I broke off, staring at the book resting on top of Erin's files. "What is that?"

"I know." She smiled grimly.

I reread the book's title. *"Embracing Tradition: The Wife Within?"*

"An early Christmas gift from Renée. It was waiting on our kitchen table, all gift-wrapped, when I got back from my medical conference in Philadelphia last week."

My eyes widened. "You gave Renée a key to your house?"

"Of course I didn't. But mere locks cannot keep her from her sainted son."

"Who's Renée?" Stella peered over my shoulder at the book while the dog gave it a cursory sniff.

Erin rubbed her temples. "My mother-in-law. Anyway, Casey, did you happen to get any interesting mail last week?"

I shrugged. "Just the usual—wedding bills, vet bills, and heating bills. Why?"

"Because David and I got a letter from the county clerk— we aren't legally married. Pastor Rick died before he signed and filed our marriage certificates. Can you believe that?"

"What?" I frowned. "How did that happen?"

"I have no idea, but his wife found a stack of unsigned documents on his desk last week when she cleaned out his office."

"Well, can't you just send it in without him?" I asked.

"No; I need his signature to make it legal, and since he's dead, I won't be getting that any time soon."

I swallowed hard. "But Nick and I—"

"I know." Erin nodded. "He presided over three weddings that weekend: me and David, you and Nick, and one other couple. And apparently, we're all still technically single."

"But *we* signed the marriage certificate!" I exclaimed. "And what about our witnesses? We have a whole churchful of people to back us up!"

Erin shrugged. "Yeah, well, the State of Massachusetts doesn't want to hear it. We have to go down to the courthouse and do the whole thing over."

"But . . ." I paused. "I didn't get a letter."

"Then you might want to give the county clerk a call."

"So Nick and I, we might not really be married? After all that?" *After he almost stood me up at the altar?*

"Hey, maybe the four of us can go to city hall together." Erin smiled. "Have a double wedding." She waited a few seconds for me to react. "What?"

"Nothing." I struggled to maintain a poker face. "I'm just shocked, you know?"

"Tell me about it." Her wry, world-weary doctor routine kicked into overdrive. "You drop tens of thousands of dollars on a wedding, you'd think you could trust the officiant to do his job correctly. I mean, what is this, amateur hour?"

I nodded dumbly, barely registering a word she said.

"You'd think *someone* at the church would've caught this earlier, but no." Erin was really getting fired up now. "I say we explore our legal options. We deserve compensation for our pain and suffering. David's cousin is an attorney in Lexington; I'll give her a call and ask if we have a case. A trio of broken-hearted brides; what jury's gonna say no to that?" She finally stopped to catch her breath. "But it'll be more sympathetic if all three of us band together. Do you know who the other bride was?"

Stella's voice quavered behind us. "Me."

7

ERIN

I still can't believe this." David reread the letter informing us that our newly minted marriage was a fraud, then glanced over at me with excitement. "Do you realize what this means?"

"I should've put all that money toward my med school loans instead of buying the froufrou wedding dress?" I tipped back my kitchen chair and grabbed a spoon out of the drawer next to the dishwasher.

"It means we have a chance to do it all over again!" My new husband (well, *almost* husband, according to the State of Massachusetts) looked thrilled about this prospect. He was definitely more optimistic and spontaneous than I (a good thing, considering that I was such a perfectionist control freak that my father joked they had to invent a new personality profile for me—type A plus), but the wedding hoopla had been as stressful for him as it had been for me. Maybe more so—after all, Renée was *his* mother.

"Honey." I stirred my yogurt. "How could you want to do all that again? Do you not remember the migraines we got over the great fondant-versus-buttercream controversy?"

"No, no, I mean let's do it right this time. The way we wanted to do it. We can go to Hawaii, just the two of us, and get hitched in our bathing suits on the beach. No hysterical bridesmaids, no stuffy country club, and best of all, no Mom."

"But we just took our honeymoon in September!" I protested. "I can't take another week off."

"Sure you can. What's Dr. Lowell going to do? Fire you?"

"He might, actually."

"Are you kidding? He loves having your Harvard Med diploma up on his office wall. Makes him feel smart by association. If he fires you, he won't be able to go around name-dropping his new partner's Ivy League pedigree. I say we pack our bags and go. Two honeymoons in four months—let the good times roll."

I closed my eyes and conjured up a vision of pristine white beaches, golden sunlight, and lush green foliage. David and I, holding hands, repeating our vows as the surf crashed over the—

Back to reality, Dr. Maye. "I'd love to, David, but we can't. I have so many new patients, and flu season started early this year—"

He dropped to one knee in the middle of the scuffed linoleum floor. "Erin, will you marry me?"

"Already did." I wriggled the fingers of my left hand at him.

He threw out his arms as if about to burst into song. "Okay, then, will you marry me again?"

The man didn't have a pragmatic bone in his body.

No wonder I loved him so much.

He clapped one hand to his heart. "I'm not getting up till you say yes. Every time you try to make coffee or open the fridge, here I'll be, right underfoot, getting gigantic bruises on my knees. So you might as well save us both the suspense and contusions and say yes now."

I sat down on the floor next to him and kissed him. "Yes."

"Yes?" He looked as elated as he had the first time I'd accepted his proposal. "You'll run away with me and commit all manner of lewd, lascivious acts on the beach?"

"I will. But you better bring enough cash to make bail when we get arrested for public indecency."

"Done."

I kissed him again. "I'll talk to Dr. Lowell tomorrow; if he'll give me the time off, we'll go."

He pressed my hand between both of his. "This is gonna be great. We'll get some time to ourselves before Mom moves in."

I froze midkiss. "Before what, now?"

His smile faltered. "Before my mom moves in."

I snatched my hand away. "I know I didn't hear you correctly. Because if you just said what I thought you just said, then I . . . then we . . ."

"It's just for a few weeks, nothing major. She's remodeling her house and—"

"Since when?"

"She got depressed after the wedding—"

"*Our* wedding? Why?"

"—and called a contractor and they're ripping out her kitchen and all the bathrooms. Pretty soon she'll have no hot water and no place to cook."

"Then she can stay at a hotel," I said flatly.

"Erin!"

"No, David. No. I have been more than accommodating when it comes to your mother's . . ."

He narrowed his eyes. "My mother's what?"

I made myself count to five. "Your mother's whims. I agreed to have the wedding at *her* country club, with *her* pastor, right before I gave up a great job and moved to *her* town. I am a reasonable woman. But this is beyond the beyond."

His tone changed from accusatory to cajoling. "You're right. I know. She gets a little carried away sometimes, but she's my mother and she's all alone . . ."

There it was: the widow card. Renée's ace in the hole,

brought out every time anyone didn't fall over themselves to cater to her every need.

"Listen. Honey." I paused, trying to find the most diplomatic way to word this. "I know she's your mother and I know she's come to rely on you since your father passed away. But we're newlyweds. We need our space."

"Agreed, but—"

I threw up a hand. "She cannot move in with us. Full stop."

"Okay, well maybe 'move in' was the wrong way to put it. She'll just be visiting for a few weeks while—"

"While they gut her entire house? Do you honestly think that's going to be a nice, neat, monthlong project? It's going to take months, David. Possibly years. What about all her bridge friends? Can't she stay with one of them?"

"She wants to be with family," he said plaintively. "She doesn't want to impose on her friends."

"Then she better get used to cold showers and takeout, 'cause she's not moving in with us."

He looked at me like I'd grown fangs and talons. "Erin!"

"What? David, try to see my side of this. Did I say anything when she cried at the rehearsal dinner because she was, quote, losing her only child forever?"

"No."

"Did I say anything when she interrupted our first dance to ask when we were going to start trying to conceive?"

"No."

"Did I say anything when she tried to kill me last Thanksgiving?"

His face turned crimson. "Would you get over that already? It was an accident!"

"An accident? I must have told her fifty times that I was allergic to peanuts. I tell everyone I meet. It's practically tattooed on my forehead!"

"She's getting older," he countered. "She forgets things sometimes."

"Yeah, whenever it's convenient for her."

He shot up into a standing position. "What exactly are you saying?"

"I'm saying she's not moving in with us! Not now, not ever."

He set his jaw. "Just because you have the MD after your name doesn't mean you get to make all the decisions."

This took me completely off guard. "Wait. What?"

"Every time we argue, you pull rank, and I'm sick of it."

"I never said anything about—"

"Yes, okay, we all know you're the exalted physician who married the lowly pharmacologist! But that doesn't mean you get to call all the shots!"

"My being a physician has nothing to do with any of this."

"Then why do you always get the final say?"

I exhaled sharply. "David, there are certain issues where a spouse deserves veto power."

"And let me guess—*you* get to decide what those issues are."

Something inside me snapped. "That's right, David. I do. I gave up my apartment in Boston and all my friends and moved all the way out here so your poor, bereft mother wouldn't have to be alone. I gave up a great job opportunity at a prestigious teaching hospital to hand out cough syrup and antibiotics."

His eyes had lost all trace of loving enthusiasm. "She's my mom and she helped pay for this house. What am I supposed to do?"

"I told you accepting that money from her was a mistake. I told you! Well, I'm only going to say this once: If she moves in, I move out."

He stared at me but didn't say anything.

"David?" I prompted.

Still no response.

I grabbed my purse off the kitchen table and headed for the garage.

"Erin, don't."

I whirled around, frightened by the rage breaking over me. "I mean it. It's me or Renée. Who's it going to be?"

He studied the linoleum. "It's not that simple."

I reached for the doorknob.

"Please don't."

I turned the dead bolt and pushed the door open.

When he looked up, his eyes were bleak and betrayed. "You promised to marry me all over again."

"Yeah, well, maybe once was enough."

8

STELLA

Sweetie, did we get any important mail recently?" I banged the front door shut behind me, which seemed to spook the dog, so I leaned down and rubbed his ears to reassure him.

Mark rushed into the foyer, looking both annoyed and relieved. "Are you ready to stop behaving like—" He broke off when he saw the dog. "What is that?"

I tilted my head, trying to look nonchalant. "A dog."

He folded his arms over his green raglan sweater. "I see. And whose dog is it, exactly?"

"He's ours." I tugged on the leash. The dog lumbered forward. "I bailed him out of the county shelter."

"You're kidding, right? Whose dog is it, really?"

I brushed past him into the kitchen. "Look at him, Mark. *Smell* him. Do you really think anyone we know would let their dog run around all matted and filthy like this?"

He glanced at the dog, who had planted himself next to the marble-topped island and was scratching away at his neck with his back foot. "Stop yanking my chain and tell me what the hell's going on."

"I'm not yanking your chain, darling." I started humming as I rummaged through the cherry cabinets for hot chocolate mix and a mug. "This is our new dog. Isn't he a cutie? I'm going to make cocoa—want some?"

"Stella. What have you done?"

I filled the kettle with water and placed it on the burner. "I took him over to that little pet supply shop on Fifth Street, and the owner helped me pick out food and dishes and toys and that sporty new collar. Her name's Casey—Casey Keating, I think. Do you know her?"

His face went ashen. "That crazy animal-rights girl who's always passing out leaflets on the evils of animal testing in front of the hospital?"

"I don't know. I guess. Anyway, she knew who you were. And of course she'd heard all about me. I'm the Paris Hilton of the Berkshires, thanks to Taylor and Marissa." I found the bag of mini-marshmallows and crammed a few into my mouth. "All the dog stuff's in the trunk, so when you get a chance, could you bring it in? Oh, and could you put the convertible top back up, too? I had to take it down to fit him in the passenger seat. I thought we were going to die of frostbite on the ride home. What do you think we should name him?"

"You're serious. You actually adopted this filthy monstrosity of a dog?"

I batted my eyelashes at him. "Don't talk that way about our *baby*, sweetheart."

His lips crimped together. "Don't start with that again."

"I'm not." I nibbled a few more marshmallows as I sprinkled cocoa powder into the mug. "You wanted to get a dog, so we got a dog. I'm just trying to be agreeable."

"You're not being agreeable; you're being passive-aggressive. I already told you, we're getting a maltipoo."

"From a breeder with a waiting list? Why should we spend a ton of money buying a designer dog when there are so many homeless animals dying in shelters every day?"

"Oh God." He shook his head. "The lunatic leaflet girl's gotten her hooks into you."

I beamed. "I'm just trying to do the right thing."

"Give it up!" He jabbed his index finger toward me. "The only reason you got that dog is to make a stand against my vasectomy. You don't want a mangy stray messing up this house any more than I do. What are you going to do when he starts peeing all over the rug? Chewing up the furniture?"

As I surveyed the spotless travertine floors, white leather sofa, and pristine Berber carpet I'd so carefully picked out, I realized he had a point. I didn't want to sacrifice my brand-new house to make a point about my biological clock. A five-minute argument was going to cost us eight to ten years of muddy pawprints and drooled-on Italian leather. Plus bloat, whatever the hell that was.

My expression must have reflected my second thoughts, because he nodded and said, "See? You know I'm right."

"Well, I can't just take him back to the shelter," I said. "Casey said that big, black, male dogs almost never get adopted."

"I will not going to have some overgrown mutt marking his territory all over my house."

"He's neutered," I protested. "Besides, he seems pretty mellow."

We both took a moment to stare at the dog, who had reared up on his hind legs and was resting his head on the counter, his long pink tongue slurping toward the marshmallows.

"You shouldn't have gotten a pet without consulting me first," Mark said.

My jaw hit the floor. "Excuse me? You're the one who put me on a waiting list for the maltipoo! I don't remember being consulted about that."

"That's different—I was trying to make you happy, not one-up you with some childish power play. Besides, maltipoos are a much more practical choice, given our family situation. Taylor hates big dogs. She says they can't be trusted."

I slammed the cocoa tin down on the counter. "So what? Taylor doesn't live here."

"Well . . ." He started choosing his words very carefully. "If we keep this dog, the girls won't want to come over very often."

My smile was even tighter than his. "In case you haven't noticed, *the girls* hate my guts. They're not coming over anyway."

"They're coming for Thanksgiving next week." He stared up at the ceiling. "And they don't hate you."

"What's that?" I cupped a hand to my ear. "I can't hear you."

"They don't hate you," he muttered.

"Ha."

"Okay, it's possible they resent you a little bit. But they'll get over it, sweetheart. These things take time."

"Everyone told me not to marry a guy twice my age," I said to the dog, who was trying to look innocent while mainlining marshmallows on the sly. "Everybody said the nanny shouldn't marry her employer's golf buddy. It would never work, they said. But would I listen? Nooo."

"What are you talking about?" The tension ebbed out of his shoulders as he uncrossed his arms and stepped forward to embrace me. "Nobody said that. And we *are* going to work. You and me—we're a team."

I let him pull me up against his chest but didn't say anything.

"I love you, Stell. We're going to have our share of fights—maybe more than our share—but I will always love you."

"Only because I'm young and pretty," I goaded.

"No." He buried his face in my hair. "Because you're everything I ever wanted and I can't live without you. Do you get that? It's not about how you look. It's about who you are."

That's what all my boyfriends had said since Alan Gilardi gave me my first French kiss in sixth grade. And most of them had been lying.

But Mark wasn't like all those other guys. He was strong and steady and solid as a rock. He'd always put me first, always given me what I needed.

Until now.

"I love you, too," I whispered. "But I still want to have a baby."

"I know." He squeezed me tighter.

"So?"

"So we'll talk about it. After Thanksgiving."

I whirled around. "We will?"

He smiled. "When do I ever say no to you?"

I flung my arms around his neck. "I love you."

"Good." He glanced over at the dog, who was watching us, his tail thumping steadily against the floor. "Now will you please do something with that dog? He's giving me the creeps."

"He's a good boy," I defended. "And if I take him back to the shelter, they'll put him to sleep. You should have seen Casey when I said I was thinking about returning him. She looked at me like I was an axe murderer."

"Who cares what Casey Nestor thinks?" He mumbled something under his breath that sounded suspiciously like "white trash," but that couldn't be right—Mark never used language like that.

"We're keeping the dog, Mark. We have to."

"We're not."

"We are."

"What about Taylor's phobia?"

"What about euthanasia?" I countered.

Mark gave me a look. "You don't even like him."

"I do so!" I insisted a little too loudly.

"No, you don't. You haven't even given him a name."

"I'm waiting to come up with the right one!"

"Casey Nestor. What a piece of work." He snorted in disgust. "That girl should spend more time worrying about her own marriage and less interfering in ours—"

"Oh, yeah." I suddenly remembered what I'd asked him when I'd first walked in the door. "That reminds me. Have we gotten any important letters lately? Like from the county clerk?"

"No," he said quickly, but his eyes gave him away. He looked guilty somehow, *caught*.

"Are you sure?" I forced a laugh. "Because Casey's friend got married the same weekend we did, and she just got a letter saying that Pastor Rick died before he signed her marriage certificate."

His face. It was the wedding night vasectomy confession all over again.

"Oh my God," I whispered. "You knew. You got that letter and you hid it from me."

He held up both hands. "Hey, nobody's hiding anything. I just wanted to wait to tell you until you'd calmed down about—"

"Your first big fat lie?" My voice came out sharp and icy. The dog lowered his head and whined.

"See?" he blustered, trying to stay on the offensive. "This is why I didn't tell you! Because I knew you'd react like this!"

"It's always my fault, isn't it?" I shot back as the dog slunk toward the foyer. "You lie, you hide things, and *I'm* supposed to feel bad? Jesus, Mark, what else aren't you telling me?"

"Nothing!"

"A crack habit? A mistress or five?"

"Stella, you know I would never—"

"I don't know anything about you!" The teakettle whistled on the stove. "All these things I took for granted . . . I was so stupid! How can I believe a word you say?"

"Because I love you." His voice was barely audible over the kettle. "I made a mistake, yes, I admit that. I shouldn't have assumed you'd remember our conversation in Bermuda. But you can trust me, Stella. Our marriage is built on love and honesty and—"

"Our marriage." I snatched the kettle off the stove and started to laugh—I couldn't help it. "Let me tell you something about our marriage, buddy—as far as the State of Massachusetts is concerned, our marriage doesn't even exist!"

"What is that supposed to mean? Are you threatening me?"

"I'm just stating a fact. Hang on to that letter as long as you want. I know the truth—you're not really my husband. Not in any sense of the word. Now if you'll excuse me, I have to go give our new dog a bath. He'll be sleeping on your side of the bed tonight. Enjoy the couch."

9

CASEY

"Hey, hon." Nick barely looked up from the televised basketball game as I came through the front door of our cozy apartment. "How was work?"

"Busy." I shucked off my bulky parka and stooped down to greet the cats, Maisy and Tate. While they jostled each other trying to get my attention, I tried to get Nick's. "Did a ton of business before noon. People are finally starting to try the premium foods, and I managed to move about half of the Kongs I ordered last week. If we keep going like this, I might be able to hire an assistant soon . . ."

But he wasn't even pretending to listen. His eyes were glued to the TV as he raised his can of Foster's to his lips.

"Honey," I said gently. "Remember when we talked about using glasses instead of drinking straight out of the can?"

"Uh-huh." He grabbed the remote and upped the TV volume.

I sighed and raised my voice to compete with the sports announcer's. "And remember how we talked about using coasters?"

"Sorry." He swiped at the wet rings on the coffee table with his sweat sock–encased foot.

I opened my mouth again, then realized that I had started to sound exactly like Bree on *Desperate Housewives*. While I hung up my coat, I tried to ignore the clutter and potato chip crumbs surrounding my husband and silently repeated sage snippets of advice from all those relationship books I'd read before the wedding. What was that question I was supposed to ask myself when I was tempted to nag my spouse? *Do you want to be right, or do you want to be happy?*

I wanted to be happy. Definitely. Happy all the way.

Except was it so much to ask to have a clean carpet, too? How hard would it be for him to use a bowl or a napkin, or—

"I fixed the shower," Nick announced, turning his attention back to me as a commercial flashed onto the screen.

"You did?" My irritation melted into relief, then guilt. See? He helped out around the house. Besides, he put in long hours at his father's law office all day. The man was exhausted. Why was I always so quick to find fault?

"Yep. Ran to the hardware store after work."

"Thank you." I unwound my wool scarf and draped it over

the coat hanger. "You're my hero. I need a hot shower like no-body's business."

"No problem." He made a vague kissy noise, then put his beer can back down on the coffee table.

Without a coaster.

"What?" he demanded when he saw the expression on my face.

"Nothing, nothing." I rubbed my upper arms. "Just warm-ing up. Hey, could you do me a favor and start dinner while I shower? What do we have in the fridge?"

"Not much." He buried his hand in the bag of chips. "We're pretty much down to yogurt and broccoli."

"You didn't get a chance to go to the grocery store?" I had planned to go on my lunch break, but he'd taken the shopping list with him this morning, insisting that he would do it.

"I went to the hardware store." He sounded offended. "I can't do *everything*."

"I know, but . . ." *Do you want to be right, or do you want to be happy?* "Okay, no problem, we'll order pizza."

"Whatever." Another handful of chips. "I'm not that hungry."

I filled the cats' dishes on my way to the bathroom, where I got undressed, pulled my hair up into a ponytail, and reached for the faucet.

"Um, Nick?"

"Yeah?"

"About the faucet? Where's the knob to turn on the hot water?"

"It broke off," he yelled.

I opened the bathroom door and poked my head into the hall. "Yeah, I'm aware of that. But you said you fixed it."

"I did. That's what the wrench is for."

I glanced over my shoulder to see a massive red wrench lying on the corner of the bathtub.

"You're kidding."

"No." He finally roused himself from the couch and came into the bathroom to show off his handiwork. "All you do is clamp this part down on the metal nub here"—he adjusted the wrench claws around the scrawny silver bar that used to anchor the faucet knob—"and turn." He twisted the wrench with both hands, unleashing a torrent of warm water. "See? And if you want it hotter, you just bring it back and twist again!" He stepped back, beaming with pride.

I did my best to smile back. "Wow. That's very . . . re-sourceful."

"Yep. The landlord offered to call a plumber, but I told him not to bother."

"So, uh, that's it? There's no plumber coming?"

"You don't need a plumber when you've got a *man* around the house." He swaggered back to the couch in his beer-stained hockey jersey.

I want to be happy, I want to be happy. "Well, thanks, honey." I climbed into the tub and made a mental note to phone the landlord in the morning.

As the hot water streamed over my tired, aching muscles, I pressed my palms against my lower back and stretched. Nick's repair job might not have been the most conventional solution, but the shower worked; that was the important thing.

This is what marriage was all about: letting the small stuff slide. All the books said so. I needed to overlook the petty crap like moisture rings on my—scratch that, *our*—coffee table and focus on the big picture. I needed to stop imposing my insanely high expectations on other people. Maybe I could even stop imposing them on myself. Nick and I could have a good marriage. Not like my parents. Not like my sister. We'd be the ones who beat the odds. The guy who wouldn't look twice at me in high school would still be with me on our fiftieth anniversary.

"Hey, did you ask your dad about brunch this weekend?" I asked when I ambled back into the family room with a makeshift towel turban on my head.

He shook his head. "Forgot."

"You work with him all day. How could you forget?"

"It's a law office, Case. He doesn't want to waste billable hours making brunch plans."

"Okay, then I'll just call your mom tomorrow."

He jerked his gaze away from the basketball game. "Do not call my mom."

"Why not? Last week, she said she wanted us to come over for brunch, and I don't want her to think I don't like them."

Big eye roll. "They know you like them. Trust me. Everyone knows you like them. We don't have to spend every single weekend eating French toast with them to prove it."

"Well, excuse me for trying to be a good daughter-in-law. You should count your blessings—what if your mom and I were fighting all the time like Erin and David's mother?"

"Then I'd get to sleep in on Sundays."

"Nick!"

"What?" He muted the television and slouched down into the sofa cushions. "It's not enough that you married me? You have to marry my parents, too?"

"What's wrong with that?"

"You have my last name, okay? You got me. I spend the whole week listening to my dad gripe about how I dropped out of law school; I should get weekends off." His blond hair flopped over his forehead as he withdrew further into the depths of the couch.

"I know you and your dad are having a hard time right now, but—"

"Yeah, we are. Nothing's ever good enough for him, and I don't need that from you, too."

I want to be happy, I want to be happy. "I understand. But family is important, Nick."

"Really? Then why don't we have brunch with *your* family on Sunday?"

I just looked at him.

"You're always talking about family time. Why can't we ever spend any time with yours?"

"You know how my family is," I said tightly. "Don't drag them into this."

"Fine. But you're the one who had to get married. You said that's what you wanted, but nothing's ever enough."

"What are you saying? I bludgeoned you into marriage?"

He shrugged. "You're the one who proposed."

"I did not!"

"You bought the ring."

"That is not fair! You asked me what kind of diamond I liked."

"Yeah, and the second I did, you dragged me to the mall, picked out a ring, and paid for it yourself."

"You said you were low on cash," I gritted out. "Should I have let you run up your credit card bill?"

"You should have waited until I asked you properly." He couldn't meet my eyes. "The old-fashioned way."

"Really." The ends of my wet hair were creeping out of my turban and soaking through my robe. "And when would you have gotten around to proposing the old-fashioned way?"

He shrugged.

"When?" I pressed.

"I would've."

"Right. If I hadn't bought this ring, we'd still be in relationship limbo!"

"Well, you got me, okay? You got what you wanted."

"Lucky me." I marched into the bedroom, pulled on clean

jeans and a sweater, and crammed my feet back into my hiking boots.

"Where are you going?" he asked as I pulled on my parka. "What about pizza?"

"Get your own damn pizza," I snapped. "The old-fashioned way."

I stomped down the stairs toward my truck. On the way I checked the mailbox. Sandwiched between the phone bill and my new issue of the *Whole Dog Journal,* I found an envelope bearing the seal of the State of Massachusetts. I glanced at the typed address, then up at the windows of our apartment, where the television's flickering glow outlined the silhouette of the man whom yes, truth be told, I had sort of proposed to.

I folded the envelope and crammed it deep into my coat pocket.

Right now didn't feel like the best time to reopen negotiations.

10

ERIN

Fat, wet flakes of snow sifted down from the darkening clouds as I locked the office door behind me and headed for the parking lot. David and I had spent a long day apart after last night's standoff—I'd checked into a hotel in Pittsfield, where I'd been so furious that I'd actually sent off an email to Jonathan, one of my friends from residency, asking him to test the waters and find out if there might still be a job for me in Boston.

God help me if any of this ever got back to Renée. *How are you two going to give me grandchildren if you aren't spending any time together? Your job is too stressful, Erin, I keep telling you. What's the point of being a doctor these days, anyway? It's all red tape and HMOs. Hurry up and start a family before it's too late. Let David wear the pants for a change.*

She was right about one thing: My job *was* stressful. My

last scheduled appointment had been at four thirty—Ava Schaltzi's chicken pox—but then Kelly Fendt had rushed into the waiting room with her toddler bundled up in a blanket. She'd demanded to see a doctor. Immediately. Christa at the front desk had been so freaked out that she'd called me away from my paperwork to deal with the situation.

"I know she's a hypochondriac, I know she's a pain in the butt," Christa had said nervously. "But she says her son has whooping cough. She says he's coughing up *blood.* I put her in exam room B."

So I'd given up all hope of squeezing in a session at the gym and agreed to assess the situation. Little Carter Fendt had smiled up at me from behind his pacifier.

"He's been coughing," Kelly reported. "All night long. He stopped breathing for a minute, Dr. Maye. I swear he did."

"Mm-hmm." I scanned his chart, then pressed my stethoscope against his chest to listen to the lungs. No wheezing, no rales, no signs of any distress. "I don't hear anything to be too alarmed about . . . let's take his temperature."

"Good idea." Kelly looked vindicated. "My husband says I'm making a mountain out of a molehill, but I know my child, Dr. Maye. A mother has a sixth sense about this sort of thing. And I can't bear to see my little boy—"

"Was it a barking cough?"

She considered this. "No, I'd say it was more of a rattly cough. I could hear it in his chest."

"Mm-hmm. No fever," I concluded, glancing at the ther-mometer. "He was coughing up blood, you said?"

"Well . . ." She fiddled with the silver chain around her neck. "He was definitely coughing up fluid. Last night."

I made a note of this in the chart. "What color?"

She hesitated. "What color?"

"What color was the fluid? Green? Yellow? Brown?"

"Oh. It was yellow, I guess. Kind of clear."

I jotted this down. "Okay. Have you noticed anything else unusual? Diarrhea? Rashes?"

"His face was very pink when we came in from sledding the other day. Oh God, what do you think it is? Whooping cough? Bronchitis? Pneumonia?"

I smiled patiently, no easy feat given the fact that this was her third unscheduled "emergency" this month. "It may just be a cold."

"Oh no." She threw up a hand. "You didn't hear him coughing last night. The poor darling was fit to die."

"Well, he is a bit congested, but he's up to date on his shots, and since he's been immunized against whooping cough—"

She lifted her chin. "Are you saying I don't know what's wrong with my own child?"

I kept my expression bland. "Has he been coughing so hard he vomits? Does his face change color?"

"No," she admitted.

"Okay, then. Try a vaporizer in his room tonight. Maybe some mentholated ointment."

Her eyes widened in horror. "Aren't you going to give him antibiotics?"

"Not yet. I'll call you tomorrow, and if he's not feeling better, we'll try a different approach."

"But he needs a prescription! I know my baby and—"

"Dr. Lowell will be on call tonight," I said firmly. "You can let us know if he gets worse or has any trouble breathing."

"He's having trouble breathing right now!" she cried, gathering up Carter, who was happily blowing spit bubbles and helping himself to a fistful of goldfish crackers from his mother's pocket. "No offense, Dr. Maye, but you're fresh out of medical school, aren't you? I'd like to see someone with a little more experience."

"Dr. Lowell's with another patient."

"I want antibiotics, and I want them now. You obviously don't understand what it's like to be a mother."

No, I didn't, I reflected as I trudged through the fresh snow to my beat-up old Toyota. Maybe if I did, I could understand the primal urge that drove Kelly Fendt and, for that matter, Renée to intervene even when it might do her children more harm than good.

I climbed into the driver's seat, turned the key in the ignition, and waited for the engine to warm up. My black loafers were soaked through with melted snow, and the hem of my gray pants was dirty from the parking lot slush. This was my wardrobe now: sturdy shoes, tailored pants. Ugh. When I first met David, I'd been wearing a black sequined tube top and an obscenely short camouflage skirt at a bar in Boston. I'd just finished my first semester med school finals, and my roommate and I had decided to kill our few remaining functioning brain cells with alcohol.

I'd been shimmying on the sticky bartop at the Cat and Canary under a strobe light, blissfully ignorant of the years of Talbot's and Ann Taylor stretching out ahead of me, when I tripped on a shot glass and stomped on the bartender's hand as he served up a frosty glass of Guinness.

"Sorry," I'd breathed, crouching down to examine the damage. "Did I break your proximal phalanges?"

He'd tried to smile through his wince. "Nothing a cast and six months of intensive physical therapy won't cure."

I winced and prodded his fingers. "Can you make a fist?"

He'd rolled his eyes. "What, are you a doctor in a red G-string?"

I'd flushed. "Oh my God. You can see up my skirt?"

"Yeah. So can everyone else."

I'd hopped down behind the bar and tugged my hem down. "You better put some ice on that hand."

He stood back and watched me fashion a cold compress out of a dish towel and the cubed ice in the cooler. "So *are* you a doctor, or do you just have a lot of practice dealing with wounded bartenders?"

"I'm a med student," I'd admitted sheepishly. "First year.

Don't tell my professors I'm administering treatment without a license, okay?"

"As long as you don't tell *my* professors about the bartending gig." He laughed at my expression. "I'm in the pharmacology program at Northeastern."

"Then why are you . . . ?"

"My fellowship doesn't exactly cover rent prices in Boston. It's either bartend or take a monthly allowance from my mother, so here I am." He grinned. "You'd understand if you knew my mom."

"And I just mangled the hands you use to do research."

"Consider it karmic payback for all the jokes I've made about physicians' handwriting." He flinched as I pressed the makeshift ice pack against his swelling hand. "With any luck, I'll be able to hold a beer again someday."

"Is there anything I can do to ease your pain and suffering?"

He leaned forward, just inside the perimeters of what I considered my personal space. "You could give me your phone number. Just in case I need my lawyers to track you down for the huge malpractice suit."

I scribbled down my name and number on a cocktail napkin.

He squinted at the writing. "I'm not even going to say anything about the penmanship."

"Wise." I struck a pose. "'Cause I have three-inch heels and I'm not afraid to use them."

"No kidding." He laughed again. "I'm David. I'd shake your hand, but I'm kind of scarred for life."

And that was that. We'd been inseparable since that night, growing closer as we swapped the bar scene for nights at the opera, camouflage skirts for preppy blazers, torrid sex in our drafty Boston apartment for lukewarm cuddling in our fixer-upper starter home in Alden.

We were fated to be together, clearly. I mean, an ass-shaking pediatrician and a martini-shaking pharmacologist? What were the odds?

As the Toyota's vents started coughing out heat, I dug my cell phone out of my purse and dialed our home number. One of us had to swallow our pride and take the first step. The situation with Renée could be worked out. David loved me, he would understand that we couldn't let his mother invade our—

"Hello?" A familiar voice picked up on the other end of the line.

I grimaced.

"Hello?"

"Renée?" I strangled out.

"Erin." From the tone of her voice, I knew she'd heard about yesterday's fight.

"Yes, hi. Listen . . . is David there?"

She took a moment to let the full force of her disapproval sink in. "He's still at the hospital."

Then why are you in our house, answering our phone?

"I dropped by to make sure he got a decent meal," she continued as if reading my mind. "Since you're swamped with work. Again."

"How thoughtful," I oozed. "But as it happens, I'm actually on my way home from the office, so—"

"Perfect," she oozed right back. "There's plenty to go around. I'm making a chicken stir-fry. With peanut sauce."

11

STELLA

"You have to help me," I begged Casey, reaching across her pet supply shop's counter to tug the sleeve of her flannel shirt. "Please. This dog—he's wrecking my house. The chewing, the shedding, and drool . . . I had to clean off the *ceiling* in the mudroom the other day!"

She flashed a totally insincere smile and handed me a flyer advertising the dog trainer who held obedience classes at the store twice a week.

I let go of her sleeve and hung my head while the dog sat by my side doing his docile *Best in Show* routine. "Listen, I get it, adopting a pet is a lifelong commitment and I can't take him back to the shelter. And honestly, I could handle it if he was just wrecking my house. But it's more than that. He's wrecking my marriage!"

Her eyebrows shot up. "This dog?"

I nodded.

"This dog sitting right here is ruining your marriage?"

We both regarded the giant black mutt, who looked back at us with his tail wagging and his eyes sparkling.

"This is just an act!" I cried. "He's not like this at home. He's like . . . like Dr. Jekyll and Mr. Hyde!"

"Really." She didn't even bother trying to hide her disdain.

"Swear to God! He chewed half the arm off our new leather sofa. He shredded my husband's first edition of *Great Expectations*. He ripped open all the down pillows in the linen closet. We still don't know how he opened the door. My husband says I have to choose: him or the dog."

"Well, may I give you some advice?"

"Please." I craned forward, desperate for some words of wisdom.

"Choose the dog." Then she gave me the same look that Taylor and Marissa had given me when Mark and I had announced our engagement. The look that said, *You're a fluffy little bimbo with a bra size bigger than your IQ and I'd feel sorry for you if I didn't hate you so much.*

Well, maybe I had to take that from Taylor and Marissa, but I didn't have to take it from Casey Keating. I put both hands on my hips and demanded, "Who the hell do you think you are?"

Her head snapped back in surprise.

"I mean it. I come in here looking for some friendly advice, and this is how you treat me? Nice customer service!"

"You didn't come in for advice, you came in to dump your dog on me."

"You're desperate for any excuse to look down on me. Yes, okay, I'm new in town. And yes, I'm a little bit younger than my husband—"

"A *little* bit?" Casey muttered.

"Hey! Let me finish. If you really cared about animals, you would help me find solutions to my problems. But you don't; you just want to feel superior and haze me because you think I'm the kind of girl you would have hated in high school."

From the look on her face, I could tell I'd hit a nerve.

"You don't know anything about me, and you don't know anything about my marriage. So you just . . . you just *shut up!*"

She blinked. "Are you done?"

I nodded, gathering up the dog's leash.

"Okay. First of all, I do care about animals."

"Well, so do I," I countered. "I love my new dog very much."

"Whatever you say. Second, you're right. I don't know anything about your marriage."

I pounded the counter. "Damn straight!"

"But when a guy asks you to decide between him and a pet, you're almost always better off with the pet."

I yanked on the leash as the dog inched closer to the treat display. "You're a newlywed, right? Would you choose a dog over your husband?"

"My husband would never give me an ultimatum like that." Her expression was suddenly unreadable. "I'm more of the ultimatum giver in our relationship."

"But if he did," I pressed. "If he said, 'It's me or the mutt that ate the sofa'? Who would you pick?"

She tucked a strand of her reddish-brown hair back behind her ear. "Ask me again on a different day."

The bell on the door jangled as Erin Maye strolled in. "Hey! Look who's here!" She crouched down and started loving on the dog. "Hey, buddy! How ya doing?"

"Not good," Casey reported before I had a chance to say anything. "Her husband's making her get rid of him."

"Really?" Erin scrunched up her face. Her cheeks and nose were bright red from the cold. "I guess I could see that—Dr. Porter doesn't strike me as much of an animal person."

I nodded. "Well, if you know anyone who wants a hyper, hundred-pound puppy . . ."

"I'd take him, but my mother-in-law's allergic."

"But it's not like your mother-in-law lives with you," Casey said.

Erin arched one eyebrow.

"*No.*" Casey gasped. "What happened?"

Erin cleared her throat to indicate that these subjects

should not be discussed in front of outsiders like me. "We'll talk. Want to go grab dinner?"

Casey shook her head. "Can't. Nick had to order a pizza last night."

"So?"

"So I want to make him a real meal to make up for it tonight. We had this stupid argument . . ." She trailed off, staring at me.

"What?" I stared back. "You might as well go ahead and talk. So what if you had some little spat with your husband? At least he's not making you get rid of your dog."

Casey brightened. "True." She turned back to Erin. "Well, we had this ridiculous fight because he replaced our shower faucet handle with a pipe wrench—don't ask—and I ended up going to the movies by myself while he had to order a pizza. So I'm whipping up a culinary feast to patch things up. Rosemary potatoes, free-range chicken, the whole shebang."

"You are so June Cleaver," Erin teased. "You're the only person I know who actually mills her own guest soaps."

"I just like to keep a clean house," Casey said.

"It's a sickness, I tell you." Erin laughed. "Drop by the office—I'll slip you some meds. The good stuff."

"Promises, promises." Casey waved her off as the phone next to the register rang.

As Casey tucked the receiver between her shoulder and ear, Erin started patting the dog again. This time, she actually bothered to make eye contact with me. "I'll ask around the office, see if anyone's looking for a dog. What's his name?"

"No name yet," I admitted.

"What should we name you?" Erin asked the dog, flapping his ears. "What's a good name for a big, black dog? Hmm. Voodoo? No, too scary. Enzo? No, too sophisticated."

"What about Cash?" I surprised myself by speaking up. "Like Johnny Cash. Wasn't he supposed to be the man in black?"

Erin looked up, surprised.

"Yes, I know who the man in black is. You don't have to be so shocked. I have three years of college, believe it or not. I'm not an idiot."

"I never said you were."

"But you think it," I challenged. "You and Casey both do. You think anyone who married a man twice her age and looks the way I look has to be a dumbass."

Erin smirked. "Who 'looks the way you look'? And what way is that, exactly?"

"Like trophy wife material." There was no point denying the truth.

For a second, I thought she'd go back to pretending I didn't exist, but she threw back her head and laughed. "A trophy wife with a smart mouth."

"Yeah, well, I'm not as ditzy as I look. That's what my mom always says."

"Nice mom!"

I sighed. "She means it as a compliment. I think."

"She should have coffee with my mother-in-law. They'd have a lot to talk about."

Our little meet-and-greet was interrupted as Casey's voice got sharper and louder. "Nick, I said I was sorry about last night . . . and then I told you about . . . well, I wish you wouldn't do that—I've already bought all the ingredients and defrosted the chicken."

"Uh-oh," Erin whispered. "He's doing it again."

"Who's doing what?" I whispered back.

"Her husband. The man can't commit to anything. Not law school, not an apartment lease, nothing. He goes through about five cell phone providers a year."

"He managed to get married," I pointed out. "'Til death do them part."

Erin looked like she had a lot to say but wasn't going to say it.

" . . . well, if that's what you really want." Casey glowered as she wrapped up her phone conversation with Mr. Commitment. "Do what you want. I'm not your warden . . . uh-huh . . . uh-huh . . . no, whatever. I'm not mad. Nope. Promise. I'm not mad. See you later. Kiss, kiss."

She slammed down the receiver with a force that startled the dog. "Son of a bitch! I'm going to kill him!"

Erin winced. "Trouble on the western front?"

"He's going to the Y to play basketball with his friends!" Casey could not have looked more distraught if her husband had just confessed to cheating on her with STD-riddled porn stars. "He knew I was planning a reconciliation dinner, and he blows me off to go shoot hoops with his buddies?"

"Men," Erin said with disgust.

"But . . ." I furrowed my brow. "You said you weren't mad."

"Ix-nay on the ontradiction-cay," Erin murmured, but she was too late.

Casey refocused all her rage in my direction. "Stella. How old are you?"

I stared at the floor. "Twenty-four."

"I've got five years on you in real time, and about a billion in life experiences. I'll let you in on a little secret to successful relationships—don't blurt out every feeling you have the second you have it."

The smug big-sister act was wearing really thin. I flipped my hair and mimicked her tone. "Lying? That's your key to a happy marriage?"

"Not lying," she corrected. "Delayed reaction. Choosing your battles. You have to decide which hills you want to defend. I myself prefer not to die on the hill of chicken and rosemary potatoes."

"And I prefer not to die on the hill of pound puppies and half-eaten leather sofas."

She finally cracked a smile.

"Oh, and the dog has a name now," I told her. "Cash. As in Johnny."

"I like it," Erin said.

"Me, too." Casey crossed the store and flipped the sign on the front door from Open to Closed. When she turned back toward us, her anger had been replaced with what seemed like defeat or resignation. "Listen, do either of you want to come up to the apartment and have dinner? I've got a lot of free-range chicken to unload."

". . . so we spend a week in Italy, have a fantastic time, and come home completely jet-lagged. I was ready to sleep for a week." Erin paused for a sip of chilled white wine. We had gathered around Casey's antique dining room table ("I tossed Nick's IKEA particleboard eyesore the second we got engaged") while she served up perfectly prepared chicken with fresh sprigs of rosemary on elegant ecru china plates (also antique). Between the intricate lace tablecloth, the white taper candles, and the subtly scented cranberry wreath hanging above the sideboard, the whole room could have been transported directly out of *Better Homes and Gardens*.

"You guys went to Italy for your honeymoon?" Casey sighed wistfully. "You are so lucky. Between paying for the wedding and renegotiating my lease for the store, we could only afford a weekend in the Adirondacks."

"Don't feel bad," I consoled. "Mark and I went to a bed-and-breakfast in Vermont."

"Yeah, but I bet it was a five-star hotel with a personal valet to run your baths and peel you grapes."

"Uh . . ." She had me there. Mark had picked the Cartwell House Inn because we were both sick of the long flights to Europe and wanted to go someplace nearby to de-stress after the wedding. He and I had already been to London, Paris, Tuscany, New Zealand, and, of course, the fateful trip to Bermuda; we'd figured that we'd go low-key for the honeymoon. "There might have been a truffle or two on the pillow each night."

"Anyway." Erin dinged her wineglass with her dessert spoon to reclaim our attention. "We come home from the honeymoon, utterly bedraggled after six hours crammed into those tiny airplane seats, we open the door to the house, and his mom is sitting in the living room waiting for us!"

"How'd she get in?" I asked.

"I still don't know. David claims he never gave her a key, so either she stole his and had a copy made without his knowledge or he gave her a copy and doesn't have the guts to admit it. I'm not sure which scenario is scarier. But she's waiting for us in the living room, and she's *cleaned.* The whole house. We had just moved in a week before the wedding, so we hadn't had time to do anything. She unpacked everything—the kitchen, the bedroom, *my vibrator—*"

Casey made a face. "Oog."

"Hang on, wait for it: she even made our bed. In the same sheets that she used when she married David's father."

"Ew," I blurted out. "I thought you said his father was dead?"

"His father is dead. But apparently, she saved their marital bedding. She wanted us to consummate our marriage on the same sheets David was conceived on."

Casey spat a mouthful of wine back into her glass. "That is disgusting."

"I know." Erin nodded.

"No, I mean, that is really disgusting. Sick, depraved, wrong on so many levels . . ."

"I know," Erin repeated. "Paging Dr. Freud."

I couldn't get the picture of threadbare, faded sheets out of my head. "Did she actually say all that?"

Erin smiled grimly. "Clearly, you've never met Renée. She said all that and more. She will not rest until I quit my job and procreate. I've told her a thousand times that I just finished my residency and I spend all day dealing with other people's sick, cranky children, which tends to muffle my own biological clock, but she's not having it. And I haven't even told you about the time she tried to kill me."

"Shut up!" I said. "She did not."

"She absolutely did. I have a severe peanut allergy, as she is very well aware, and what do you think she tried to slip into every single side dish last Thanksgiving?"

"Really?" I breathed.

"David had to stab me in the thigh with my EpiPen on her dining room floor."

"Maybe it was an accident," I said.

Erin and Casey exchanged that superior, knowing look again. "So naïve."

"I'm not naïve!"

"Honey, does your mother-in-law live here in town with you?"

"Mark's mom died before I met him," I admitted.

"You are *so* lucky." Erin held out her wineglass to Casey for a refill.

"Yeah, you are," Casey seconded. "You hit the jackpot. New house, luxury hotels, no mother-in-law . . . if it weren't for the dog, your marriage would be perfect."

I took a tiny sip of wine.

"If Nick and I had the kind of money you and Mark have, we wouldn't have to worry about my business all the time. He could stop working in his dad's office. All our problems would be solved. We'd never fight again."

Erin doubled over in a sudden coughing fit.

"What?" Casey blushed. "It's true."

"Did I say anything?" Erin croaked. "No. But let's face it: Every marriage has problems."

"If it weren't for Renée, you and David wouldn't have issues," Casey said. "You guys are made for each other."

Erin developed an intense interest in the tablecloth's lacework.

I glanced down at my flat, empty, nonpregnant belly. "My marriage isn't perfect, believe me."

Casey snorted. "Please. Your biggest problems are like, 'Should we go to St. Thomas or St. Croix for Easter?'"

I opened my mouth to correct her but couldn't force out the words. How could I admit that everything was going wrong with Mark? That saying "I do," might have been the biggest mistake of my life?

"So what are you guys going to do?" I asked softly. "About the marriage certificate screwup? You're both going to get remarried?"

"Of course," Erin and Casey chorused.

"Yeah, me too," I agreed quickly.

"I mean, it would be pretty sad if Nick and I couldn't even last three months." Casey's laugh sounded forced.

"How pathetic would it be if I let a bunch of hand-me-down sheets break up my marriage?" Erin added.

"I'd definitely do it all over again," Casey said.

"Me, too." Erin nodded.

"Good." I looked around the table. "We're happy. We're all happy."

"Yep."

"Absolutely."

"Never been better."

There was a long pause.

I cracked first. "Mark had a vasectomy and didn't tell me until our wedding night."

Casey covered her face with her hands. "I pressured Nick into getting engaged, and I'm pretty sure I'll never be good enough for him."

Erin tipped back her chair and sighed. "My husband's morphing into a spineless mama's boy, and I have no idea what happened to the alpha male I married."

"This sucks," I said.

"Amen, sister."

"Why is marriage so hard?" I wondered.

"And why can't we be honest about it?" Casey threw in. "It's like you have to have the perfect relationship and if you ever go to bed mad or think about what might have happened if you'd stayed single, you're a failure."

"Do you wish you were still single?" Erin asked her.

Casey nibbled her lower lip. "Not exactly. But I wish Nick had proposed the right way. I wish I didn't always have to take the initiative."

"I sometimes wish I were still single," Erin admitted.

My turn. "I wish . . . I wish Mark wanted to have children. Or that I didn't. I wish I had someone to talk to about what's really going on."

"You can talk to us," Casey offered.

"Right. You guys think I'm a superficial little tart."

"What?" Erin feigned shock. "We do not!"

"Well, not anymore," Casey amended. "Turns out, we're just as screwed up as you are."

"Thanks." I topped off my wine.

Casey raised her glass. "Here's to honesty."

"And friendship," Erin added.

I held my glass up next to theirs. "And surviving the first year of marriage without killing anyone."

Clink.

12

ERIN

What's up with kids all getting sick on major holidays? Is it a plot? A preschool conspiracy? As the newest physician in the practice, I had to be on call for Thanksgiving, and the phone hadn't stopped ringing since five a.m. There'd been a six-month-old spiking a high fever, a kindergartener who'd managed to wedge half a wishbone up his nose, and a four-year-old who'd needed stitches after her big brother stabbed her with an icicle "by accident." And, of course, no on-call shift would be complete without a panicked visit from Kelly Fendt—her son had come down with what she swore up and down was spinal meningitis and turned out to be a spectacularly uninteresting runny nose.

As I climbed into my car, I tried to focus on the many positives of my job. True, when I chose pediatrics as my specialty,

I'd imagined I'd stay in Boston, working on challenging hospital cases and contributing to cutting-edge medical journals. I hadn't anticipated the hassles of billing paperwork, insurance pre-authorization, and everyone looking askance at my modest Toyota and wondering aloud why a doctor couldn't afford a more luxurious ride (two words: student loans).

But I was still making a difference. I'd salvaged Thanksgivings for those local families, who could now go back to mashing potatoes and stirring gravy instead of having to haul their distressed children all the way to the ER in Pittsfield.

I didn't need the latest technology or the chance to treat exotic diseases. I would be happy here, because I had David.

Right?

Just this week, in an effort to placate me after our argument, he had told Renée that she would have to delay her home remodel until spring so that he and I could have some more "honeymoon time," and then she'd have to split her visit between us and her sister in Florida. To sweeten the deal, he'd insisted that we were having Thanksgiving dinner at our house this year. She'd whined and wheedled and guilt-tripped, but he'd stood his ground: She could come to our house or spend the holiday with her friends. At last, he was getting it. I needed him to be on my team.

What a guy.

Right on cue, my cell phone rang, and I answered with a smile. "Hey, love."

"How goes the battle?" I could tell from his voice that he was smiling, too.

"Good. I'm done here—at least for now—and I'll stop and pick up dinner on the way home."

"Great. My mom called and demanded to bring something, so I told her she could bake one of her famous apple pies. She'll be over in about an hour."

"Okay, see you soon. Love you."

"Love you."

Fifteen minutes later, I pulled up next to the White Birch Restaurant and packed the boxed turkey and side dishes into the backseat of the Toyota. Someday, when I'd worked my way up the totem pole, I'd be able to stay home and cook Thanksgiving dinner like a normal person, but for now, the kitchen staff at Alden's only gourmet restaurant would have to do.

"Just throw everything in the oven at three-fifty and warm it up," Steffi, the restaurant manager, instructed. "Put the turkey in a roasting pan for about an hour. The side dishes should go in for about twenty or thirty minutes. If you have any questions, feel free to give us a call."

"Thanks, but I think I'll be okay." I laughed. "Even I can't screw up precooked food."

She shook her finger with mock severity. "Can't that cute husband of yours help you out around the kitchen?"

"Elaborate meals aren't his thing," I explained. "He makes great cocktails, but when it comes to food, all bets are off. If he had his way, we'd be sitting down to frozen burritos and SpaghettiOs."

"Just like the Pilgrims and the Indians." Steffi waved goodbye as I got into the driver's seat. "Have a wonderful Thanksgiving, Dr. Maye!"

"I will!" I waved back. "We're doing low-stress holidays this year!"

Renée's huge white Cadillac was parked in the driveway, blocking my access to the garage. I double-checked the clock on my dashboard, grabbed the boxes full of turkey and fixings, and hurried up the front walk to lean on the doorbell.

"Oh good, you're finally here." Renée flung open the door and invited me into my foyer. She was wearing huge diamond earrings and a festive seasonal sweater emblazoned with a turkey sporting a Pilgrim's hat. "What happened? Did you get held up at the clinic?"

"No." I stared at her, bewildered, while David took the boxes out of my arms and gave me a quick kiss on the lips. "I thought you weren't coming over until later."

Renée squeezed my forearm. "Well, here I am, dear! You're just in time. Go wash up and take your place at the table. We're all ready to eat."

A cursory glance at the table confirmed that this was, in fact, the case. A steaming brown turkey glistened on our new silver platter, which was surrounded by baskets of rolls, dishes of peas and sweet potatoes, stuffing, cranberry sauce, etc. Three place settings of the china and crystal Renée had insisted we register for completed the Rockwellian tableau.

I gestured helplessly to the white boxes I'd handed off to David. "But I brought dinner."

She steered me toward the bathroom. "Yes, dear, and I know you had the best intentions, but it's really not Thanksgiving unless everything is homemade."

"You were supposed to bring pie," I stammered. "Pie."

"Well, you know me, I get a little carried away with my cookbooks!" She laughed merrily. "Delusions of Julia Child! I was going to stop with the pie, really I was, but then that pesky Henry Reynolds showed up at my door and invited me to have Thanksgiving dinner with him at a fancy restaurant in Lenox."

"You should have gone," I bit out.

"A restaurant? For Thanksgiving? Never! Besides, you know I can't abide that old codger. He's been making eyes at me for two years, but he's just not my type. Too jowly. And always winking and making dreadful puns. I did feel sorry for him, though, spending the holiday all by himself, so I thought I'd whip up a few things for him."

"Then why are they all on my dining room table instead of his?" I demanded.

"Oh, his daughter invited him to her house in New Hampshire and he decided to go at the last minute." Renée opened the door to the guest bathroom and shoved me toward the sink. "Now let's go, Mrs. Schmidt. Scrub up!"

"It's not Mrs. Schmidt. It is Dr. Maye." I looked to my husband for support. "David?"

"She didn't change her name, Mom," he said, hunching up his shoulders. "We've been over this."

"We have?" She shook her head. "Funny, I don't remember. Well, no need to put on airs around me, darling—we'll both be Mrs. Schmidt when we're in this house. And soon, you'll have a baby, and then you'll have the most important title of all: Mommy."

I turned on the faucet full blast and lathered my hands with vigor. "This is our first married Thanksgiving and I want to host it."

"You are, dear." This time, she actually patted me on the head. "We're in your house, aren't we?"

"Yes, but you cooked the meal, set the table, brewed the coffee . . ." I trailed off as I gazed past her, down the hall, to the open door of the guest room. "What is that?"

Renée feigned innocence, but I knew from the expression on David's face that something had gone horribly awry with our united front.

"Is that luggage?" I threw down the hand towel and charged into the guest room, where stacks of suitcases and an ancient steamer trunk blocked the path to the bed.

"I got a little carried away," Renée tittered. "I tried to

take only what I really need, but you know I always over-pack."

There was enough luggage here to keep Elizabeth Taylor outfitted for a month. I whirled around to find David skulking in the doorway, head hung low. "You said you talked to her!"

"I did," he mumbled. "But . . ."

"I already hired the contractors, and the renovations start tomorrow." Renée clapped her hands together. "Isn't it exciting!"

"You moved in," I said flatly. "This morning."

"Now don't worry, Erin, I know you newlyweds need your privacy. I'll stay out of your hair." She tilted her head. "Considering the hours you work, that shouldn't be too hard."

"You moved in," I repeated.

"Surprise!" She bustled back toward the kitchen, humming a happy tune.

"What the hell?" I hissed at David, who looked like he was suffering a massive internal hemorrhage. "I go to work for four hours and she moves in lock, stock and barrel?"

"I tried to say no, Erin." His eyes beseeched mine. "I know what we agreed. But she has nowhere else to go and she's my *mother*."

"She has other places to go, David, you know she does. What about her sister in Florida?"

"Try to understand," he said. "I'm her only child. And she did give us money for the house . . . She won't be here forever."

Only till she dies. That was the horrible thought that popped into my head. She was going to live with us until she keeled over dead—or I did. Actually, I was probably the more likely candidate, given Renée's culinary assassination attempts. The entire Thanksgiving dinner was probably marinated in peanut oil.

Renée's lilting voice drifted into our white-hot battle of wills.

"Come on in and sit down, kids—dinner's getting cold. David, why don't you say the blessing? Oh, we have so much to be thankful for!"

13

STELLA

"How do we know if it's defrosted enough?" I gazed down at the pale turkey in the roasting pan. "How will we know when it's done?"

"Right here." Mark pointed out a little red plastic dot on the side of the bird. "That pops out when the internal temperature gets high enough."

"Okay." I sighed dutifully and started squirting herb butter and white wine all over the turkey. "If you say so. You sure you don't want to just hit the White Birch and let them deal with all this prep work?"

"Don't worry so much, sweetheart." He rubbed my shoulders with his strong, capable hands. "We'll all pitch in and make dinner together. You, me, and the girls. Who knows? Maybe you and Taylor will end up bonding over the whole thing."

I had woken up drenched in sweat last night, dreaming that Taylor had managed to get me alone with the electric carving knife, but I just smiled sweetly and got back to the bird, which Mark had insisted on soaking in a gourmet sea salt brine that cost as much as a week's worth of groceries. "Now what about the gaping hole in the middle? Do we put stuffing in there, or what?" I peered into the disemboweled body cavity.

He laughed and shook his head. "You wouldn't make much of a chef."

"Nope," I agreed cheerfully. "Cooking is not my thing."

My thing, as we all knew, was kids. But we had agreed to call a truce for Thanksgiving; to pretend, in the fine tradition of our WASPy upbringings, that we looked forward to opening our house to hellish dysfunction and long-simmering feuds. (Also in fine WASPy tradition, we had stocked up on plenty of gin and tonic.) His daughters were coming, and we had to prove that we were deliriously happy and that our May-December (or as Mark liked to say, "more like May-October") marriage was getting stronger every day.

The truth was, we hadn't discussed the letter from the county clerk since that fight in the kitchen. We both knew that bringing up the state of our union was bound to set off another round of extreme fighting about the baby issue. So we skirted the issue and remained carefully, painfully polite with each other.

And Cash was staying. Since my meltdown in Casey's

apartment last week, the dog had refused to leave my side. He curled up under my chair while I ate breakfast, camped outside the bathroom door and whined while I showered, and snuck up onto the bed to sleep between Mark and me at night.

"It's the rescue dog honeymoon phase," Casey had explained when I mentioned this to her. "He's just come out of a scary transition from the shelter and he wants to make sure you're not going anywhere. It's just like having a houseguest—for the first few days, they're quiet and accommodating, but after a few months, they're rummaging through your medicine cabinets and drinking the last Diet Coke without asking."

"All I can say is, if this is the 'honeymoon phase,' we're in trouble when he starts to get comfortable," Mark had grumbled. "And I don't want him in our bed anymore—that's a sacred space for the two of us. Not to mention all the shedding—you know, *you're* the one who insisted on the white sheets. If we had gotten a maltipoo—a little, nonshedding maltipoo—we wouldn't have these problems."

But the big, dramatic "it's the dog or me" ultimatum had turned out to be an empty threat. I took it as a very good sign. If he could compromise on the dog issue, he could compromise on the baby issue, right?

"*Down,* Cash." Mark shoved Cash's head away from the turkey as the dog propped his front paws up on the counter. "Down."

"You don't have to get violent," I huffed, crouching down to scratch Cash's ears.

"Stella. Please. That was hardly violent. I just don't want this mongrel getting dirt and slobber on my kitchen counter."

"He's not a mongrel, and he's not dirty," I defended. "I just gave him a bath last night."

"Yes, I noticed the profusion of black fur clogging the Jacuzzi drain. And point of information, sweetie: Cash is, by definition, a mongrel."

"Well, so what?" I asked hotly. "He's a good boy and he loves us—"

"He loves *you,*" Mark corrected.

"Maybe he'd love you, too, if you weren't constantly shoving him and—"

The doorbell chimed, startling both of us. Cash bounded for the door, barking up a storm.

"See?" I said, checking my reflection in the freshly Windexed microwave door. "He's a good watchdog."

"He's a legal liability on our homeowner's insurance," Mark retorted. "Not to mention an egregious bed hog." He grabbed Cash's collar, dragged him into the laundry room, and shut the door. "No bark," he warned as Cash started to whimper.

Then we clasped hands, plastered toothy grins on our faces, and threw open the front door. "Hiii! Welcome to the new house! So glad you could make it!"

Taylor and Marissa stood on the stoop, making a big production of shivering despite their cashmere scarves and thick wool coats.

"Daddy, I'm freezing!" Marissa exclaimed, swooping into her father's embrace. She had inherited his wavy brunette hair and aristocratic cheekbones, but she had her mother's stunning green eyes and flawless skin. Not that I'd ever met Brenda. But I'd seen pictures—Taylor had made sure of that.

As Marissa moved on from Mark to give me a meek, formal "Happy Thanksgiving," Taylor swept into the foyer, not bothering to close the door behind her.

"Hmm." Her calculating brown eyes raked over the chandelier, the artwork, the baseboards that Cash had been gnawing on yesterday. "I like what you've done to the place."

This stunned me into responding. "Thank you."

"There's only so much you can do to customize these McMansions, but you've done a decent job." She nodded appraisingly. "Given the shoddy construction and the clusterfuck architecture, this place doesn't look half bad. I mean, it's nothing like our old house on the Hill, but they just don't build 'em like that anymore."

Ah, yes. The house on Spruce Hill, Alden's ritziest neighborhood for local bigwigs and wealthy summer people. The house that Mark had deeded to Brenda during the divorce.

Marissa's eyes got huge as she glanced toward Mark, but Taylor just sauntered down the hall, taking off her coat and scarf as she went. Since I'd seen snapshots of her as a child, I knew she'd been born a brunette like Marissa, but now she had bleached her hair platinum, and that, in addition to her willowy height, preppy sense of style, and deep-rooted self-confidence . . . well, quite frankly, she scared the bejesus out of me.

Mark ignored the McMansion dig and forced a good-natured chuckle. "All right, girls, roll up your sleeves! We're all going to help Stella with dinner. Won't that be fun?"

Marissa waited a few beats before murmuring, "I guess" and handing me her coat.

"You invited us over to do scullery work?" Taylor sniffed. "Daddy. You know I'm not the culinary type."

"Well, neither is Stella." he said. "It's her first time making Thanksgiving dinner, and we're all going to help. We're starting a new tradition around here—egalitarian holidays. Why should the hostess have to do all the work?"

"I don't know," Taylor snickered. I could hear her opening cabinets in the kitchen. "Maybe because she's the *hostess?*"

Mark squeezed my hand. "Taylor Lillian Porter . . ."

"What's in here?" Taylor asked. One second later, she started to shriek. "Agh! Ow! Oh my God, Daddy, get it off me! *Get it off me!*"

We sprinted into the kitchen to find Taylor pinned to the travertine tile floor beneath Cash's massive front paws. He panted up at me and wagged his tail proudly.

"Good boy," I mouthed while Mark and Marissa rushed over to pull the dog off my stepdaughter.

"Ick!" Taylor wiped at her face. "I've been slimed! Since when do you have a vicious attack dog?"

"Sorry, I should've warned you." Mark lapsed into full divorced-father guilt mode. He didn't ask her why she'd felt entitled to peer into every last nook and cranny of a house that didn't belong to her. He just handed her a clean white dish towel and kept groveling. "That's Stella's new dog."

"*Our* new dog," I corrected. "Cash. He loves meeting new people."

Marissa looked like she might start giggling, then decided against it.

"Well, your dog owes me a new sweater." Taylor scowled down at her argyle knit. "And a facial." She wiped off the drool, along with most of her lipstick, blush, and eyeliner.

"So sorry," I said. "He just doesn't know his own strength. Now who wants to help me peel potatoes?"

"I do!" Mark volunteered.

"Okay, and who wants to chop celery for the stuffing?"

Dead silence.

I tried again. "What about making the gravy?"

"Can't." Taylor matched my simpering smile. "I'm a vegetarian. I don't touch meat products."

"Since when are you a vegetarian?" Mark demanded.

"For years, Daddy! Duh. Don't you know anything about your own daughter?"

Marissa glanced at Taylor as if to ask permission before venturing, "I'll help with the gravy."

"Thank you," I said gratefully. "Okay, Taylor, that leaves you with the squash and the dinner rolls."

She pointedly examined her French manicure and said nothing.

I tried to remember that I was married now, a grown woman of twenty-four who should not have to resort to middle-school mind games to deal with Taylor. Even though we were almost the same age, I was her stepmother. It was wrong to feed her rivalry for Mark's affections. I needed to take a step back and try to feel some compassion. I should try to feel . . . maternal.

"Okay." I stepped in just as Mark started to lecture Taylor about the importance of family teamwork. "It's okay. She wasn't expecting kitchen duty. It's fine, Mark, really."

Mark looked relieved. Taylor looked homicidal.

"She can set the table. Come on, I'll show you where we keep the china." I led Taylor into the dining room.

She crossed her arms over her chest and sulked.

I inhaled. I exhaled. "Taylor. Babe. Work with me. I'm try-ing to be nice."

She slitted her eyes and lowered her voice. "Don't bother. You fooled my father, you may have even fooled my sister, but you're not going to fool me. I know what you are."

"Hmm." I nodded, trying to stay calm and analytical. "I'm sorry to hear you're upset."

She looked ready to claw our mahogany dining room table with her sharpened nails. "I bet you are."

"But eventually, things will get better between us. Someday, maybe we can be friends."

"Death first." She slammed open the china hutch, snatched up a delicate, platinum-rimmed plate, and brought it down hard on the table. Shards of china flew everywhere, including into the palm of her hand.

The conversation in the kitchen halted. Cash started barking furiously.

"Whoa! Everything okay in there?" Mark called.

Taylor glared at me for a moment, then started crying. "I dropped a plate, Daddy—it was an accident, I swear. But my hand's bleeding and I feel dizzy and oh, can't someone please put that dog outside? He's giving me a headache."

Mark shot into the dining room. "You feel dizzy? Your head hurts?"

"Uh-huh." Taylor stuck out her bottom lip and clutched her injured hand to her chest.

Marissa raised her eyebrows as she looked from me to Taylor, but she didn't say anything.

"Maybe you hit your head on the tile when the dog knocked you over," Mark suggested. "Maybe you're getting a concussion."

"He has a name," I interjected. "Cash."

Mark turned to me, irritated. "Well, do us all a favor and put *Cash* out in the backyard, okay?"

"It's frigid out there." I pointed to the flurry of snow falling outside the window.

"He's got a fur coat, he can take it." Mark put an arm around Taylor's shoulder and steered her into the guest powder room. "Sit down right here, honey, okay? Now follow my finger . . . look up, look down . . . do you feel like you're going to throw up? Do you hear ringing in your ears?"

Ten minutes later, Taylor had secured her place as queen bee, curled up on the half-eaten white sofa with a chenille afghan, a cup of chamomile tea, and the TV remote. "Daddy," she called.

Mark once again abandoned his potato-peeling duties and trotted off to wait on her. Two minutes later, he popped his head around the doorjamb. "Listen, Stell, can you take over for me for a few minutes? *It's a Wonderful Life* is on and Taylor wants me to watch with her."

I looked up from the diced celery in disbelief. "You're not serious?"

"I used to watch it with the girls every year when they were little, and ever since the divorce . . ." He shrugged. "It means a lot to her. I'll only be a few minutes. Just until the commercial break."

"Daaaddy!" came the high-pitched wail from the next room.

"Fine." I gripped the chef's knife and resumed chopping. "Go ahead. Whatever."

Two minutes later, Taylor called, "Hey, 'Rissa! Come here a sec!"

Marissa's face turned bright red as she glanced from the sauce simmering on the stove top to me.

"Marissa! Hurry! It's your favorite part!"

"Go ahead," I said, waving her toward the door. "Go. Don't feel bad. I'll just . . . do everything myself."

And I did. While *It's a Wonderful Life* segued into *Miracle on 34th Street* (another fond childhood favorite, as it turned out), I slaved over the turkey and the trimmings. I let Cash out of the laundry room and he sat loyally by the stove, waiting for me to reward his patience with munchies. Three hours later, the turkey was dry, the potatoes were lumpy, the stuffing was singed, and the gravy had congealed into a brown paste, but dinner was as ready as it was going to get.

"Okay, you guys!" I yelled toward the family room. "Dinner is served."

All I heard in response was the sweeping violin from the movie's sound track. So I set the table and arranged the food artfully on the starched linen tablecloth. Even Casey would have been proud of my presentation.

"Hel-looo! *Dinner is served!*" I hollered down the hall.

Still nothing.

Trying to think charitable, holiday-appropriate thoughts, I marched into the family room. Mark, Marissa, and Taylor were watching the TV with slack-jawed fascination while snacking from a plate of cheese and crackers they'd somehow smuggled in from the kitchen, presumably while I'd been on a bathroom break.

I gasped. "You've spoiled your appetites!"

"No, no," Mark assured me, brushing crumbs off his sweater. "We just needed a little something to tide us over. Because, uh, everything smells so good."

"*So* good." Taylor smirked. "I gather you charbroiled the turkey. Very nouvelle cuisine."

I dug my fingernails into my palms. "Let's just eat, okay?"

"Okay." Mark nodded. "As soon as this scene is over."

I snatched the remote out of Taylor's hand and snapped off the TV. "Now."

Mark couldn't have looked more shocked if I'd slapped him. "Stella!"

"What? I've worked very hard to make a nice dinner for us, and I would like us to please sit down before it gets cold." I paused, searching for one of those academic phrases he was forever throwing around. "I.e., right now."

In the long pause that followed, we heard it—the clinking of china from the dining room.

"What the hell?" Mark led the charge down the hall, where we found the shredded turkey carcass lying on the rug, the bowl that had previously contained mashed potatoes empty, and the bread basket overturned. Under the table, Cash rolled over onto his back, wagging his tail as he licked his chops.

"My food." Tears flooded into my eyes. "My dinner. All my hard work."

Behind me, Taylor started to snicker.

"Oh, sweetheart." Mark put one arm around me. "I'm so sorry."

This just made me tearier.

He cleared his throat. "But, you know, I did ask you to put the dog outside."

14

CASEY

When the doorbell rang on Thanksgiving Day, my heart soared as I ran to answer it. Nick had come back! He'd finally decided to put me first! Finally—we could start behaving like a real married couple.

"Hang on," I called as I wrestled with the shiny security chain. When I finally got the door open, I found . . ."*Erin?*"

"Hi." She was leaning against the porch railing wearing loose black pants, her puffy green parka, and a scowl that suggested she'd chugged a whole quart of vinegar on the ride over.

"Uh-oh. What happened?" I stepped back into the entry-way and motioned her inside.

The scowl deepened. "Thanksgiving with Renée. That's what happened. Listen, I'm sorry to barge in unannounced like this, but if I stayed in that house one more second, I was going to do something that would cost me my medical license. And my family's in California, and all my other friends are in Boston, and I don't want them to know that David and I are . . . well, that we're spending Thanksgiving like this."

"No problem. Think of me as the newlywed halfway house." I shut the door and held out a hand for her coat. "Did Renée start with the peanuts again?"

"I didn't have time to find out." Erin's hands shook a bit as she shucked off her parka. *"She's moving in."*

My eyebrows shot up to my hairline. "I thought you said David—"

"He talked to her. I talked to her. Everyone talked to her, but there's no stopping the mother-in-law from hell. Our guest room is filled with her luggage right now. And once she's in . . ." Erin shuddered. "We'll never get her out."

"Wow."

"Yeah. She wins." Erin's eyes were bleak. "I lose. She's got my husband, my house, my Thanksgiving dinner . . . it's all over."

"You're in shock." I walked her over to the sofa and made her sit. "But it's not over between you and David. Everything's going to be fine."

Erin shook her head. "No, you don't understand. Once Renée's in the house with us . . . I'd heard all those clichés about you don't just marry the man, you marry his whole family, but . . ." She slumped back into the cushions. "The power. The evil. My God, I had no idea."

There was only one appropriate response to this. "I'll make coffee." While the Colombian roast brewed, I arranged some of my homemade Christmas cookies on a hand-painted seasonal plate and brought them out to Erin.

"You need to eat," I said firmly.

"I can't."

"You have to." I thrust the plate toward her. "Come on now—have a gingerbread man. One hundred percent peanut-free. You need your strength to plan your counterattack."

While Erin nibbled the arms off a gingerbread man, I sat down on the ottoman next to her. "I'm glad you came over. Thanksgiving just isn't the same unless I get to play hostess."

She stopped nibbling and looked around. "Hey. Where's Nick?"

I folded my hands primly in my lap. "Detroit."

She waited for me to elaborate, and when I didn't, she ventured, "Is there something you want to tell me?"

"No." I laughed bitterly. "I have the perfect husband, haven't you heard? I landed the catch to end all catches. He just happens to prefer spending Thanksgiving in Michigan to spending it with his wife."

"But I thought you two were going over to his parents' house?"

"We were. But then his friends called up yesterday morning and said they had extra tickets for the Lions game in Michigan today and anyone who wanted to see 'football history in the making' should pile in for the road trip."

Erin whistled. "Oh boy."

I smiled pleasantly. "'Oh boy' is right."

She handed the cookie platter back to me. "I think you need these more than I do."

"He hasn't even called to check in since he left. It's a ten-hour drive, and I know he brought his cell phone."

"Well . . ." She took another bite of gingerbread to stall. "You know how guys are. Maybe he just forgot?"

I snorted. "Has David ever forgotten to call you on a major holiday?"

Erin shrugged. "It's never been an issue. Ever since we moved in together, we've spent the holidays together. Us and Renée."

"At least he doesn't leave you to explain to his family why he couldn't be bothered to show up for your first married Thanksgiving. His mom and dad are *livid* that he took off; I tried to smooth things over, but they just went off on this rant about how he hasn't been the same since he quit law school."

"They sound lovely."

"No, they are, actually, but Nick was supposed to get his JD and take over his dad's firm and marry Julia, his girlfriend from law school, and instead, well, he quit after his second year and married me. It's a little embarrassing for them."

Erin cocked her head. "Why on earth would they be embarrassed?"

"Because I'm, you know."

"What?" she prompted.

"You know." I lowered my voice. "White trash."

"Casey, don't be ridiculous!"

"Says the woman with the Harvard MD. It's easy for you to laugh, sure, but I grew up in a trailer park with my mom, her assorted live-in boyfriends, no dad, clothes from Goodwill, and a sister who slept with literally every single member of the football team. The Nestor girls are legendary in this town, and not in a good way."

Erin shook her head. "But you're not your mom or your sister. Just because they made mistakes—"

"Let me ask you something. You're a fancy Ivy Leaguer like Nick's parents; is my family the kind of family you'd want *your* child marrying into?"

She couldn't maintain eye contact. "Your family doesn't make you who you are."

"But they're part of the package. You said it yourself—you don't just marry a person, you marry their whole family."

"I can see how it would be hard to grow up in a small town like this with a family like that, but don't you think you're being a little too sensitive? I mean, look at you now! You're a pillar of the community! You went to college, you own your own business, you do volunteer work for the local animal-rescue groups—"

"I married a nice boy from a nice family," I finished for her. "Only problem is, he's too good for me and everyone knows it. Including him."

"Is that what you really think?" Erin asked incredulously. "Nick Keating is too good for you?"

"Let's look at the facts: I initiated moving in together. I'm the one who kept bringing up marriage. I had to . . ." I wanted to confess that I'd sort of had to propose to him, but that sounded too pathetic, so I said, "I had to buy my own engagement ring."

She helped herself to a chocolate macaroon and jabbed it toward the tiny diamond sparkling on my left hand. "You paid for that?"

"Pretty much." I gnawed the inside of my cheek. "He was paying off a lot of debt at the time, and—"

"And *he's* too good for *you?*" Erin spewed a few cookie crumbs in her vehemence. "Do you hear yourself?"

I started to shake this off, saying, "You don't know the whole story," but she was having none of it.

"Casey, I don't care how hunky he was in high school. That was twelve years ago. He should be down on his knees kissing your feet!"

"We balance each other out," I insisted. "I'm controlling and judgmental. He's a free spirit. I'm incredibly hard to live with—"

"And he's not?"

I thought about the pipe wrench on the rim of the tub.

"I guess," I said grudgingly. "I just always wanted him so much. He didn't even look at me when we were teenagers; I was twenty-seven when he finally asked me out—"

"When he finally smartened up, you mean." Erin snorted.

"He had just moved home after he left law school and happened to be driving by when my truck got a flat out by Waronoke Pond. He stopped to help me change the tire, and he looked at me and I looked at him . . . it was straight out of a movie, I tell you." The memory still made me smile. "I knew exactly who he was, of course, but he didn't remember me. He didn't realize we'd gone to school together until I told him, on our third date. I was so thrilled to finally be with him—"

"Okay, you need to stop with the hero worship. If you aren't an equal partner in the relationship, you're screwed. Reality check: he's just a *guy*. A cute guy, I'll give you that, but a *guy*. With plenty of faults and questionable commitment to his marriage."

"Not true." I shook my head. "Nick would never cheat on me. I worry about a lot of things, but that's not one of them."

"He doesn't have to cheat to check out of the relationship," she pointed out. "He's in *Detroit*. What did he say when he found out you guys weren't legally married?"

I leapt to my feet. "Coffee's ready! Would you like cream and sugar?"

"Don't insult me with these transparent diversionary tactics. What did he say?"

"Not much, actually."

Erin furrowed her brow. "Did you guys already make it official at the courthouse? Jeez, you're so efficient."

"No, we haven't made it to the courthouse yet." I retreated to the kitchen.

"Wait!" She jumped up and followed me. "What is going on with you?"

I turned my back on her and stared into the cupboard at the orderly rows of matching blue mugs. "Here's the thing. I haven't exactly told him yet."

I heard her sharp intake of breath.

"Don't be all—" I imitated her scandalized gasp. "It was hard enough getting him down that aisle the first time. And now whenever we have a fight, whenever we have to scramble to pay the rent and the heating bill and the lease on the store, he breaks out the same old line: *You're the one who had to get married.*'"

She made a face. "And why do you want to be legally bound to this guy, again?"

"Because I love him!" I exploded. "And he loves me. In our own twisted way, we make each other happy."

Erin looked like she was struggling to hold her tongue.

"And don't give me that look," I added. "Because yes, we are happy. Or we were, anyway. Before the wedding."

"If you say so."

"I do say so." I poured piping hot coffee into the mugs, spilling a bit with uncharacteristic clumsiness. "I can handle my own husband. Besides. Don't you have your own faux marriage to save?"

Erin wrapped both hands around her coffee mug as if trying to absorb the warmth through the ceramic. "Don't remind me. Listen, have you eaten yet?"

"Nope. I made a pumpkin pie for Nick's parents, but his mom was going to cook most of the meal."

"I'm starving," she declared. "Absolutely famished."

Suddenly, I was starving, too. "I have a homemade lasagna in the freezer," I volunteered.

"Sounds delicious."

While we were waiting for our makeshift Thanksgiving dinner to defrost in the oven, we flipped on the TV and watched the tail end of *Miracle on 34th Street*.

"Just think," Erin said, tucking her stocking feet up under her on the couch. "All over America, normal, happy families are watching this and getting along and eating turkey and stuffing."

"No, they're not," I replied. "They're all bickering and criticizing each other and sneaking secret gulps of booze in the garage. There's no such thing as a normal family."

As soon as Erin heard the words "bickering and criticizing," she sat bolt upright. "Oh, crap, that reminds me—I have to call my parents." I excused myself to the bedroom to give her some privacy while she dialed her cell.

I collapsed into the smushy down comforter on the bed and mulled over what Erin had said. Maybe she had a point. What was more important: marriage or football?

The frustration that had festered inside me all day surged into fury. Who did he think he was, anyway?

I grabbed the cordless phone lying on the nightstand and punched in Nick's cell phone number. He didn't bother to pick up, but that was fine: I could say my piece to his voice mail.

"Hi, honey, how's your trip?" My tone stayed relentlessly upbeat. "I'm calling to give you some news: remember how you didn't want to get married? Well, surprise, you're not! Legal glitch, blah, blah, blah, long story short, we're still technically single! And you get to stay that way, you lucky boy! You always manage to get your way, don't you? I'll have your things packed and waiting on the porch when you come home."

Then I hung up, wrenched off my diamond engagement ring and gold wedding band, and slammed them into the nightstand drawer.

"Casey?" Erin called from the front room. "You okay in there?"

"I'm fantabulous," I announced, storming down the hall to show off my newly naked left hand. "I just broke a few of the chains that bind me."

"Viva la revolution." She raised her fist in solidarity. "Now let's eat. Is the lasagna ready yet?"

We both jumped when we heard the knock at the door.

"Who's that?" Erin whispered.

"I have no idea," I whispered back. "But it better not be Nick."

"Well, it *really* better not be David. Or, oh my God, what if it's Renée?"

"Casey?" wailed a thin little voice on the other side of the door. "Are you home? Please be home, oh please, please, please."

And then we heard a deep, resounding woof.

"Stella?" When I yanked open the door, Cash raced in, nearly knocking me over.

"Yeah, it's me." Stella trudged in behind the dog. Her face was smudged with flour and she smelled of charred meat.

"What happened?" Erin asked, staring at the pair of suitcases resting on the stoop.

"Marriage happened," Stella snapped. "Wedded bliss. Happily ever after. What a crock."

"You left Mark?"

"Hey, something smells good. Are you making pizza?"

Erin and I exchanged a look. "Lasagna," I said. "And if you need a place to stay, you're more than welcome to hole up here for a few days."

"Thank you." She heaved a mighty sigh. "I'll start looking for an apartment tomorrow morning, but I don't know how many building managers will be working the weekend after Thanksgiving."

"An apartment?" Erin repeated. "It's that bad?"

Stella swallowed hard and nodded. "I can't stay with him. And I can't go back to New York—everyone will smirk and say they told me so."

"Who would say that?" I asked.

"*Everyone* would say that. Everyone's been dying to say it ever since Mark and I announced our engagement. And I can't afford rent in Manhattan; I'd have to live with my mother in Westchester County, and even if I could stand living with my mother and listening to her lecture me about the sanctity of marriage every single day, she has to sell the house anyway to pay my father's legal team—"

"Whoa, okay, slow down. You can stay here as long as you need to," I assured her. "There's only one problem—I'm not allowed to have dogs in the apartment. I can sneak one in for a few hours every now and then, but the landlord will freak if he finds out Cash is staying here long-term."

"I can take him," Erin blurted out.

Stella narrowed her eyes. "But you said your mother-in-law had allergies."

Erin's grin was diabolical. "Oh well."

Stella blinked. "I see I'm not the only one who had a horrible Thanksgiving."

I stepped out to the porch to drag the suitcases in. "Make yourself comfortable. You want coffee? Cookies? Lasagna?"

"Lots of everything, please." She rubbed her temples. "And do you have any wine?"

"We definitely need wine," Erin agreed.

"One bottle of wine, coming right up."

"Perfect." Stella sighed. "We'll drink a toast to the end of my marriage."

15

ERIN

It's on, Renée, I thought as Casey waved, then pulled her truck away from the curb in front of my house. *You want my husband? You want my guest room? You'll have to fight me for it.*

"Let's go," I whispered to the hulking black dog beside me. Cash and I crunched through the thin layer of black ice that coated the flagstone path leading up to the front door. Renée's Cadillac was still monopolizing the driveway, but the house windows were dark—David and Mommy Dearest must have given up on me and gone to bed. "You got my back?"

Cash snuffled loudly in response, which sent me into paroxysms of giggles. After polishing off two bottles—maybe three; I'd lost track—of wine, along with most of the lasagna and an entire pumpkin pie, Casey, Stella and I had regained a sense of humor about our Thanksgivings. We'd spent the evening parked in front of the TV, flipping between schmaltzy, soft-lit holiday specials and ESPN, where we had watched the recap of the Detroit Lions football game while Casey yelled obscenities until the neighbors downstairs started jabbing the ceiling with a broom handle. We had all turned off our cell phones, the better to elude the men who had somehow duped us into believing they were marriage material. Despite the inauspicious start to the day, I'd ended up having a marvelous time. So marvelous that Casey had to drive me home.

While I dredged the bottom of my purse for my house keys, I fantasized about my next husband. He would be tall and good looking, of course; smart as a whip with a compassionate spirit and a beguiling European accent. His name would be . . . Hugh, perhaps, and his parents would live overseas. Hugh would whisk me away to a penthouse overlooking a grassy park with cavernous walk-in closets and separate, his-and-her bathrooms. We would never stoop to petty quarrels over who mixed in the recyclables with the trash or how, despite repeated reminders, someone could forget to rinse his beard trimmings out of the sink every single morning.

Yes, life with Hugh would be grand. But before I could track him down and start my new life, I owed it to myself to make a last stand for my marriage. If I left David, it would be on my terms, not Renée's.

The dog whined and pressed his nose into the crack between the door and the jamb as I tried unsuccessfully to connect the key with the lock.

"Shhh," I admonished, swaying on my feet. "I'm going as fast as I can."

Finally, I managed to jam the key into the dead bolt, but before I could twist it, the door burst open.

"Erin?" David's silhouette was barely visible through the dark shadows in the entryway. "Where have you been?"

Before I could answer, the dog muscled his way in and streaked down the hall.

"Cash!" I cried, as David flattened himself against the wall.

"What the hell was that?" David sounded panicked. "Did you find an *animal* out there?"

"Oh, relax, it's just a dog." I couldn't keep the note of disgust out of my voice. *Hugh* would never freak out about a harmless domestic canine.

"Are you sure? It looked like a wolf!"

I shook my head and stepped into the house. "David. Come on. When's the last time you saw a wolf prowling around our front yard? Besides, Cash is way too big to be a wolf. He's a mix between a Great Dane and a Newfoundland, as far as we can tell, and he's Stella Porter's new pet."

"Well, what is it doing in our house?" he demanded.

"I told her we'd dog-sit for a few days."

"Why would you tell her that? You know my mom has allergies." He paused, sniffing my breath. "Where have you been? Have you been drinking?"

"A little bit," I conceded. "My call hours ended at five, so spare me the sanctimony. Did you and your mother have a nice dinner?"

"Help!" Renée started screaming upstairs. "David! Somebody! *Help!*"

"Oh my God, it's mauling her!" David bolted across the living room, tripped over the rocking chair, then picked himself up and pounded up the stairs. A few seconds later, the screaming stopped as yellow lights flooded the landing.

I kicked off my boots and headed for the kitchen to slug back a big glass of water and some ibuprofen to head off tomorrow's hangover.

Before I even made it to the cupboard next to the sink, the bloodcurdling screams started up again.

"No, no, *nooooo,*" Renée wailed. She didn't sound like she'd been mauled. Rather, she sounded like she was about to maul someone else.

"Erin," David called. "Would you come up here, please? Right now?"

"Of course, honey." I fished one of the dog biscuits Stella had given me out of my pocket and padded upstairs to lure Cash out of Renée's room.

"*Right now.*" David sounded like he was two seconds away from a nervous breakdown.

"I'm coming," I snapped back.

"That isn't a dog, it's a demon!" Renée was screeching as I arrived at the doorway to the guest room. "A demon from hell that she conjured up to torment me. All I've ever done is love her! I've treated her like my own daughter and—" She broke off as I waved from the hall.

Cash trotted over and collapsed at my feet. "What seems to be the problem?" I asked.

David was holding his head in both hands. "The dog . . ."

I reached down to scratch behind Cash's ears. "Did he startle you, Renée? I am so sorry."

My mother-in-law looked unexpectedly old and frail in a flowered flannel nightgown. Her hair stuck out at odd angles, and her face, usually powdered and lipsticked to perfection, looked pale and vulnerable. "No, the dog did not *startle* me. He jumped into my bed and tried to kill me while I slept. And then he . . . he . . ."

"He what?" I struggled to swallow back a yawn.

She pointed imperiously toward the middle of her bed.

My eyes snapped open. "Oh."

"Yeah," David said.

Nestled in the folds of the blue-and-yellow plaid duvet was a steaming pile of dog feces.

"Well." I dusted off my hands and started toward the bed. "Let's get this out of your way. I'll get you some fresh blankets."

Renée's face had taken on a purplish tint. "That is the most filthy, disgusting, vile thing I have ever seen in all my born days! This is why I always told you, David, dogs do not belong in the house. Didn't I tell you?"

David looked at me. "Now what?"

I shrugged. "Now I wash the sheets and we go to bed. What else can we do?"

"You are taking that dog back to Stella's tomorrow," he declared.

"I can't."

His face was starting to get a little purple, too. "What do you mean, you can't?"

"I can't," I repeated, bundling up the blankets and heading for the basement door, Cash right on my heels. "I'll explain the whole thing later, but Stella needs us to take care of the dog for a few days."

David followed me, leaving Renée to gnash her teeth upstairs. "Then fob it off on Casey. She's so crazy about animals, let her take care of this unhousebroken beast!"

"Okay, firstly, Casey's not allowed to have dogs in her apartment. Secondly, his name is Cash and he *is* housebroken. He just had a long day and he got a little too excited."

"He shat in my mother's bed!"

"And I'm sure he feels awful about that. Let's talk about this in the morning, okay? It's too late to do anything about it tonight and I'm dead on my feet."

A series of loud, pointed sneezes punctuated the tension crackling between us.

"My mother is allergic," he seethed.

"I'll bring home some Zyrtec samples from the office," I offered.

He glared at me.

"David," Renée called. "David, I need you."

"Go ahead." I shooed him away. "I'll be up in a few minutes."

"This is not over," he warned before stomping off to minister to the hapless victim.

I opened the patio door and unfurled the blanket, dumping Cash's little indiscretion on the back lawn, then wadded the soiled linens into the washing machine. While I waited for the laundry to cycle through, I flopped down on the sofa and propped my head up against a throw pillow.

Four hours later, my cell phone rang, jerking me out of a sound sleep. I was still on the sofa, bleary-eyed and cotton-mouthed, but no longer buzzed. Though I was no longer technically on call, I picked up my phone, checked the Incoming Call number, and groaned.

"Hello?" I mumbled into the receiver.

"Oh, thank God," said Kelly Fendt. "I was praying you'd be there. Listen, Dr. Maye, I know it's late, but I have to see you. It's an emergency."

·　　·　　·

Cash greeted me at the door when I dragged myself home at six a.m. "Hey buddy, you still up?" I left my coat on the entryway floor and slogged upstairs to bed.

"Good morning," I whispered to David, stripping down to my panties and slipping his soft Northeastern T-shirt over my head. "Good night."

He lifted his head from the pillow and fumbled for the alarm clock. "Where'd you go?"

"Kelly Fendt," I said, which was all the explanation he needed.

"Jeez, what was wrong with the kid this time?"

"Nothing. She was convinced his appendix was about to burst because he kept fussing and rolling onto his right side in his crib."

David rubbed his eyes. "And?"

"And I told her to go to the ER in Pittsfield, but she started wailing and carrying on that the ER docs wouldn't know her son's quote-unquote, 'history.'"

"Honey. Kelly Fendt is a lunatic. You know this. You've told me this many times."

"I know, but she's very convincing. So I met her at the office and did an exam, and when I told her it was probably just gas pains, she threatened to sue me for malpractice."

His head plopped back down. "See? Lunatic."

"She kept clutching my hand and begging me to help her, and I knew Dr. Lowell would have a conniption if I blew her off, so I went with her to the ER."

"Seriously?"

"I had to, David. She was hyperventilating and shaking like a junkie."

He looked appalled. "Okay. She may be a lunatic, but you're worse for letting her manipulate you every time."

"Yeah, yeah. So we went to the ER for a surgical evaluation. Just to cover everyone's ass."

"What was their diagnosis?"

"Gas pains." I sighed. "Everything looked normal. The woman is a classic case of Munchausen's. That poor kid is going to grow up to be an OCD, agoraphobic hypochondriac who's never kissed anyone for fear of germs. Either that or a strung-out heavy metal guitarist who eats live reptiles onstage." I peeled back the covers and crawled into bed. Cash followed suit, hopping into the middle of our queen-sized bed and sprawling out next to me.

David's head popped back up. "Excuse me. Why is that dog in our bed?"

"I dunno." I was half-asleep already. "Maybe Stella and her husband let him sleep there."

"Well, we'll have to untrain him." David leapt out of bed, which proved to be a major tactical error—the dog stretched out his long legs and settled into the warm nest of David's vacated blankets.

"Come on, dog." David grabbed Cash's collar and pulled. "The bed is for people only. Off you go."

Cash gave him a disdainful look, closed his eyes, and exhaled loudly.

"Off! Off!" David pulled and pushed and waved his arms, but to no avail. Cash started snoring. "Get up and help me, Erin. Erin?"

"Shhh," I said, pulling David's pillow over my head. "I'm sleeping. We'll deal with this later."

"You're just going to lie there and let a dog take my rightful place in our bed?"

But I was sinking gratefully into a tranquil haze where histrionic mothers and intrusive in-laws and incendiary piles of dog poop didn't exist.

When I woke up at noon, the phone was ringing and Cash was still snuggled up beside me. I could smell the sharp tang of fresh coffee drifting up from the kitchen, and David was nowhere in sight. I rolled out of bed and opened my closet, scowling at the neatly hung rows of earth tones and pleats and sensible loafers. Nothing bright, nothing flashy, nothing remotely appealing. Where was the camouflage miniskirt when I needed it?

When I came downstairs to the kitchen, David and Renée were huddled around the newspaper, sipping coffee and grousing about the pothole in front of our house that the town council refused to fix until spring. They looked up disapprovingly as I swanned in wearing jeans and the only relic I could find from my bar-dancing days: a tight black sweater cut indecently low.

"Who was on the phone?" I asked, praying that Kelly Fendt hadn't gotten hold of my home number.

Renée frowned as if she'd just swallowed a spoonful of sodden coffee grinds. "Just that pesky Henry Reynolds, wanting to know if I had a good Thanksgiving. I told him that my husband has been dead five years, my son barely spoke a word to me after I slaved all day in the kitchen, and my daughter-in-law stomped out before we even sat down, then came home drunk with a filthy animal that . . . well, how *could* I have a good Thanksgiving?"

I ignored all the barbs and instead teased, "I think someone has a crush on you."

She sniffed. "Nonsense. I've told him a hundred times I'm not interested."

I poured myself a huge mugful of java. "Then why'd you give him our phone number?"

Renée rustled the newspaper and refused to respond.

"Did *he* have a good Thanksgiving, at least?" I prompted.

"I didn't ask," she said sourly.

"Where's your new best friend?" David demanded.

"Still sleeping." I crossed over to the table and kissed the top of his head. "Where'd you end up last night?"

"The couch," he grumbled. "We're giving that dog back to Stella today."

"Can't do it," I replied brightly.

"Erin." David shot a sidelong glance at Renée, who was

clearly fascinated by the argument brewing between us. "You have to."

"The only thing I have to do today is shop," I said.

Renée was aghast. "On Black Friday? Have you lost your mind?"

"Just my fashion sense. I need some cute clothes like nobody's business. Casey's picking me up in twenty minutes. We're going to the mall." I hitched up my jeans and told Renée, "I'm going to get you the best Christmas present ever."

"Erin . . . ," David warned.

"Have a good day, sweetie. And don't forget to walk the dog."

16

STELLA

So did Nick ever call you back?" Erin asked Casey as we browsed the Macy's makeup counters. We had already torn through the lingerie and coat sections like a tornado, and now we had moved on to lipstick.

"I have no idea—I turned off my cell phone and unplugged the land line." Casey's voice was badass, but her eyes looked miserable. "He can stay in Detroit till spring thaw, for all I care."

"So I take it you still haven't told him you're not legally married?" Erin pressed.

I turned to Casey, my mouth open. "You haven't told him yet?"

"Oh, I told him. On his voice mail. And then I told him hell would freeze over before I'd remarry him." Casey set her jaw. "Forget it. I already called our landlord, and the locksmith is coming on Monday. It's *my* apartment. I'm the one who signed the lease."

"Surely he'll be back by Monday," Erin said, dabbing a bit of blush onto the apples of her cheeks.

"Who knows?" Casey rubbed a mauve lipstick sample on the inside of her wrist. "Maybe he'll take a road trip to Mexico to celebrate his return to bachelorhood. Maybe he'll run off to Anna Delano's house and shack up with her. But you know what? I don't care."

"Maybe you care a little," I said gently, replacing the mauve lipstick with a wine-red shade. "Here, this is more your color."

"I don't care!" She smeared the red lipstick on top of the mauve with bright-eyed fury. "I don't! If he doesn't want to be with me, no one's got a gun to his head. Let him run off with Anna—she's wanted him since eighth grade. *She* can do all the cooking and cleaning and turn off *her* shower with a wrench. I'll find someone better, someone who really appreciates me."

"Like Hugh," Erin said dreamily.

I frowned at her. "Who?"

"Nothing." She stared down at the blush palette.

"Give me that." I took the blush away from her. "Stay away from oranges, okay? You're a summer. You want pinks and lavenders."

"I hate pick and lavender," she protested. "I want blacks and reds. And leopard print."

"Don't you work in a medical office?" I reminded her. "Like, with infants?"

She rolled her eyes. "Not for work. For after work."

"For all the fancy nightclubs in Alden?" Casey said dryly.

Erin shifted her weight from foot to foot. "I used to be cute, okay? I was the party girl of my med school class. I was notorious!"

I managed to keep my mouth shut as I looked her over: severe, shoulder-length brown hair, faded jeans, and her puffy parka. No makeup, no jewelry except for her wedding rings, and flat, roomy loafers.

Erin caught me staring. "What?"

My gaze zoomed back to the nail polish samplers. "Nothing."

"What? You think I'm boring, don't you? Old and boring and blah."

"No, I don't."

"Yes, you do! Every guy who walks through this store looks at you. You! No one even notices Casey and me."

"Hey," Casey protested.

"Well, it's true," Erin insisted. "No sense denying it. Stella looks like Angelina Jolie's little sister and we . . . and I . . ." She sucked in giant gulps of air. "I'm just *stuck* here. Forever."

"Oh, boy." Casey grabbed her arm and towed her through the crowd toward the exit. "Existential crisis time."

"It's okay," I said as Casey plowed ahead, parting the crowd like a bouncer. "Deep breaths."

"I'll never get out," Erin wheezed. "It'll be me and Renée and Kelly Fendt and the petty office politics and my drafty used car until I drop dead."

"No," I promised. "You can leave anytime you want. You're from Harvard Med—any hospital would kill to hire you."

"That's what I thought, once upon a time." She tumbled forward into the jewelry counter. "But then I emailed one of my coworkers last week, asking if the hospital might want to hire me, and I never heard back. That means no. That means he asked and he doesn't want to hurt my feelings. I left the fast track and I can never go back."

Casey's ears pricked up. "'He'?"

"Oh," I said, nodding. "Hugh, right?"

Erin laughed. "No, Jonathan. We were residents together, we dated for about two weeks and now we're like brother and sister. David hates him."

"Is he good looking?" Casey persisted.

"Casey. What'd I just say? Brother and sister. Besides, I'm married."

"No, you're not," Casey pointed out. "None of us are. And just because you don't want a perfectly good eligible doctor doesn't mean I don't. I'm back on the market, girl. I am on the *prowl!*"

Erin and I both stopped and stared at her.

"What?" Casey put her hands on her hips. "I am."

"Your husband's only been gone twenty-four hours," I pointed out.

"For the last time, he's not my husband. I need a new man."

Erin was getting pretty worked up, too. "I need a new job. What have I done? What have I done?"

Seeing Erin's distress, a multipierced teenage sales clerk rushed over and asked, "Are you all right, ma'am? Do you need me to call someone?"

"Oh God," Erin keened, closing her eyes in despair. "She ma'amed me."

"We're fine." Casey flashed the clerk a confident smile, then half-dragged Erin out to the food court.

Hundreds of surly, slow-moving Black Friday shoppers, all carrying bulky shopping bags, pressed in on us.

"Coming through." Casey pushed through the crowd with the calm authority of a paramedic. "Excuse me. Coming through." She swooped in on a wobbly table littered with napkins and ketchup packets just as another pair of women stepped up to claim it.

"Hey!" exclaimed a blonde in too-tight jeans. "This is our table!"

"Yeah, we got here first," agreed a snub-nosed redhead who looked like blondie's sister. "And we've been on our feet all day—got up at four thirty this morning to hit the sales."

"Sorry." Casey shrugged as she sat down in one chair and

slung her shopping bags into the other. "But to the swift goes the race."

The blonde and the redhead exchanged exasperated glances but started stalking someone else's table as Erin and I shuffled up.

"Sit." Casey shoved a chair toward Erin with her foot. "Stella, you go get her some ice water."

"I don't need ice water," Erin insisted. "I just need my old life back. Me and David, living in the city. With Renée on the other side of the state."

"Ice water, stat," Casey repeated, as if she were the MD instead of Erin. "Maybe you better get some chocolate ice cream, too."

"No ice cream." Erin crossed her arms. "No dillydallying. I'm going to go buy a leopard-print thong. Maybe a matching garter belt, too."

Casey looked at her for a moment. "Erin. You realize that putting on exotic underwear isn't going to magically transport you back to Boston."

Erin didn't say anything.

"And you realize that it's not going to get your mother-in-law out of your house? Or make you twenty-one again?"

"I don't need water," Erin insisted. "I need air. I'm suffocating."

I darted over to the fast-food counter with the shortest line and ordered the largest ice water they had, which turned out to be a plastic cup roughly the size of a wading pool. When I fought my way back to the table, Erin and Casey were deep in conversation.

Erin was gesturing helplessly, her eyes bleak. ". . . I thought I was going into this with my eyes wide open. We were mature, we finished school, we had our finances in order, we talked about goals . . ."

Casey nodded. "I know! Nick and I went to all these couples retreats—well, one; I signed us up for three, but he refused to go back after the first one—and I read all these books on what to expect before, during, and after the wedding."

I tried to join in, but the two of them were on a roll.

"It wasn't just about the white dress and the diamond ring," Erin continued. "I was serious about it. I still am."

"Yeah, but no one ever tells you what happens after the honeymoon," Casey finished. "How could they? You can't understand what it's like until you're knee-deep in it."

"And if you're on the outside, you have no idea what it's like on the inside," Erin said. "And then you end up at the mall on the day after Thanksgiving, having a nervous breakdown at the Clinique counter and trying to fill the gaping holes in your life with leopard-print thongs. Pathetic."

I cleared my throat. "I'm back. Here's your ice water."

"Thanks, Stella." Erin smiled absently up at me, like she was the major-league player and I was the bat boy. Then she went right back to Casey. "And they say it gets worse when you have children—the in-law drama, I mean."

"You can't think like that," Casey said firmly. "You have to take it one day at a time or you'll go nuts."

I fidgeted, unable to contribute. It was too late for me to take anything one day at a time. Everyone who warned me not to rush into marriage had been right. I was a failure, and for the rest of my life, I would have to live with the reality that my choice of a husband—legal or not—had been a mistake.

"I think I'm going to get some ice cream," I announced, keeping my head down as I turned away from the table. "You guys want anything?"

They waved me away, and as soon as I got in line at Ben & Jerry's, a young mother queued up behind me, pushing a double stroller containing what I assumed were twins—a boy and a girl, both with defiant cowlicks in their soft brown hair. The boy was humming to himself and kicking the stroller in time with his tune. The little girl was drifting off to sleep, her thumb in her mouth as she stroked her cheek with her plump little fingers.

A quick look at the mom's ring finger confirmed that she was married. Probably to a guy her own age, who'd come into the marriage without any ex-wives or hateful daughters or secret vasectomies.

I stepped out of the line and into the crowd, trying to put as much distance between myself and those twins as I could. But the mall's corridors were packed with shoppers, and after two minutes of mincing along at a glacial pace, I lost patience and ducked into the nearest store, a froufrou bath boutique full of scented shower gels and organic soaps.

Inhaling deeply, I willed my tense shoulders and clenched fists to relax. Aromatherapy—that's what I needed. As long as I was in here, I should pick up some lavender bath oil and a sea-weed face mask. Then I could go home, fill up the Jacuzzi . . .

But wait. I couldn't go home and fill up the Jacuzzi because I didn't live there anymore. I'd have to go back to Casey's, rinse out the bathtub, turn on the faucet with a wrench, and hope the hot water didn't run out, which Casey had warned me it often did.

I leaned forward to sniff a red-striped block of peppermint soap when I heard Taylor's voice. Right behind me.

"You should have seen her, Mom. Crying over the slimy re-mains of the turkey. The whole thing was hilarious."

"Well, your father never was one to help out in the kitchen," replied an amused, cultured voice with a hint of a Boston accent. "Remember the time I put him in charge of the appetizers and the fire department had to come out?"

Taylor giggled. "I think the whole neighborhood remem-bers. But honestly, she's worse than he is! Thank God their dis-gusting dog ate the whole dinner."

"Don't be catty, sweetpea." But the tone was indulgent.

I froze, my face inches away from the scented soap, afraid that if I turned my head even an inch to the side, I'd be recog-nized.

"Well, anyway, that's the last Thanksgiving I'll have to spend with *her*." Taylor sounded overjoyed. "They had a huge fight right in front of me and Marissa—about the dog, of all things—and she packed a bag and left. What a hag."

"Lots of people have fights over the holidays—I'm sure they'll work it out."

"Daddy doesn't think so," Taylor announced triumphantly. "He says she's gone for good and he knew it was coming all along."

"Really." Her mother sounded skeptical. "He said that?"

"Yep. He was as mad as she was, maybe madder. I swear, if he'd had a bottle of champagne in the house, he would've opened it."

My eyes started to water from the overpowering smell of peppermint.

"Good-bye and good riddance. That's what he said. And she deserves it! Like he didn't give her everything she ever asked for. That gigantic diamond ring, for starters. I can't even believe how much he spent on that thing. He said he was going to buy me a new car last summer, but as soon as *she* came along . . . And they didn't even last six months."

"Hmm." The other voice was still skeptical. "Well, she's young, you know. Very young."

"Not that young," Taylor shot back. "She's the same age as me, and I know enough not to have tantrums just because some stupid turkey didn't turn out perfect."

"Well, it's your father's marriage, not ours. So really, it's none of our business."

"Ha! My family, my business. She's a *nanny*, Mom. It's so clichéd. And she's not even that pretty."

Taylor extended her forearm to spritz a sample of body splash on her wrist. A blast of vanilla-scented chemicals assaulted my nostrils.

I started sneezing and couldn't stop. My eyes squeezed shut as I braced myself against the counter with one hand and tried to cover my mouth with the other.

"Ugh," Taylor said loudly. "It's so inconsiderate to go out in public if you're sick. Stay home and keep your germs to yourself." Then she looked up from her vial of vanilla long enough to meet my eyes. "Holy shit."

"My sentiments exactly." I crossed my arms, rocked back on my heels, and took a good, long look at the woman who'd been married to my husband before me.

Brenda Porter had the long, reddish hair, porcelain complexion, and regal composure of a titled English lady. Her face looked like one of the old oil portraits hanging in the Clark Art Institute in Williamstown. In her well-cut black trench coat and knotted silk scarf, she looked like the kind of woman who'd never made a fool of herself or raised her voice—not even when giving birth to her demon spawn. Mark told me she'd been standoffish and hated to try new things, but as I looked at her, I was consumed with envy. She'd been with the man I loved, and look how much better she'd handled herself. *She'd* held on to him for fifteen years. *She'd* always kept her home warm and inviting, with no anarchist dogs. *She'd* convinced Mark to have babies (even if they had turned out to be demon spawn).

Basically, she was everything I wanted to be when I grew up, and I really had to fight the urge to cram the entire bar of peppermint soap down her throat.

"Well, speak of the devil." Taylor turned to her mother with a smug little smirk. "Mom, this is Stella, Dad's new—and soon-to-be ex-wife."

"How do you do." Brenda extended her right hand.

Taylor looked pointedly at my left hand. "I notice you're still wearing the diamond."

"Oh my God." My voice was sharp. "Why are you so obsessed with this little piece of rock?"

"There's nothing little about it." Taylor fluffed her hair. Brenda didn't encourage her daughter, but she didn't make any move to intervene, either. "You could put someone's eye out with that thing."

"Don't give me any ideas."

Taylor lifted her chin. "See, Mom? I told you she was immature."

"*I'm* immature?" I squeaked with outrage. "I'm not the one who ruined Thanksgiving!"

"You're the one who burned the entire meal, then let the

dog eat it all, then started screaming and left your husband. So actually, I'd say you *are* the one who ruined Thanksgiving. Plus, you robbed me of my rightful convertible."

"Here." I grabbed my engagement ring and yanked it off. "Here! If a car means that much to you, then here! Take the damn thing and go cash it in!"

I slapped the diamond into her hand, hoping the ring's prongs might nick a vein or two.

Taylor tried to shove it into her coat pocket, but Brenda stopped her. "Taylor, you can't take this."

"Oh yes, she can," I said.

"She can't." Brenda handed the ring back to me. "Taylor, you go on ahead. I'll meet you at Crate and Barrel."

Taylor shot me a venomous death glare, then stomped off toward the door. My cheeks burned with shame as I visualized her and Brenda sitting around the breakfast table with Marissa tomorrow, cackling about my public meltdown.

"Stella." Brenda patted my arm and gazed into my eyes with what almost looked like compassion. "Like it or not, we have something in common: we both married Mark. I lived with him for fifteen years."

"So what are you saying?" I crossed my arms defensively. "You know him better than I do?"

"No." But she was obviously lying. "I'm merely saying I have some insight into how he handles relationship problems."

"And?"

"And you might want to hold on to that ring. The first year of marriage is hard, particularly when you're married to Mark, but he adores you, Stella."

I shook my head. "But Taylor just said . . ."

Brenda laughed softly. "Champagne and 'good riddance'? Taylor has a flair for the dramatic, but she's not always a stickler for factual accuracy. Here." She pressed the ring into my palm. "Mark and I have kept in touch since the divorce, and he's dated a lot of women. But you're special to him. He loves you very much."

I paused. "Shouldn't *he* be telling me this?"

"Confrontation has never been his forte. I know I shouldn't meddle, and I'm sure you don't appreciate it." She adjusted the strap of her purse. "Children have a way of complicating things between a husband and wife."

No kidding. I nodded and opened my mouth, but nothing came out. What was the appropriate way to thank your husband's ex-wife for marriage advice?

Before I could string a sentence together, Brenda pivoted on the heel of her immaculate black boot and followed Taylor into the crowd.

Still reeling with shock, I squeezed my engagement ring, then slipped it back on my finger. He adored me. He missed me.

He refused to have children with me.

I wandered up and down the aisles, breathing in the heady blend of spice and florals, and picked out a bottle of lavender bath oil. Just in case.

As the clerk rang up my purchase and handed me my receipt, my cell phone started to ring. Mark.

17

CASEY

So did you call Mark back yet?" I asked Stella, who was fondling her cell phone while pretending to be engrossed in a cable broadcast of *White Christmas*.

"No." Stella stared at the phone as if she could force it to ring again via psychic powers. "I want to, but—"

"But what?" I prompted.

"But nothing's really changed between us." She snuggled back into the throw I'd knitted from soft Irish wool and tucked her feet up underneath her. Stella had been camped out in my apartment for the last two days, cocooned in flannel pants, Mark's old sweater, and multiple blankets, leaving the sofa only for bathroom breaks. And she still looked like Jennifer Connelly, damn her.

"Well, you need to get up and find something to do," I advised. "This whole sitting-around-doing-nothing routine? Erin says it's a one-way ticket to Prozac Junction."

"I went shopping with you guys," she pointed out.

"Yeah, on Friday. And ever since we got back from the mall, you've been sprawled out on that couch like a beached whale."

Stella scowled. "Are you calling me fat?"

"Only if a size four is fat."

"Okay, then." She helped herself to another double chocolate chip cookie and stroked Maisy the cat, who had curled up next to her. "I miss Cash. He's the worst dog ever, but he's sort of growing on me. I hope Erin's taking good care of him."

"Why don't you go visit him? Man problems plus a vegetable state of inactivity equals serious depression," I warned again. "Take it from someone who's been there."

She dragged her glassy gaze away from Bing Crosby and Rosemary Clooney for a second. "Is that why you've been so busy this weekend?"

"I just like a clean home."

"Yeah, well, there's clean and then there's totally obsessive. You, my friend, have crossed the line."

"What? I've just been trying to get the place presentable for company."

"You reorganized the silverware drawer." She started on another cookie. "You took a toothbrush to the grout on the bathroom floor."

"You weren't supposed to see that."

"Have a seat." Stella patted the couch cushion next to hers. "Join me on my journey to Prozac Junction."

I shook my head. "I have to get up early tomorrow to open the store. Inventory. And before I go to bed I should wash the towels, scrub the sinks, put together the grocery list—"

"Casey." She covered her ears. "Stop. You're making my head spin. Sit your butt down and travel to a magic, black-and-white wonderland of Christmas carols and cute guys in uniform."

I walked over to the sofa and tried to sit down, but as soon as the backs of my legs touched the cushion, I bounced right up again. "I can't. I can't sit still. I have to stay busy."

Stella gave me a look. "This is about Nick, right? Has he called yet?"

"No."

"Have you packed up all his stuff?"

I glanced down the hall toward the hamper, where Nick's dirty socks and boxers still mingled with my whites. "No."

She clapped her hands. "Then let's go, girl, he'll be home any minute, right?"

"It's not that easy. Nick and I . . . it's complicated. I know that sounds like a cop-out, but I'm not ready to give up on him yet. This isn't like you and Mark; it's not an all-or-nothing issue."

"Uh-huh."

"And we're never going to solve our problems if I change the locks and make him sleep out in the snow."

"Didn't you say his parents live like five miles away?"

"That's not the point." I bristled. "He's my husband—well, sort of, anyway—and I can handle him. People change, you know. It happens."

"Uh-huh."

The phone rang, saving me from the rest of this conversation. "See? That's probably him right now!" I snatched up the cordless phone on the kitchen counter. "Hello?"

"Casey?"

It took me a full five seconds to recognize the voice. "Tanya?"

"Yeah, it's me. Listen, I know we haven't really talked for awhile—"

"What happened to your voice?" I asked, hurrying into the bedroom and closing the door behind me. "You sound hoarse."

"I've had a long day. Brett left me."

"Again?" My sister's two-year relationship with her live-in boyfriend could best be summed up in two words: train wreck.

"Yeah. We had a huge fight last night. He'd been drinking a little too much and I'd been working overtime a little too long, and you know how that goes. I yelled at him for not being supportive of me and the boys, and he said I'm never happy and he can do better than me."

I sank down onto the bed. "Tanya. You don't have to take this crap from him."

"But I love him." Her voice cracked. "And I keep thinking, if I can't make it work with him, then who can I make it work with?"

Someone who's not a selfish, lying jackass? "Stop beating yourself up. You can do so much better."

"No, I can't." Her voice went flat as she pulled herself together. "I can't. And I know you told me not to come crying to you with the same old problems—"

"It's okay," I soothed. "I just wish you wouldn't let him do this to you over and over again. Brett's a lost cause. He's never going to change."

I remembered what I'd just told Stella: *"People change. It happens."* As much as I disparaged my sister for clinging to a man who took advantage of her blind devotion, wasn't I guilty of the exact same thing?

Tanya sounded empty and defeated. "I just keep thinking, maybe if I'd tried a little harder, if I hadn't nagged him so much . . ."

"It's not you," I said crisply. "It's him. Forget about him and move on. You'll be better off."

"That's easy for you to say—you've got Nick."

I didn't reply.

"I mean, look at my life and then look at yours." Her laugh was low and wistful. "No wonder you didn't want to spend Thanksgiving with us."

My cheeks burned with shame. "Tanya—"

"No, I didn't mean it like that. I just . . . I'm glad you're happy. And I understand. If I married a guy like Nick and had a marriage like yours, I wouldn't want to deal with our family, either."

Ten years had gone by since high school, and Tanya and I were still exactly the same: the Nestor girls who were never quite good enough, who never fit in. While my sister went on and on about how lucky I was to have snared the Golden Boy, I finally admitted that the qualities that most embarrassed me about her were the ones I still struggled with myself. I'd distanced myself not because she hadn't changed since childhood but because I was afraid *I* hadn't.

I heard call waiting click on Tanya's end of the connection.

"Oh, gotta go," my sister said. "That might be Brett."

"So what if it is?" I asked, incensed. "I thought we just decided—"

"Call you later, Case. Love you!" She left me with a dial tone.

I sat on the bed for a few minutes, replaying the conversation I'd just had. Tanya and I might be more similar than I wanted to admit, but that didn't mean we had to continue down the same path.

"Hey, Stella," I yelled, opening the bedroom door. "Get in here and help me pack up Nick's stuff!"

She peeked in, eyes wide. "What happened to 'He's my husband and I can handle him'?"

I reached into the closet and pulled out a stack of Nick's jeans and folded shirts. "This *is* how I'm handling him. I'm mad as hell and I'm not going to take it anymore. Grab that duffel bag and throw his shoes in."

Stella started to laugh when she saw the inside of our closet. "You color code your wardrobe?"

"Less jawing. More packing."

"Remind me never to work for you."

"Come on," I teased, "you're such a natural with dogs."

She nibbled her lower lip. "Speaking of work, I'm going to have to find a job now. Do you think there are any families out here who need nannies?"

"Only the summer people," I said. "But you could apply at some of the preschools, right?"

"Yeah. Back to the minimum-wage world." Stella looked less than enthusiastic about that prospect. "My mom's going to be *pissed*. When I tell her I left Mark . . ." She shuddered. "Pray for me."

"She wants you to give the marriage a try?"

"She wants me to stay married long enough to void the prenup," Stella corrected. "Ten years."

I had to laugh. "Oh please. No one is that mercenary with their own child."

"That's what you think."

We both froze at the distinctive sound of snow tires crunching over the icy parking lot in front of the building. I peeked out the bedroom windows to see a tall, shadowed figure emerge from the passenger side of an SUV.

"Is it him?" Stella whispered, though obviously Nick couldn't hear us from outside.

I nodded.

"Did you put the chain lock on the door?"

"I think so. Maybe."

We raced down the hall to the front door. My heart pounded in time with the muffled thunks of footfalls on the stair treads.

Keys jangled, the doorknob turned, and Stella and I leapt back from the threshold as the door jerked open a few inches, impeded by the small brass chain I'd slid into place.

"What the . . ." Nick peered through the crack with one eye. "Casey?"

I tried to sound casual. "Yes?"

"Open the door; it's cold out here!"

I stood motionless, torn between wanting to stand my ground and wanting to fling open the door.

"Casey?" Nick mashed his face into the crack of the door frame. "Who else is in there?"

"Stella Porter," I said crisply. "She's staying here for a few days."

He snorted. "Since when are you friends with Stella Porter? I thought you said she was a—"

"Never mind her," I said quickly. "I want to talk about us. I take it you got my voice mail?"

He paused. "The one about not being married anymore?"

"Yes, Nick, that one."

"Yeah, I got it."

"You got that message and you didn't bother calling me back?"

"Yes, but—"

"You were gone for four days! Including Thanksgiving! And you didn't call me once!"

"I was trying to give you some time to cool off!"

"I am cooled off!" I shrieked.

"It's not like I was doing lines of coke at a strip club, Case, it was just a football game."

"For four days!" I repeated. "For all I knew, you were lying dead in a ditch."

He stamped his feet on the welcome mat. "Okay. I see your point. You're right. I should have called."

I practically dropped dead of shock. "Did you just say I'm *right?*"

"Yeah." His eye reappeared at the door. "I was a tool, and I'm sorry. Now will you please open the door?"

I considered it for about half a second. "No."

"Casey." His teeth started chattering. "Seriously. I'm dying out here."

"That's not really my problem, is it?"

"Look, it's been a long couple days, and we're both upset," he said. "But I love you and we'll work it out. Let's sleep on it and talk everything over tomorrow."

That's probably exactly what Brett had said to my sister.

"No. I'm through talking to you. I'm sick of being the one who always has to compromise."

He paused. "*You* always have to compromise?"

"That's right! I have to do everything myself because when I wait for you to do it—"

"Are you kidding me? You have to do everything yourself because you can't stand it if everything doesn't happen on your secret timetable!"

I started pushing the door shut, nearly severing his nose.

"Wait! No! I know I haven't been the man of your dreams lately." Nick pushed back against the door. "But I'll make it up to you. I've been thinking a lot since you left me that message. I need to make some changes."

I wrapped my arms around my torso. "Yeah, you do."

"And I will, honey. I swear. We'll start over."

"You have to make more of an effort," I warned him.

"I will."

"You have to take the initiative."

"Done."

I nibbled my lower lip. "You have to go down to the courthouse with me—tomorrow—and get married again."

Silence.

"Nick?"

I looked at Stella. Stella looked at me.

"Nick?" I raised my voice.

"Can't we please talk about this tomorrow when we're both feeling a little more—"

"Cop-out," Stella intoned.

"Excuse me," Nick said. "This is between me and Casey."

"Well, are you going to marry her or not?" Stella had become the curfew-obsessed, overprotective father I'd never had.

"It's none of your business!" Nick exclaimed.

"No, go ahead and answer," I told him. "I'd really like to know. Are we getting married again or not?"

Another long silence. Then: "We already got married once."

"That means no," I translated.

"That does not mean no!" Nick insisted.

I hugged myself tighter and asked, "Well, does it mean yes?"

"It means we'll talk about it tomorrow. *Alone*."

"Goodnight, Nick." I slammed the door.

18

ERIN

"Today was a good day," I announced to David when I arrived home from the office on the Monday after Thanksgiving. "The waiting room was full of kids who picked up nasty bugs over the holiday weekend, but none of them belonged to Kelly Fendt."

David looked up from the newspaper. "Do you think she finally decided to listen to reason? Or just switched pediatricians?"

"Hey. Whatever. I'm not about to look a gift horse in the mouth." I dropped my bulging leather tote bag on the kitchen table, then glanced around. "Where's the dog?"

David returned his attention to the paper. "In the basement."

"David!" I hurried across the kitchen toward the basement door. "It's cold down there, and damp! How long has he been down there?" I heard pathetic whining and scratching; the second I turned the knob, Cash heaved his considerable weight against the door and came barreling out. He circled the table at top speed, slipping and sliding on the freshly waxed linoleum (thanks, Renée).

"Hey buddy!" I kneaded the loose skin at the scruff of the dog's neck. "Poor thing, locked up in the dark all day." Cash threw himself on his back, begging for a belly rub. "Honestly, David, what were you thinking?"

David hunched over behind the folds of newsprint. "It wasn't my decision."

"Don't try to pin this one on your mother. It's your house!"

"Yes, and she's our guest and the dog scares her."

I put my hands on my hips and regarded Cash, who was wriggling upside down, all four feet pedaling in the air while his tail thumped against the cabinet with the rapid-fire precision of a machine gun. "This dog scares your mother?"

Only the top of David's hair was visible over the Arts and Living section. "She says shelter dogs are unpredictable. And after what happened Thursday night . . ."

I rolled my eyes. "You guys are going to have to get over that. Thursday night was a fluke. He was in a new place with new people; he had an accident. If you must blame someone, blame me for not making sure he did his business before I took him inside. He had a bowel movement. He didn't rip out her jugular."

"I see your point," David conceded. "But my mom says—"

"I washed the blankets, I said I was sorry, what more does she want?" I frowned, surveying the unusually quiet house. "Where is she, anyway?"

"At her bridge club. The roads were icy, so Henry Reynolds offered to give her a ride."

I shook my head. "That man is a glutton for punishment."

My so-called husband finally lowered the newspaper, took off his glasses, and started rubbing his forehead. "She says she doesn't want to be alone with the dog while you and I are off at work. She says he growled at her."

"Really."

"Yes. Now, I grant you that she can sometimes be a little, uh . . ."

"Insane?" I suggested.

"*Oversensitive,*" he amended. "But it's possible, Erin. He could have growled. We don't know anything about his history, or why his owners gave him up. Honey, sometimes dogs just snap, you know? They'll be fine one minute, and the next . . ."

"What'd she do, sit you down and make you watch *Cujo* on your lunch break?"

"Honey, you know I'm on your side. But I'm not going to call my mother a liar and force her to spend all day with a dog that terrifies her. I'm just not." He held up a hand when he saw my expression. "And luckily, this doesn't have to start another huge fight between us, because he's not even our dog."

"That's right," I said hotly. "He's Stella's, and I promised her I'd take good care of him. And barricading him in the basement all day—where we store all kinds of paint cans and chemical cleansing agents that could poison him, by the way— is not taking good care of him." I stalked back toward the mudroom and grabbed his leash. "Come on, Cash, you deserve a walk."

"Erin . . ."

"What?" I clipped the leash onto Cash's collar, then looked expectantly up at David. "What?"

His hazel eyes were bleak. "Please don't be mad."

To my surprise, I realized I wasn't angry. The initial flash of irritation had passed and left in its wake something much scarier: resignation. "I'm not mad," I told him, pulling on my leather gloves. "But I'm not stupid, either. This is the way it's always going to be with Renée. You're always going to side with her."

"That's not true," he protested, but I cut him off.

"Apparently, I have to decide if a three-way marriage with you, me, and your mother is something I can live with. At the rate we're going, we might as well bring her down to the court-house to sign the marriage license right under my name."

"Is that a threat? You're not going to remarry me now?"

"I don't know," I said slowly. "I love you, but there's a reason they say three is a crowd."

When I returned from the walk, my mood had improved and my biceps were aching from trying to rein in Cash, who pulled like a sled dog on the leash. A maroon Oldsmobile was parked on the curb by our mailbox, so I could only assume that Renée had returned from her bridge club with the long-suffering Henry Reynolds.

"Hello," I called as Cash tugged me through the doorway.

"Oh Erin, dear, you're back." Renée rushed into the entryway to give me a hug and kiss, after which she made a big show of cowering from Cash, as if his fangs were dripping blood. "Just in time to meet Mr. Reynolds."

"Call me Henry." A stocky, affable man in his sixties stepped forward to shake my hand. In his preppy khakis and brown leather bomber jacket, he looked a little like a New England version of Harrison Ford—so why did Renée spurn him every time he asked her out?

"Pleased to meet you." I yanked the leash as Cash sprang up on his hind legs and nuzzled Henry's neck. "As is the dog."

Renée's hands flew to her face. "Oh my word, David, do something! Better put him back in the basement."

"Nonsense." Henry playfully cuffed Cash's muzzle. "He's a good boy, barely out of the puppy stage. Aren't you, boy? Aren't you?"

Cash wagged his tail so hard that he toppled sideways onto the carpet.

My mother-in-law hid behind David, peering over his shoulder.

"Don't worry, Renée, he'll be fine." Henry laughed, then winked at me. "Women, eh?"

I smiled back. "Tell me about it."

"Well, it was nice to meet you, Erin. Renée never mentioned that her son was married—"

I shot David a look.

"—but I'm sure we'll run into each other again soon." He turned back to Renée. "A pleasure, as always, madam. And if you change your mind about that movie on Friday . . ."

"I won't." Renée didn't crack a smile. "But thank you for the ride."

"Jeez, Mom," David admonished as he closed the door behind Henry. "Why won't you give the guy a chance?"

"He seems nice," I chimed in. "Very mellow."

"Mellow. Bah." Her mouth puckered. "I don't date, David, you know that." She surveyed our home with a satisfied smile. "I have everything I need right here. Now, I have a surprise for you." Renée looped her arm through David's. "Henry gave me a gift certificate to the White Birch. Dinner for two."

"Aw, that's sweet," I said. "When do you think you'll go with him? What about this weekend?" Maybe I could slip Henry a few extra bucks to keep her out all night, and David and I could break out the new lingerie I'd bought on Black Friday.

Her eyebrows snapped together. "I told you, I don't date. He's not the first male to try to turn my head with baubles and trinkets. Presents like this are entirely inappropriate."

Foiled again. "So you gave it back to him?"

"Of course not."

David nodded wearily. "So what are you proposing?"

Renée pressed the gift certificate into his hand. "I'm proposing that you two newlyweds have a date night."

He gaped at her. "Really?"

She beamed. "Of course. You've hardly had a moment alone together since I moved in, and I know how you love the duck at the White Birch. Now run upstairs and change."

I tried not to look stunned. "Wow, Renée. Thank you."

"You're welcome, darling." She reached up to pat my cheek. "It's the least I can do. You've been such a gracious hostess."

Try as I might, I couldn't detect the slightest trace of sarcasm in her voice. So I raced up after David, who took the stairs two at a time.

"Can you believe this?" He charged into our walk-in closet and grabbed the first jacket and tie he saw. "You, me, the White Birch . . . and best of all, no Mom!"

"I know." I took my time selecting a black wool skirt to pair with a clingy blue top that Stella had helped me pick out at the mall. "This is really nice of her."

He yanked his sweater off over his head. "She's probably going to use this as leverage to guilt-trip us for the next year, but who cares? Tonight, I get you all to myself. Alone at last!"

"Mmm." I threw him a saucy grin. "Maybe it's time to test-drive my new black lace thong."

"Does this mean you forgive me for banishing Cash to the basement?"

"I might."

"What if I promise to let him lie around in our bed all day, watching soap operas and eating bonbons?"

I laughed. "Maybe I'll go commando."

His hands slid down to my hips. "We could just skip dinner and you can have your way with me right here in the closet."

He kissed me, I kissed him back, and just as we were about to start rolling around on the carpet, Renée's voice drifted in: "David? David, I need you."

"Damnit." He broke away and headed toward the stairs, clutching his shirt and tie in one hand. He paused in the doorway, turning back to me with a hot, carnal stare he hadn't given me since we left Boston. "Meet me downstairs in five minutes or I'm coming back up to finish what we started here."

I fished a black bra out of my underwear drawer. "I'll see what I can do."

In record time, I changed, swept my hair up into a French twist, and dabbed on perfume and eyeshadow. Exactly five minutes later, I was shrugging into my long black dress coat in the front hall. "Be good," I told Cash. "We'll be back soon."

David rounded the corner, and I caught his hand in mine. "This is really great of your mother to do. Really generous. I know I've said some bitchy things these past few weeks, but I may have misjudged her, I admit it . . ." I broke off when I saw his expression. "Oh no. What now?"

Before he could answer, Renée strolled up behind him. She had her coat on, and a fresh coat of lipstick.

Son of a . . . "What a surprise, Renée," I choked out. "Are you going out, too?"

She clutched her sequined black evening purse. "Well, dear, I wanted to stay home and let you kids enjoy yourself—"

"And we appreciate that," I cried. "We do! So we're just going to—"

She shook her head sadly. "But I can't stay here." Her voice dropped to a sepulchral whisper. "I forgot about the dog."

"Honestly, Mom, the dog will be fine," David snapped.

"You say that, but you weren't here when he growled at me." Renée fluttered her eyelashes like a Southern belle who'd laced her corset too tightly. "I won't feel safe all alone with him."

Inspiration struck. "You could ask Henry to come over," I suggested. "I'm sure he'd be glad to protect you."

Her face was like stone.

"Renée." I forced a smile. "I know you and Cash got off to a bad start, but he's a pussycat, I promise. Casey gave me some chew toys for him—we'll just toss him a few and he'll be good as gold all night."

My mother-in-law and I locked gazes in a staredown for a few seconds before I relented. "Okay, okay, you can put him down in the basement if you're really that scared."

"But what if he got out somehow?" She tugged her collar up around her chin. "Imagine if you came home and that dog had killed me. How would you feel then?"

A deafening crash came from the next room, followed by a series of frenzied yelps.

I skidded into the kitchen on my high heels to discover that Cash had overturned the stainless steel trash can and was strewing coffee grounds, banana peels, and empty yogurt containers all over the floor.

"You see?" Renée crowed. "He's a menace. Who knows what he'll do next?"

David ran his hand through his hair as he surveyed the wreckage. "That's the spirit, Mom. The glass is half-full."

"I'm only thinking of you, dear. You and your safety. Now come along, let's go to dinner. The reservations are for seven thirty."

I picked up a sodden paper towel and dropped it back in the trash can. "Reservations?"

"I called while you were getting dressed," she cooed. "To make sure we'd get a good table."

"Well, we can't leave until I clean this up." I pushed up the sleeves of my new shirt. "It's Monday night; we're not going to need reservations."

David rested his hand on my shoulder. "Don't worry, hon. I'll take care of this."

My mother-in-law tapped her foot and glanced at her watch. "Well, *I'm* ready to go. I'm positively famished."

David got that familiar, dazed look in his eyes. He had shut down and tuned her out. It was his only defense after a lifetime of Renée.

This is what the entire evening was going to be like. So much for date night.

"Why don't you two go on ahead," I ground out. "You and David go have dinner and I'll stay here with the dog."

"Really? You wouldn't mind?" From the way her face lit up, I knew that this had been her plan all along. Damn. She was shrewd, I had to give her that. "Come on, David, start the car."

But David dug in his heels. "I'm not going anywhere without Erin. I'm not leaving my wife to pick up garbage while you and I have dinner, and that's final, Mom." He loosened his tie. "We'll go to the White Birch another night."

"But . . ." Renée put on a pouty face.

"Why don't you start dinner while Erin and I clean up the mess?" David asked.

"I've lost my appetite," she snitted, then marched upstairs.

"Alone at last," I remarked as the guest room door slammed. "Just what we wanted."

I bent down to scoop up a handful of eggshells and glanced at the piece of paper lying underneath them. How many times had I told Renée: recycle, recycle, recycle. Then I noticed the hospital letterhead on the paper.

Dear Dr. Maye:

Dr. Witkowski has informed us of your ongoing interest in our facility. We are pleased to inform you that we

have several openings on our general pediatric service
and would be happy to speak to you at your earliest
convenience . . .

A job offer. They were asking me back to Boston, to the hospital I'd turned down when David and I had decided to move out to Alden. But why was this letter in the trash?

"David." I handed him the stationery. "Did you see this?"

He scanned the text. "Dr. Witkowski? What is *Jonathan* doing telling them you want to move back to Boston?"

"I emailed him when we had that big fight last week and—"

"Of course you did." His eyes flashed. "The minute we have a problem, you go running back to Jonathan. Typical."

"David! Give me a break. I did not go running back to anyone. But yes, I have been thinking about that job offer I passed up in back to Boston, and I emailed him—"

"He's still in love with you," David accused. "He's always had a thing for you!"

"Okay, now you're just talking crazy." I waved the letter at him. "And you didn't answer my question. Did you see this and throw it out?"

He looked insulted. "No. I don't open your mail. Although maybe I should start, seeing how you and Jonathan are sending love notes to each other."

I didn't even dignify that with a response. "Well, if you didn't throw it out, who did?"

Both of us looked up toward the guest room.

"*I knew it!*" I hissed. "That woman has absolutely no boundaries. She won't be happy until I'm barefoot, pregnant, and chained to the stove. Actually, she'll probably make me live down in the basement with the dog."

He squeezed my shoulder to calm me. "We don't know what happened, so let's not rush to judgment."

My jaw dropped. "You cannot be serious."

"Even if she did throw that letter out—and we don't know that she did—I'm sure it was a mistake. She's getting older, she gets confused."

"She's sharp as a tack and she's out for blood!" I cried. "Don't you dare take her side on this!"

He was getting that blank, autopilot look again. "I'm not taking sides, Erin."

"That's the problem! You need to take a side, and it needs to be mine. She intercepted my job offer and threw it out without telling me!" I knew I should lower my voice, but how could he not see what a huge deal this was?

"Well, you told Jonathan Witkowski you'd move back to Boston, so I guess we're even."

I grabbed his jacket lapels and pulled his face closer to mine. "Stop that, David. Jonathan has nothing to do with this. This is about you, me, and Renée. She can't treat me like this in my own house. You need to decide who you're going to be with: her or me."

The top stair creaked. "Is everything all right down there?" Renée called.

I glared at David and whispered, "Tell her. Tell her she cannot do this to me."

"David?" Renée's voice got louder. "Are you all right?"

"Tell her," I begged.

"Everything's fine, Mom," he called back. "Don't worry."

I let go of his lapels and took a giant step back.

He reached out to catch my hand. "Don't get upset, honey. Give me a chance to—"

"I've given you enough chances." I put my coat back on and snatched up the dog's leash. "Pack up your chew toys, Cash. We're done."

An hour later, I knocked on Casey's door.

"Beat it, Nick!" she called from inside the apartment. "I said no and I meant it!"

I knocked again. "It's not Nick. It's me!"

The door swung open. Stella and Casey peered out.

"Hey." I tried to look cheery, surrounded by suitcases and one very jazzed-up dog. "Do you guys have room for two more?"

19

STELLA

"Listen, Mom, I have to tell you something and you're not going to like it." I had Casey's apartment all to myself on Tuesday afternoon, and the time had come to break the bad news to my mother. "Mark and I are still having problems and I don't know what's going to happen. I moved out on Thanksgiving."

My mother choked as if I'd just said I had leprosy. "Stella, no!"

I took a deep breath and kept going. "I know you're disappointed—"

"Not disappointed; I am *ashamed*. Marriage is a sacred vow. You do not just give up when the going gets tough."

I curled deeper into Casey's cushy sofa, gnawing the inside of my cheek. "We haven't given up yet, but . . ."

"You made promises! In front of your friends, family, in front of God . . ."

"But the pastor never signed the marriage certificate. I told you before, Mom, Mark and I aren't even legal."

"Well, you hunt down that slipshod pastor and you make him sign it, missy."

"He's dead."

She started wailing, a thin, reedy swan song of despair. I hadn't heard her this upset since my father's arraignment.

"You can't leave him, Stella! You'll get nothing in the divorce!"

"Well, really, there can't be any divorce without a marriage," I pointed out. "I'll try to work things out, I really will, but—"

The wailing got louder. "Who's going to take care of you?"

"Well." I sat up straight. "That's what I wanted to talk to you about. I put in applications at a bunch of child-care centers."

"Stella, please." She sniffed. "No one's going to hire you as an au pair after you ran off with your last employer's poker buddy."

"I'm not trying to be an au pair. I'm talking about teaching preschool."

"*Teaching preschool?*" As if my diagnosis had just progressed from leprosy to bubonic plague.

"Well, assistant teaching, anyway. Until I can finish my

B.A. The pay's not great, but I was thinking I could do that during the day and maybe take classes at night. I have this friend who's a doctor, who offered to help me if I sign up for some science classes."

"A female friend or a male friend?"

"Female."

"Then what good is she?"

"She's smart, Mom. She went to Harvard. Anyway, she and I were talking, and you know, I might want to get my nursing degree. There's a real shortage of nurses out here, and I could specialize in pediatrics."

"Oh my Lord. Do you have any idea how much nurses make?"

"A lot more than assistant preschool teachers," I guessed. "My friend says—"

"Enough about your friend! Is *she* married to a nationally renowned heart surgeon?"

"No, her husband's a pharmacologist. Although, actually, it turns out they're not really married, either. They got married over Labor Day weekend, too, the day after me and Mark, and they had the same pastor. And he didn't sign their marriage license either, which turned out to be a good thing because she just left her husband last night."

"Then she's not the best person to be going to for marriage advice, is she?"

And you are? My mother had looked the other way for

years while my dad had taken off for "business trips" and come home reeking of expensive cigars and cheap perfume. She and I both knew what had really gone on at all those conferences in Vegas, golf weekends in South Carolina, and lavish retirement parties on rented yachts, but neither of us ever said a word.

I closed my eyes. "What do you want from me, Mom?"

"I want you to go home to your husband and work this out."

"But how? There's no way to compromise about babies—either you have them or you don't. You can't have half a kid."

"Do you love him?"

I didn't answer.

"Well? Do you?"

I curled back into the pillows. "Yes."

"All right, then. He loves you, Stella. His face when you walked down that aisle—love like that doesn't come along every day."

"But he lied to me," I whispered. "On purpose. A lot."

"Maybe he'll change his mind about children." Her tone brightened. "Maybe you'll get a medical miracle."

"I don't think so."

"Or . . . well, I don't know how to phrase this delicately, but Mark's not going to live forever, you know."

"Mom!"

"Well, you have to be practical. He *is* thirty years older than you, and his family has a history of heart disease."

"So what are you saying? Wait till he croaks, then take his money and run to the sperm bank?"

She didn't say anything.

"Forget it!" I waved my fist in the air. "I don't care what everybody thinks—I didn't marry him for money, and I'm not staying with him for money. *I am not a ho.* I am going to be a pediatric nurse."

"Stella—"

"No! Don't argue with me! I can take care of myself!"

"You're going to miss that big house and all your fancy clothes," she warned.

"I'd rather have a baby than a designer wardrobe."

"You'll be lonely without Mark."

"No, I won't. I'll have my trusty dog to keep me company."

"You have a dog?"

"Kind of." I flinched as I tasted blood in my mouth—time to ease up on the cheek-gnawing. "I'm sorry, Mom. I know you think I'm screwing everything up. But I have to do what's right for me."

She broke out the heavy artillery. "This is going to *kill* your father. Why don't you just move back in, wait a year, see how it goes?"

I knew if I went back to Mark, I'd never get up the nerve to leave again. I had to make a last stand, and it had to be now. "That's not fair to either of us."

"Give it six months!" she cried, sounding like an auctioneer.

"Mom. Please try to be on my side."

"Well . . . at least if you become a nurse, you might be able to meet another rich doctor."

"Right. Way to look on the bright side."

When Mark opened the door, he looked like I felt—sleep-deprived and pale. He'd tried to hide this from me by putting on an obnoxiously red sweater vest that he knew I hated, but I wasn't fooled.

"Hey," I said, suddenly wanting to reach up and stroke the stubble on his cheek. "You look . . ."

He half-smiled. "Yeah. You, too."

"I just need to pick up a few of my things. I've got some boxes in the car—oh, I guess you'll probably want the car back, won't you?"

He cleared his throat, then said gruffly, "Keep it."

I shook my head. "No, that wouldn't be right. Just give me a few days to find something else; I'll look through the auto classifieds tonight—"

"Keep it. Please. What else am I going to do with a little BMW convertible? Drive around and advertise my midlife crisis?"

I finally cracked a smile. "You could always give it to Taylor."

He started to laugh. "God, she'd love that."

"I saw her the other day, at the mall," I confessed.

"I know." He got serious again. "Brenda called."

"Oh. Well, she was really nice about the whole thing. It

could have been pretty awkward," I babbled, very aware that I should shut up but unable to stop the stream of verbal diarrhea. "I mean, the new wife runs into the ex-wife, worlds collide, could get tricky, but she—"

"You're still wearing your rings." He reached out to examine my hand.

I stared down at our entwined fingers. "So are you."

"Of course I am." His voice was thick. "I'm not the one who left."

"I left because I had to, not because I wanted to."

"I love you so much, Stell. I'll always love you."

And now I was crying. Crap. "I'll always love you, too. But that's not enough. We don't want the same things."

He tugged me closer, until we were pressing together. "Don't leave."

I turned my face into the scratchy nub of his sweater, letting the wool soak up my tears. "But I can't . . . you don't . . . I want a baby, Mark. I can't explain it. If I could talk myself out of it, I would, but when I see a mother with a stroller, my whole body hurts."

"That's exactly how I've felt since you walked out on Thanksgiving," he murmured. "My whole body hurts."

"Why does it have to be this hard? Why do I have to pick one or the other?" I started to hiccup as I cried.

"You don't." He tucked my head in the crook between his neck and shoulder. "Not right now."

"Maybe not today, but someday, and every minute we spend together just makes it more and more—" *Hiccup.*

"Sweetheart, don't cry."

I breathed in his clean, cedar scent and cried harder. "I miss you so much."

He hugged me tighter.

"I—*hic*—hate that we can't stay like this forever."

"Don't leave," he repeated, kissing the top of my head. "We can make this work. I'll do whatever it takes."

"But you said—"

"You're the most important thing in my life. If having a baby is what it takes to make you stay, then . . ."

I blinked up at him through wet, spiky eyelashes. "Then what?"

He grazed my temple with his thumb. "Then I'll call a urologist tomorrow and make an appointment."

"Really?" My hiccup echoed through the foyer.

He laughed even as his eyes misted up. "Really. Anything. Just stay."

I threw my arms around his neck. "I'll stay."

He scooped me up, carried me to the bedroom, and started our second honeymoon.

20

CASEY

Nick walked into my store at noon on the dot. "Let's go, Case, I'm taking you to lunch."

I'd spent the whole morning trying not to get my hopes up, trying not to let my heart leap into my throat every time I heard the bells on the shop's door jingle. Nick Keating wasn't one to come crawling back.

But here he was, tall and handsome in his suit and tie, tracking slush all over my freshly mopped floors.

"Wipe your feet, please," I said, blasé as could be.

He didn't move. "Casey. Come on. We have to talk."

I tried to pretend I was Stella for a minute—confident and gorgeous and used to hunky men demanding lunches with me. "I have nothing left to say to you."

"Well, I have some stuff I have to say to you." He scowled.

"If this is about rest of your personal belongings, don't worry. I'll have them piled in the parking lot and ready to move by the end of the week. Including that ratty brown armchair."

"Okay, first of all, that armchair is not ratty, it's comfortable."

"Fine. Including that *comfortable* brown armchair."

"But this isn't about the armchair."

"Then what?" I spread my arms wide. "What could we possibly have to talk about?"

He glanced from one side of the shop to the other. "Not here. Can't you close for an hour?"

"No." I took a seat on the stool behind the counter. "I'm not going to play by your rules any more. So say what you have to say or move along. I have a business to run here."

He recoiled. "Jeez, when did you get so—"

"When did you stop loving me?" I demanded, jumping back off the stool. "And why did you marry me if you didn't?"

"What are you talking about? You know I love you."

"No, you don't. Actions speak louder than words, Nick, and someone who loves me would not treat me the way you do."

He nodded. "If this is about Detroit—"

"It's about Detroit and the engagement ring that I had to buy myself and the wedding you tried to back out of and I should have let you." I flattened my palms on the countertop. "You want out, I'm letting you out."

He started toward me. "I don't want out."

"Well, that's too bad, because I do." I stared at the ceramic bowl full of dog treats next to the register. "I've waited long enough for you to love me the way that I love you. I thought if I worked hard enough, I could make this marriage work, but I can't. I can't do everything."

"No one's asking you to do everything," he said. "But you never let me do anything at my own pace. You push and you push and you push—"

"Because you'd never do anything otherwise! How can I ever trust you again when you've made it blatantly obvious that you don't want to be married to me?"

Understanding dawned. "This is about what I said when you locked me out of the apartment."

"That little detail about not wanting to go to the courthouse to make it legal? Yes, Nick, this is about that."

"Well, I wasn't about to get into our personal lives in front of Stella Porter! Since when do you even like her?"

"That's not the point! You had your chance and you blew it!"

"You're being ridiculous," he stormed.

"*You're* being ridiculous!"

He turned around, stalked toward the door, then turned back around and stalked over to me. "Do what you want. You always have and you always will. But just so you know, I'm sick of you making all the decisions."

"Well, guess what?" I glanced at the ceramic bowl again,

itching to throw it. "I'm sick of you digging in your heels all the time."

"Push, push, push!"

"Dig, dig, dig!"

"Nothing's ever enough for you," he accused. "You're supposed to love *me*. Not the basketball jock I used to be, not the lawyer I was supposed to be, not my dad, not my mom, not the neat, constipated little life you decided we need to have . . . *Me*."

"I do love you!" I yelled. "Or I did, anyway, until you decided we didn't need to be married anymore."

And then he broke out the oldest, nerve-splittingest line in the history of men: "Marriage is just a piece of paper."

His eyes widened when he saw my face, and he took a step back toward the door. "Okay, what I meant was—"

"This is not about a piece of paper," I strangled out. "This is about you and me."

"Yeah, but—"

"And if you loved me enough, you'd have no problem committing to me. You'd give me a ring, you'd give me your heart, and you wouldn't make me beg for it."

"If *you* loved *me* enough, you wouldn't demand everything before I was ready to give it to you," he countered.

"Three years," I reminded him. "Long time."

"Second date." He crossed his arms. "You started talking about names for our future children."

I wrenched off my ring and threw it at him. It hit his jacket and bounced onto the black rubber mat by the door. "Get out."

"Casey, wait. I'm sorry."

"Too late." I headed over to the door and yanked it open. As I did, I noticed a pedestrian strolling toward the store, and I panicked. The last thing I needed was the Alden rumor mill cranking out reports about Casey Nestor brawling with her perfect husband in broad daylight.

"Can't we work this out like adults?" Nick asked.

I could barely hear him. "Nope. We're through. End of discussion."

"Can't we even—"

"Fine! Use the back door, then!" I lunged behind him and propelled him past the display cases, through the back room, and out the back door into the alley.

He didn't dig in his heels this time. He let me shove him out and slam the door behind him.

Good, I told myself, dusting off my hands as I headed back through the shelves of kitty litter and Nylabones. Out with the old and on with my life. Stella and Erin were right; we weren't in high school anymore. This social outcast deserved better.

The door chimes jangled again, and I heard a familiar voice call, "Casey?"

"Coming!" I slapped on a smile and headed out to say hello to my sister.

•   •   •

"Hey." Tanya didn't come all the way through the door; she just poked her head in. "You got a second?"

"Of course." I beckoned her in. "Come in, come in, you'll turn into a Popsicle."

She edged inside, clasping and unclasping her hands in front of her. Her long blonde hair fanned down to cover half her face. "How are you, Case?"

"Great," I lied. "How about you? What happened with Brett?"

"Oh fine. We made up. Everything I said on the phone the other night—forget that. We're fine now. Better than ever."

I nodded and kept my editorial comments to myself. "How are the boys?"

She laughed. "The usual. Driving me crazy. Getting into trouble every chance they get."

"Bring them by sometime," I offered. "I'd love to take them to the movies or something."

"They'd like that."

We smiled at each other until the silence turned awkward.

"So, um." I drummed my fingernails on the counter. "What else is going on?"

"Not much. The store's slow, so the manager told me to take off early, and since the boys are still in school, I thought I'd stop by. Haven't seen you much since the wedding."

"I know." I shrugged helplessly to indicate circumstances beyond my control. "We've been so busy."

"Getting settled." She stared at the floor. "I know how it is." In her tennis shoes, baggy pants and blue smock from her cashier's job at the supermarket, Tanya bore no resemblance to the bold, brassy bad girl she'd been in high school. She looked . . . exhausted, really. Exhausted and rail thin.

"I'm starving," I said. "Do you want to go grab some lunch?"

"Oh no, I didn't want to put you out, Case. I just wanted to catch up for a few minutes. See how you're adjusting to married life." Her smile was a little wider this time. "You and Nick are so cute together. And you had such a beautiful wedding."

Regret stabbed through my heart. "It would have been even more beautiful if you'd been my maid of honor."

Her smile vanished. "Naw, but it was nice of you to ask."

"I wish you'd said yes."

"Oh, you know I couldn't get time off work to do all those fun, bachelorette things. Hell, I couldn't even make it to your shower." She looked away. I strongly suspected that she hadn't felt comfortable facing down the catty soccer mom coven at Nick's mother's house. And she'd been right—she wouldn't have fit in. But I should have encouraged her to go, anyway, instead of accepting her refusal with a secret and shameful relief that she wouldn't be there to remind the Keatings who I really was and where I came from.

"Well, if it makes you feel any better, Danni was a horrible maid of honor."

Tanya grinned. "She's always been a jealous little bitch—

she can't stand that you got married before her. But why would that make me feel better?"

Because I've been a horrible sister to you and I pretend our family doesn't exist. "You'll be maid of honor at my next wedding, okay?"

"Knock it off. You and Nick'll be together forever. You're the Nestor girl that made good."

"Yeah. How about that. Let's get lunch, okay?"

She was tempted, I could tell, but she'd gotten into the habit of denying herself even the smallest indulgences. Her indecision made me ache for the wild, carefree girl she used to be. "Come on, Tanya, my treat."

"Well, I guess I could go for a burger."

"Screw that. I'm taking you to the White Birch."

"The White Birch?" She paled. "Oh no, that's too fancy. I'm not dressed."

"It's lunch," I assured her. "Casual."

"But . . ." She played with the ends of her hair. "Someone might see us."

"So what? We're not doing anything wrong."

"Uh-uh." She seemed to be on the verge of a panic attack. "The White Birch is okay for you because you're married to Nick Keating, but me . . ."

"You're my sister," I said gently. "You deserve the best. And so do I."

"But . . ."

"No buts. We're going, I'm buying, and you're going to have a big juicy steak and a piece of pie."

"Chocolate cake," she corrected.

"But of course. Let me grab my coat and I'll close up shop for an hour."

I was halfway across the room when she squinted at the floor and picked up the ring I'd thrown at Nick. "Casey?"

I kept walking. "Yes?"

"What's this?"

"We'll talk," I promised. "At the White Birch."

"Everyone's staring at us," Tanya whispered as the host showed us to a booth in the back of the restaurant.

"No, they're not." I held my head high, daring anyone to look at my sister the wrong way.

"Okay, then, everyone's staring at *me*. This place is so snooty."

I slid into the booth and accepted the menu the host offered. "No one is staring," I chided her. "Why would you say that?"

She started rearranging the silverware at her place setting. "I don't fit in here."

"Well, neither do I."

She ran her index finger over the tines of her fork. "Yeah, you do, Case. You're a White Birch kind of woman now. And I . . . well, I'm the girl who slept with everyone else's boyfriend in high school, and I always will be."

She knew. She knew I was ashamed of her, and worse than that, she thought she deserved it.

"Hey. Listen." I waited until she met my eyes. "Fuck 'em. Anyone who can't see the amazing woman you grew up to be—they're the one with the problem. Not you. You have nothing to apologize for."

She went back to tapping the fork tines.

"Can you help it that you were born irresistible and good-looking?"

One corner of her mouth tugged up. "No."

"That's right. So let them be jealous and judgmental. We're above that sort of thing. Now what do you want to eat?"

She smoothed back her hair as the waiter approached. "Let's start with dessert."

"Excellent idea. Two pieces of chocolate cake, please," I said, before the server could even get his pen and pad out.

"Okay." She settled back against the rich leather upholstery, finally starting to relax. "So why was your engagement ring on the floor?"

I brought her up to speed on the legal status of my marriage and the fights I'd had with Nick. ". . . but turns out, it's all for the best, because I don't even want to be married to him anymore."

She looked horrified. "Don't say that!"

I forked up a big bite of cake. "He doesn't love me enough. No amount of compromise or counseling is going to change that."

"But you and Nick are meant to be. You have to get back together!"

"Why?" I demanded. "Why do we have to?"

"Because you . . . I mean, you put so much work into marrying him."

"Too much work." I gave her a pointed look. "Marriage is supposed to be a partnership. I'm not going to be any guy's doormat."

"But you . . . but he . . ." She gestured wildly. "You're meant to be!"

"I'm not going to settle, Tan, and neither should you. We're the Nestor girls, damnit."

She made a face. "I wouldn't brag about that."

"I would. Speaking of which, what are you doing for Christmas this year? I'd like to make dinner for you and the boys. It's time I did something with *my* family, for a change."

21

ERIN

"So you and Mark are going to give it another try?" I asked as Stella, Cash and I strolled down Fifth Street, enjoying an unusually warm December day. "Good for you."

"Yeah." Stella paused to let Cash sniff a street sign pole. "He goes to the urologist on Monday."

"Well, best of luck. I really mean that." I tucked my chin into my red knit scarf. "Hopefully, at least one of us can salvage her marriage from the smoldering wreckage."

Stella sighed. "David still hasn't called?"

"Oh, he's called. Called, emailed, sent flowers to my office." I stepped sideways to avoid the steady drip from the icicles melting on the awnings. "But he hasn't kicked Renée out of our house, and that's the only thing that matters."

"You seem pretty calm about that."

215

"I guess." I exhaled slowly. "I don't want to give up on us, but we can't go on like this. Not to be all *Dynasty* about it, but he has to choose me or Renée, and right now, he's choosing Renée. She couldn't drive this wedge in between us if he wouldn't let her."

Stella tugged Cash along as we crossed the street. "So what are you going to do?"

"I haven't decided. For now, I'm going to continue to take advantage of Casey's hospitality, and I'll call and get some specifics about the job offer in Boston. Just in case."

"You're really thinking about moving back to Boston." She whistled. "Does David know?"

"No."

"He's going to go ballistic."

I pulled out my ChapStick and reapplied. "Yeah, well, at least then he'd be showing me that he cared."

"Ouch."

"My friend Jonathan is coming out this weekend to talk about the whole thing. His girlfriend, Simone, has a condo in the city, and she's going to do an endocrinology rotation at UCLA for a few weeks, so I could house-sit for her while I look for my own place."

Stella squinted at me through the bright afternoon sun, taking in the set of my jaw. "Look at you. So cool and rational."

That was me—good old type A plus. Never a moment's doubt. Always on the ball.

Now if only I could stop waking up at three a.m. to sob uncontrollably while flipping through our wedding photographer's proofs.

I gazed at the wreaths and garlands and twinkling white lights adorning all the storefronts. "It'll be good to get back to the city and start working crazy hours again. Holidays are hard, especially with my family over on the West Coast." I sucked in a lungful of cold, damp mountain air. "But I'll volunteer to be on call for Christmas, and that'll keep me busy."

Stella placed her mittened hand on my shoulder. "It's okay to be sad, Erin."

"I know."

"It's not healthy to just work all the time instead of feeling your feelings."

"I am feeling my feelings." At three a.m. "I'm excited to get back to the hospital, that's all. If I move back to Boston, I mean. Which still isn't for sure."

"Uh-huh." She rolled her eyes.

"Don't patronize me. I patronize you, not the other way around, remember?"

"Whatever. Anyway, Mark and I are going away for Christmas. After what happened at Thanksgiving, we thought we were better off leaving town."

"Where are you going?"

Stella grinned. "Belize. We're renting a little bungalow on the beach. I'm packing my bikini and a ton of sunscreen, and that's it. I'm just going to lay out on the sand and read and make out with Mark all day."

"Mmm. Sounds heavenly."

"And who knows? If everything goes well with this urologist, maybe I'll even bring back a little souvenir."

I had serious doubts about Mark's vasectomy reversal, both as a physician and as a friend, but I kept these to myself. "Do you think Cash will be good with a baby?"

"Probably—he likes kids. Little girls, especially. Even Mark finally admitted he's a sweet dog." Stella laughed, and I tried to be happy for her—genuinely happy—and fight through the sour aftertaste tainting my thoughts. Why didn't *my* husband (well, faux husband) love me enough to rearrange his life priorities? Why couldn't *I* get a happily ever after with a big red bow on it? Maybe you had to have fairy-tale-princess looks to get the fairy-tale-princess life. Hmph.

As we approached the drugstore, I remembered I'd used up the last of Casey's conditioner in the shower that morning. "Hey, can you wait here for a second? I have to run in and grab a few things."

"Sure." She bent down to pry open the dog's mouth and extract out a candy wrapper he'd managed to snarf up. "Meet you at the park around the corner."

"Be there in five minutes." I hurried into the store and cruised past the displays of seasonal candy and holiday cards to the hair-care aisle. While I scanned the shampoo labels and tried to ignore the falsetto, boy-band rendition of "Little Drummer Boy" blaring through the sound system, I told myself that I didn't care about spending Christmas alone. So my marriage was spiraling down in flames. So my family was on the other side of the continent. December 25 was just another day on the calendar, just another block of twenty-four hours on the long, slow, inevitable march toward death.

I was fine with it, really. No seasonal depression here.

"Dr. Maye!"

I came face-to-face with the only thing that could make this afternoon worse: Kelly Fendt.

"Hi!" I tried to sound as friendly as possible, given the fact that she'd threatened a lawsuit last time I'd seen her. "How are you?"

"Fine. Just picking up a few little stocking stuffers." She was pushing Carter along in a top-of-the-line stroller with tires that looked rugged enough to scale Everest. "I heard about you and your husband; how are you holding up?"

News of the breakup had swept through town like an arctic cold front, aided by Renée and her bridge buddies, who had concocted a grossly distorted version of events. "I'm okay," I said. "Thanks for your concern."

"I can't imagine how hard it must be, bumping into your ex everywhere you go." She leaned forward, hungry for scandal.

"Actually, I might move back to Boston, so that won't be an issue."

"You are?" She reached down to wrestle a can of mousse out of Carter's chubby little fist. "But you can't! Who's going to take care of my baby?"

"Dr. Lowell's a top-notch pediatrician."

"But he's not *you*!" What happened to all the hand-wringing and the accusations of criminal negligence? "He doesn't know Carter the way you do. He doesn't listen the way you do."

He doesn't cave in and take your hysterical, middle-of-the-night pages the way I do.

"You'll be in very good hands," I promised her. "And if you're that worried, I can give you the name of—"

"Well, since you're here right now, would you mind taking a quick peek at Carter? He's developed a rash over the past day or so, and I just know it's something awful."

I glanced at my watch. "Mrs. Fendt, I'm sure he's fine."

She angled the stroller, blocking my escape route. "Oh, can't you just look? Pretty please? Just to give me peace of mind?"

"I really can't do an exam in the drugstore—"

"I promise I'll make an appointment next time." She held up her hand, as if swearing on the Bible. "I know you think I'm ridiculous, but I'm begging you. Just look at his hands."

Ridiculous was right. But apparently, she planned to hold me captive in the shampoo aisle until I obeyed, so I knelt down and took Carter's hand in mine, carefully turning it palm side up. Given the previous allegations of whooping cough and appendicitis, I was expecting the rash to turn out to be nothing more than chapped skin, but to my surprise, little bright red spots dotted the toddler's palm and wrist.

"See?" Kelly sounded triumphant. "A rash! Looks like someone pricked him all over with a pin, poor baby."

I frowned down at the red dots, then rested the back of my hand against Carter's forehead. He giggled, spewing graham cracker crumbs on my pants. "Has he been running a fever?"

"No."

"Has he lost any weight? Has he been acting listless?" I asked, as Carter amused himself by trying to bite my fingers.

"No, he's been bright-eyed and bushy-tailed. It's all I can do to keep up with him." She peered down over my shoulder. "There was one weird thing, though. He got a bruise on his shoulder yesterday when his grandma picked him up. He bumped up against her glasses—barely touched them—and look." She picked Carter out of the stroller, peeled off his fleecy orange anorak, and tugged down the neckline of his sweatshirt to reveal a large, purple bruise. "I've never seen him bruise like that."

I turned my attention back to the rash, pressing my finger down against the child's wrist to see if the skin would blanch under pressure. The dots remained bright red. "Hmm. Carter was in my office a few weeks ago, right? With the flu?"

"Yes." Kelly looked chagrined. "And I know I might have overreacted, Dr. Maye, but I swear this time is different."

"Well, I'm not—"

"I swear!" She pulled Carter up against her chest and rocked him. "I'm not freaking out over nothing this time!"

I got to my feet and touched her coat sleeve. "You're right."

"I am?" Her expression oscillated between victorious and horrified. "Oh my God, what's wrong with him? Is it measles? Is it smallpox?"

"I can't be sure, obviously, without doing some bloodwork, but those red spots look like petechiae. Between those and the bruising, I'd suspect a blood problem called ITP—basically, an abnormally low platelet count."

Kelly sagged against the shelf. "He's got a blood disorder?"

"Maybe," I emphasized. "And don't worry, almost all kids with this bounce back to normal in a few months. ITP sometimes shows up in children who have recently gotten over a cold or stomach bug, and when their bodies make antibodies to fight off the infection, the antibodies cross-react with the antigens in the blood platelets."

"But . . . what does that mean?" Kelly grabbed my hand and squeezed until my fingers went numb. "Why him? What do I do now?"

"Go to the ER and ask to speak with a hematologist. They should run a CBC with a differential." I pulled my cell phone out of my tote bag. "Here, I'll call ahead and talk to the ER attending."

"My baby." Kelly handed Carter over to me as if I were going to personally walk him down to the hospital. "My baby."

"He'll be fine, Mrs. Fendt." I strapped Carter back into the stroller and smiled confidently. "Everything will be fine. Go get him checked out, and call me tomorrow if you have questions." I surprised myself by leaning over to give her a hug. "Don't worry. I know you're scared, but he'll be fine."

"But . . ." She spread her arms out. "He's my whole world."

"I know," I said. "You're doing a good job. He's happy, he's healthy, he's got a great mom who loves him."

Kelly blinked back tears even as she smiled. "That's true. No one else could possibly love him as much as I do. No one."

I felt a pang of empathy for Carter's future wife, whoever she might be. And then I had a flash of sympathy for Kelly herself. She was right—no one else would be able to love her son the way she did. Maternal love might get a little crazy sometimes, but it was the purest, strongest human bond. Kelly would have to stand on the sidelines and try to hold her tongue while her son made mistakes and got hurt and fell in love with women who might not always treat him well. I wondered if that was how Renée had felt when David had married me—as if her whole world had been walking down the aisle in a tuxedo, leaving her behind. The thought was almost enough to make me feel sorry for my mother-in-law.

Almost.

22

STELLA

"Want to order Chinese?" I asked Erin on Thursday night as we sacked out on the new sofa Mark had bought to replace the one Cash had mangled.

"Eh." She didn't look away from the gritty detective drama on the television. "Not hungry."

"But you have to eat." I used my sternest nanny tone. "You've lost like five pounds this week."

"Good." She stuck out her bottom lip stubbornly. "The divorce diet. I'll be nice and slim when I start dating again."

"You're going to get sick," I warned. "You're eating dinner whether you like it or not, so you better decide what you want."

"I told you, I'm not hungry."

"Okay, imagine I put a gun to your head and told you

I'd kill you if you didn't eat something. What would you eat?"

She smirked. "I'd grab the gun out of your hand and tell you I'd kill *you* if you didn't stop harassing me."

"Erin."

"Okay, fine, I'll have some cereal if it'll get you off my back."

"Cereal is not a meal," I said primly.

"You're pushing your luck," she said, reaching down to scratch Cash's exposed belly.

"Fine." I headed to the pantry, found an unopened box of Special K, and poured some into a bowl. "But I'm getting Chinese."

"Bully for you." Erin stretched her arms over her head and yawned. "Where's Mark, anyway?"

"Still at the hospital."

"And the big doctor's appointment is Monday?"

"Yes, ma'am. Dr. Saris in Eastover. Mark says he's the best urologist around here, and if he doesn't work out, we'll go to New York."

"Full speed ahead, huh?"

I nodded. "We're making it legal, too. I'm meeting him at the courthouse tomorrow after I get off work." Despite Mark's assurances that he could provide for me and any children that we might have, I had decided to go ahead and accept a part-time job at a highly rated preschool run out of a local church.

I missed working with kids and besides, I thought this would be a good way to get involved in the community. Now that Erin was threatening to relocate to Boston, Casey would be my only friend in Alden, and between her store and her see-sawing relationship with Nick, she didn't have a lot of time to socialize right now.

"You're starting a new job on a Friday?" Erin asked.

"Yeah. I was supposed to start Monday, but the girl who's leaving came down with strep throat, so they asked me to start tomorrow instead."

"Well, take some vitamin C before you go in—those kids are riddled with germs," she advised.

"Hey, look who's handing out nutrition advice. The woman who won't eat."

She spooned up some cereal and crunched furiously to prove me wrong.

"So what do you think I should wear to the courthouse to-morrow?" I asked. "I have a cream wool suit, but I'm worried that would be cheesy."

"It's only cheesy if you wear it with white fishnets and a blusher veil."

"Okay, but do you think I could get away with carrying a bouquet?" I asked. "Nothing over the top, just a few stems of lily of the valley. For good luck."

"I think you should wear and carry whatever you want," Erin said firmly. "There's nothing wrong with wanting to celebrate remarrying—or marrying, whatever, you know what I mean—your husband."

I got carried away in the moment and asked, "Do you want to come and be a witness? You can sign our marriage certificate and . . ." I trailed off when I saw her expression. "Sorry. That was totally insensitive."

She set aside the cereal she'd just started to eat. "I appreciate the thought, I do, but I don't think I can handle any more weddings for a while."

The doorbell rang, and Cash leapt to his feet and barked.

"Who's that?" Erin yelled.

I shrugged. "I have no clue. Unless the delivery guy at the Chinese place is psychic."

Erin grabbed the dog's collar while I peeked through the glass pane on the side of the front door.

The man on my doorstep looked like a Tommy Hilfiger model: tall and blonde, with a very cute butt evident under his jeans. I didn't recognize him until he turned his face toward me.

"It's Nick!" I turned to Erin for guidance.

She stopped short. "Nick as in Casey's husband Nick?"

"That's the one."

"Well, what is he doing here?"

"I don't know!"

"What does he want?"

I glanced back toward the doorstep, where Nick was starting to look a little impatient. "Beats me."

"We can't talk to him," Erin decided. "It violates the girl-friend code of ethics."

"Well, he knows we're in here. We can't just leave him out there."

"Sure we can. Casey would want it that way."

Nick rapped on the window and pantomimed turning the doorknob.

"Can't we just see what he wants?" I asked.

"If you insist." Erin planted a hand on her hip. "But this better be good."

I put on a stony expression before opening the door. "Can I help you?"

"Hey." Nick scuffed his feet on the ridged black mat on the stoop, shaking the snow off his hiking boots. "Is Casey here?"

"Nope," I said. "Sorry."

He turned to Erin. "I went to your house first, but David wasn't home and his mom said you had probably run off to Vegas with a snake oil salesman, whatever the hell that is."

"Nice." You could practically see the smoke coming out of Erin's ears. "Did she also tell you that she *eviscerated* my marriage and left it to bleed to death?"

"Uh, no." Nick quickly diverted his attention to me. "But I know Casey's been hanging out with you a lot lately, and she said you and Mark had gotten back together—congratulations, by the way."

"Thanks," I murmured.

"So I hoped she'd be here."

"She's at a movie with her sister and nephews." Erin stepped up next to me, still hanging on to Cash, who wriggled frantically in an attempt to greet the visitor. "We'll tell her you stopped by."

"Wait." Nick wedged his boot into the foyer before Erin could close the door all the way. "Please."

"You're a pushy one, aren't you?" Erin gave him her snottiest Ivy League stare. "Cash, sic 'im."

But Cash failed miserably as an attack dog. He leapt into Nick's arms as if they were long-lost war buddies.

"Oof. Friendly dog." Nick gently set Cash down, then mopped off his face with his coat sleeve.

Erin barged back into the conversation, her tone icy. "Speaking of dogs . . . why are you here?"

Nick flinched. "I guess I deserve that."

"Yes, you do." Erin was just getting warmed up. "You might think you're too good for her, but let me tell you something, pal—"

"Erin." I cleared my throat. "Calm down. Let's just hear what he has to say."

"I will not calm down!" Her voice broke. "I am *sick* of these men who think they can do whatever they want and don't care who they hurt." She burst into tears and ran for the guest bathroom. Cash followed her and scratched at the door until she let him in with her.

The click of the lock echoed through the foyer, followed by muffled sobs and sympathetic canine whining.

"Sorry," I whispered, leading Nick toward the kitchen. "She's had a rough week. We all have. Try not to take it personally."

"Oh, I'd say it's pretty personal." He nodded as I offered him a cup of the French Roast brewing in the coffeemaker. "And she's right. I haven't exactly been Husband of the Year."

"Well, I wish I could help you, but Casey's not here."

"Out with her sister, huh?" He rubbed his chin. "That's new. Since when does she hang out with Tanya?"

"You'd really need to ask her. I don't know all the details, and I don't want to get in the middle of her marriage—"

"That's the problem!" He put the mug down on the counter and appealed to me with outstretched hands. "There's nothing to get in the middle of. She won't take my calls, she won't let me in the apartment—it's like I don't even exist. I ran into her at the grocery store last night, and she looked right through me." He seemed on the verge of tearing his hair out. "I want this to work; I'll do anything!"

"Well, if I see her, I'll tell her you stopped by."

He hung his head. "So you won't help me?"

"Help you what?"

"Win her back."

"No, I don't think it's a good idea to get involved."

"But I can't live like this." He hitched up his jeans to prove his point. "I can't sleep, I can't eat, I'm falling apart." He froze when he noticed my face. "What?"

"Nothing." I coughed.

"No, go ahead. I can take it. What?"

I rested the back of my head against the cabinet. "Maybe you need to stop thinking about how *you* feel about this and start thinking about how *she* feels."

"But how am I supposed to know how she feels when she won't even look at me?"

Boys. Honestly. "That whole not looking at you thing? That's a clue."

"Well, she's pissed, I get that, but—"

"Why do you think she locked you out of the apartment?"

He wrinkled up his forehead. "Besides being pissed?"

"Yes. What do you think put her over the edge from being annoyed to changing the locks and pretending you were never born?"

"Is this a trick question?"

"No, Nick." I couldn't keep the exasperation out of my voice. "She gave up hope. She accepted the fact that you're never going to love her the way she needs to be loved."

"Because I went to Detroit for Thanksgiving?"

"No. Although that was a pretty dickhead move. It's what you did *after* Thanksgiving."

"But all I said was—"

"She wants you to notice her."

"I do notice her."

I raised an eyebrow. "What was she wearing at the grocery store yesterday?"

"Give me a break! No guy remembers that kind of stuff!"

"When was the last time you gave her flowers for no reason? When was the last time you cooked dinner for her or wrote her a really gushy love letter?"

"Uh . . ."

"See? She wants to be treated like the prom queen. Like she's the only woman in the world and you'd rather be single for the rest of your life than date anyone but her."

He mulled this over for a minute. "The thing is, though, she's way better than the prom queen. When we were in high school, Anna Delano was prom queen, and she wasn't half as pretty as Case. She was mean, too, really mean. She and her friends used to corner Casey in the girls' bathroom and—"

"And you dated this chick?"

"When I was seventeen. I didn't know any better."

"Okay, then. You need to show Casey that she's much more important to you than this other hag ever was. Whatever you did to get Anna Delano, you need to do something ten times as spectacular for Casey. She's your wife."

"Not until she marries me again," he said stubbornly.

"Which she's never going to do unless you stop being such an ass and romance the hell out of her."

•   •   •

After Nick left, I knocked on the bathroom door. "Erin?"

The sobs had stopped, but I could still hear her sniffling.

"He's gone," I called. "You can come out."

The door opened and Cash galloped into the foyer at top speed, sniffing the floors for any trace of Nick. Erin followed, her eyes bloodshot and her nose red.

"How you doing?" I asked softly.

"I'm okay." Her smile wobbled. "I shouldn't have yelled at him like that. I just needed to let it all out, and he was an easy target."

I shrugged. "He'll get over it. Besides, he had it coming."

"So what'd he want, anyway?"

"Oh, he finally figured out he screwed up his life and now he wants a bunch of women to fix it. The usual." My stomach growled. "So listen, are we getting Chinese or what?"

She blew her nose. "Okay. Sounds good. And Stella? I'd be honored to go to the courthouse with you and Mark tomorrow."

I covered my heart with my hand. "Really?"

"Really."

23

CASEY

The flowers started arriving at nine a.m. on Friday morning. Roses, poinsettias, irises . . . every hour, on the hour. Ted, the delivery guy from Florrie's Flowers, walked into my shop with a new bouquet. Ted and I developed a chummy rapport as the morning went on.

"Here's another one," he announced at noon, hefting a glass vase full of pink tulips onto the counter. "Nice. Spendy. Tulips are tough to get this time of year."

"Thanks." I glanced around the shelves, trying to figure out where I could fit another lavish arrangement. The smell of rawhide and kitty litter had been overpowered by sweet, rich florals. "They're beautiful."

"Yeah, well, wait till you see the one o'clock delivery." Ted tapped his pen against his clipboard. "It'll really knock your socks off. Hope you like Casablanca lilies."

"I do, but I feel awful for you, having to trek back here every hour. Why don't you just drop the whole order off at once?"

"Can't. Your husband left very specific instructions—he wants 'em delivered one at a time, all through the day. Either you're a very lucky woman, or he must've done something really bad."

I smiled sweetly. "He's not my husband."

Ted winced. "Must've been really, really *bad.*"

"You have no idea." I waved good-bye as Ted headed for the door, then sternly ordered Cash to "Leave it" as he wandered up and started sniffing the tulips. Stella had asked if she could leave the dog with me for the day while she worked at the preschool, and I'd said sure. He was a good dog (well, he tried, at least) and I needed the company.

"Mr. Basketball Star thinks he can make me forget all about the last six months with a few dead plants," I said to Cash. "But we're not so easily bought, are we?"

Cash licked his chops and fixed the poinsettias with a hopeful stare.

"Forget it, those are poison. I told your mom I'd take good care of you." He trudged over to the dog bed behind the counter and curled up to pout.

"I know, you're so deprived." I straightened up as the door chimes tinkled and Mindy Janowitz walked in. Tall, blonde, and a size six even after having two children, Mindy still looked like the cheerleader she'd been in high school. She was married to one of Nick's high school buddies and had no doubt heard all about the war raging in the Keating household.

"Hey, Mindy, how's it going? Did your dog like the grain-free kibble?"

"Oh yes, she loved it. And her ear infections cleared right up." She paused, looking expectantly at me.

"Good." If she was waiting for me to volunteer some new gossip to spread around town, she was going to be disappointed. "So what can I help you with today? I just got in some great all-natural training treats. They're made with liver and free-range chicken . . ."

She appraised the bouquets with the practiced eye of a long-time marital mercenary. "Wow, these are gorgeous, Casey. Are they from Nick?"

"Yeah."

Her eyes widened. "So that's how he got permission."

I blinked. "For what?"

"To go deer hunting with Rick and Gil down at the pond."

I felt like the top of my skull was about to blow off. "Nick went *deer hunting*? Like, with a *gun*? Are you sure?"

Her grin vanished. "Uh-oh. I thought you knew."

"Where the hell did he get a gun?" I demanded. "And why isn't he at work?"

"God, I'm sorry; I thought you knew. Me and my big mouth."

"I will kill him." I seethed. "*Kill him.*"

"Okay, well, gotta run. Bye!" Mindy fled out the door and around the corner.

I grabbed the vase of roses and dumped it in the trash can

with a crash that roused the dog from his nap. Then I snatched the card out of the arrangement of tulips, preparing to call the florist and cancel all afternoon deliveries.

But before I could pick up the receiver, the phone rang.

Stay calm, be professional. "Good afternoon, Alden Pet Supply."

"Casey? It's Nick."

I hung up. Thirty seconds later, the phone rang again. I let the call go to voice mail. But the phone kept ringing. And ringing. And ringing.

Finally, I let my rage get the better of me and snatched up the receiver. "*What?*"

"Don't hang up!"

"Give me one good reason why not."

"Because I love you?" He sounded like a man on his way to the gallows.

"Are you asking me or telling me?"

"Casey, come on. Don't do this."

"You have thirty seconds to make your case," I snapped. "After that, I am taking the phone off the hook."

"Did you get my flowers?" he asked.

"Yes, actually, I did. But all the flowers in the world aren't going to make up for what you're out doing right now."

Silence.

"Uh-huh." My voice shot up about two octaves. "I ran into Mindy Janowitz. She told me all about your little bonding trip with the guys."

He exhaled slowly. "I know it sounds bad—"

"Yeah, it does. So you might as well tell me. Did you blow Bambi's mom away yet?"

"I'm not shooting anything," he insisted. "Swear to God."

"Oh please. You honestly expect me to believe you took the day off work and headed into the woods with a rifle, but you're not shooting anything?"

"That's right."

"So the rifle's for self-defense? Against the deer?"

"No." He was getting surlier by the second. "I came out to Waronoke Pond because I needed some guy time. To think about stuff. I needed to get out of my parents' house. My dad's driving me crazy. And yeah, I borrowed a rifle from Rick because that's what you're supposed to have when you go hunting. But I'm not shooting anything!"

"Nick. How stupid do you think I am?"

"I don't think you're stupid, Case; I'm telling the truth. I'm sitting here in the tree stand, talking to you on my cell phone while Rick and Gil are off tracking some wily ten-point buck! How could I talk on my cell phone if I was trying to sneak up on a deer?"

Hmm. A decent point.

"I'm going to prove myself to you," he insisted. "What do you think all the flowers are about?"

"Guilt." I paused. "And your desire to continue eating my homemade apple crisp."

He laughed. "Your apple crisp is pretty damn good. But that's not why I want to stay married to you."

I cut him off before he could even start down that road. "Forget it, Nick, no. And any chance you had of saving this relationship died a gory death when you went out in the forest to slaughter innocent animals."

"For the last time. I am not slaughtering anything, except my dignity. I am sitting here on the tree stand, freezing my butt off and thinking about you. I miss you. Please take me back."

"Stop," I said softly.

"You want me to beg? Fine, I'll beg. I don't care! Rick and Gil are miles away by now, it's just me and my cell phone in the middle of nowhere. So fine, Casey, I will beg for you if that's what you want." I heard the rustling of bulky winter clothing and the creak of old wood. "Here I am, getting down on my knees—"

The explosive crack of a gunshot thundered through whatever he'd been about to say.

I pressed the phone close to my ear. "Nick?"

He didn't respond.

"*Nick?*" The roar of blood in my ears drowned out the silence on the other end of the line.

I commenced hyperventilating. Cash trotted over to investigate.

"Nick?" Shouting into the receiver hadn't gotten me any results so far, but maybe if I kept getting louder, my luck would change. "Are you okay? Answer me, Nick. *Answer me!*"

There was a faint, faraway groaning noise from his end of the line. My heart started beating again. He wasn't dead.

Yet.

"Come on." I clipped a leash onto Cash's collar, locked up the store, and dashed out to my truck. "We're going to Waronoke Pond. Let's hope there's some tracking dog in you, buddy."

I found Rick Janowitz's red SUV parked by the side of the road near the trail leading to the pond. Muddy footprints were tracked through the snowbanks piled by the trail's entrance, but the warm temperatures over the last few days had melted much of the snow on the ground.

"Okay." I let Cash take a good sniff around the SUV. "There's the scent you're looking for. Do your thing."

He looked up at me blankly.

"Come on, let's go! Time's a-wasting!"

More blank staring. He sat down and whined for a treat.

"No, Cash, it's not snack time. We need to find Nick. Find Nick!" I tugged the leash and started down the path toward the pond. "He's got to be around here somewhere."

We loped toward the pond, stopping to investigate every time Cash showed interest in a new scent.

"Did you find him?" I crouched down to see what the dog was pawing at.

A gray squirrel streaked out from under a gnarled tree stump, and the leash snapped taut as Cash strained to pursue him.

"No!" I cried, dragging the dog back to the path. "This is life and death, and you're chasing after some stupid squirrel? Let's go!"

When we reached the frozen pond, there was no sign of Rick, Gil, or Nick. I scanned the foliage but couldn't find any sign of the tree stand.

So I did what any reasonable woman would do under the circumstances. I started screaming at the top of my lungs.

"Nick!"

His name echoed through the cold, still valley.

"Rick! Gil! Anyone! Hello?"

Cash joined in, howling along in a low, mournful dirge.

I shushed him and cocked my head, listening. But there was nothing. Just me and the dog and the fading afternoon sunlight that would soon give way to darkness.

A whimper escaped my throat. What if I couldn't find him? What if he was all alone out there, bleeding to death and thinking I didn't care enough to look for him?

Cash yipped and jerked the leash so hard that he broke free of my grasp. I watched him disappear over the ridge, my terror snowballing into hopeless panic.

Okay. Okay. Stop freaking out and think. *Maybe racing around the woods screaming bloody murder isn't the absolute best way to approach this. I should call someone. Erin. She'll know what to do. She can call the fire department or the EMTs or some-*body *and have them organize a search party.*

I fished my cell phone out of my pocket and scrolled through the directory until I found Erin's number. Ever the go-to girl, she picked up on the second ring.

"Hello?"

"Thank God." I breathed a sigh of relief. "Are you at work right now?"

"No, I'm down at the courthouse with Stella and we're having a little problem. Well, in actual fact, it's more of a big problem."

"Okay, well, I need your help," I told her. "Nick's lost in the woods. And I think he might have been shot."

"Oh my God, who shot him?"

"I'm not sure; he may have shot himself. But anyway, I can't find him and I need you to—"

"He tried to kill himself because you won't take him back?"

"No, no, it was an accident," I explained in a rush. "I think. I don't know what actually happened because I can't find him. All I know is that he and his friends were hunting out by Waronoke Pond and he—"

Woof, woof, woof!

I cupped my hand over the cell phone. "Shut up, Cash, I'm trying to do your job here!"

Woof, woof, woof!

And then I heard it: the thin, strangled moaning drifting over from the other side of the ridge.

"Hang on," I yelled into the cell phone. "Stay on the line, okay? Stay on the line."

I scrambled up the face of the slope, slipping in the mud. When I reached the top, I saw Cash standing over a body. A body encased in camouflage and bright orange accents, with limbs sprawled out at awkward angles.

"I found him," I reported to Erin.

"How is he?" she asked.

"He's not moving." I fell twice more in my haste to get down the other side of the ridge. When I reached Nick, his eyes were closed and his breathing was labored, but he was alive.

"He's breathing," I said. "And I don't see any blood."

"None at all? Well, that's good. If he got shot, you'd expect to see blood."

"Hang on, I'll turn him over and check his back." I reached out to flip him onto his side, but Erin stopped me just in time.

"No! Don't move him. If he's got a spinal injury, we don't want to jostle him around."

"Well, what should I do?" I made a concerted effort not to start hyperventilating again.

"Stay with him." She had her ER voice on, brisk and authoritative. "Give me directions to the pond and I'll call an ambulance."

"And what am I supposed to do in the meantime? He could be dying here! Should I cover him with my coat or splash water on him or give him mouth-to-mouth or *what*?"

"Casey. It's okay. Help is on the way, I promise. Just try to keep him awake; the paramedics will be there before you know it," she promised. "Now give me directions."

Nick's eyes fluttered open and he muttered something I couldn't make out.

"Wait," I told Erin. "He's trying to say something."

"Ask him if he can wiggle his toes," she suggested. "Ask him if he knows what year it is."

"Pr . . ." He wet his lips and gasped for air.

"What is it, honey?" I rested the back of my hand against his ashen cheek.

He looked at me as if he had never seen me before. His eyes absolutely caressed me. "Prom queen. You're the prom queen."

I dropped my hand from his cheek. "That's Anna Delano, Nick. Not me."

"Prom queen," he insisted, before his eyes closed again.

"What'd he say?" Erin wanted to know. "I didn't catch that."

"You better tell that ambulance to hurry," I said grimly. "He must have fallen right on his head."

24

STELLA

"Who was it?" I asked as Erin snapped her cell phone shut. "Is everything okay?"

"Nick is semiconscious in the woods talking nonsense." Erin stood up from the scratched metal folding chair in the courthouse corridor and pulled on her parka. "I have to call an ambulance and then I'm going to go meet Casey by Waronoke Pond."

"What can I do to help?" I asked.

"Well, Casey has the dog with her, so I'm going to drop him off at your house on the way to the hospital, okay?"

I nodded, unzipping the inside pocket of my purse and handing over the spare key.

She clapped both hands on my shoulders. "Are you going to be all right?"

"Sure." I tried to sound like I meant it. "Absolutely."

"Because you know I'd stay with you, but . . ."

"Erin, go. Give me a call when you know how Nick's doing."

She was already halfway down the hall, barking orders into her phone. As she rounded the corner, I sank back down into my chair.

The warm-eyed administrative assistant stationed in the office across the hall threw me a sympathetic smile. "He's still not here?"

I tilted my head back against the cool white wall. "Not yet."

It had taken me three hours to reach that conclusion; three hours of forced laughter, cold cups of coffee, and increasingly stilted chit chat. Erin had put up a good front—she'd never mentioned that she had used half a sick day to meet me here, and she'd remained cheerful throughout the afternoon—but by hour two, we had run through our entire stock of hilarious child-care stories, and a dark undertow of dread had seeped through our forced enthusiasm.

Mark wasn't going to marry me.

The man who loved me more than I ever thought possible, who had just last weekend convinced me to move back in with him, wasn't going to come through. He was going to let me down when I needed him most, and I had no idea why.

He was the one who insisted we meet here to make our vows official. He was the one who said we owed it to ourselves to fight through the rough patches and recommit to being happy. And we *were* happy—at least, I was. Just last night, the two of us had stayed up late baking gingerbread men and decorating them like doomed famous couples (Charles and Diana, Romeo and Juliet, even an emaciated Paris and Nicole). We'd kissed and flirted like we had on our first dates. I'd really felt like we were back on track.

So where the hell was he?

I tried to keep the faith. Something must have come up, right? Mark wouldn't leave me hanging like this; he hated to disappoint me. (Hated it so much that he'd gloss over little details like ten-year-old vasectomies rather than deal with them head-on.)

This was different, I told myself firmly. I wouldn't give up on him.

At quarter to five, the administrative assistant started making apologetic noises about needing to close up for the night. "I'm sorry, miss, but you might as well head home," she said. "All the judges have already left for the weekend."

"Okay," I said. "I know." But I didn't want to leave. As long as I remained here on my uncomfortable little folding chair, I could stay in limbo between being married and single.

I took the long way home, stopping to get a pedicure at the new strip mall off Route 7. Then I hit the grocery store, the video store, and the gas station, where I topped off my car's three-quarters-full tank. And still no word from Mark.

Should I drop by the hospital to see Casey? Or would I only be in the way?

The most sensible course of action was to put on my big-girl panties, go home, and deal with Mark and whatever he might have to say. No more avoidance. No more pretending. I put the car in gear and ten minutes later, I pulled up in the circular driveway.

As I climbed out of the car, I noticed that the front windows were completely dark. Erin had said she'd drop by with Cash, but I didn't hear the usual barks and snufflings on the other side of the door.

"Hello?" I stepped into the foyer and hit the light switch. "Mark?"

No answer. The house was silent; my footsteps echoed off the high ceiling as I headed toward the family room.

"Cash?" I tried. "Here, doggie, doggie."

The hush took on an ominous chill. I thought about what had just happened to Nick. Hurt, stranded, alone in the woods. What if something terrible had happened to Mark? An accident, a break-in?

My worry crested into hysteria as I reached the doorway to the kitchen. Glistening puddles of red liquid were smeared across the floor, tracked through with Cash's huge paw prints. I pressed my fingers into one of the wet stains and recoiled as I confirmed my worst fear: blood.

Fresh blood coated the Travertine tiles, the upholstered

kitchen chairs, even the throw rug by the patio door. The sheer volume of gore made my stomach lurch. Someone must have hemorrhaged all over the kitchen, and very recently, so why was the house dark? Why wouldn't anyone answer me?

"Mark?" My voice was barely a whisper. "Mark, please."

I hadn't realized how hard I was trembling until my purse fell off my shoulder and the keys clattered out of my hand.

If this were a horror movie, you could bet your buttered popcorn that a crazed serial killer would be lurking in the basement, just waiting for me to change into a see-through negligee and creep downstairs to check out the boiler room. Well. I hadn't grown up watching Wes Craven marathons on cable for nothing. I was getting the hell out of here and calling 911 before some psycho leapt out of the shadows.

But Mark . . . The trembling resumed as I stared at all the blood.

You can't help Mark if you're dismembered under the floorboards. Run. I hauled ass for the front door, grabbing the fireplace poker and brandishing it like a baseball bat.

I made it all the way to the foyer before I saw it: A clear plastic squeeze bottle nestled up against the first tread of the white carpeted staircase. The bottom of the vial had been chewed off, but the cap was still on. And it was red.

The visions of serial killers dancing in my head faded away and the poker dropped to the floor as I realized I was looking at a mangled bottle of red food coloring. Mark and I had several different shades of icing to frost the gingerbread cookies last night. We must have left the bottles out by the sink. Easy prey for an agile counter-surfer like Cash.

I raced back into the kitchen to reexamine the forensic evidence. The smears had started to dry, but I licked my index finger, ran it through the red, took a deep breath, and touched it to my tongue. No salty tang. No coppery aftertaste.

I threw the shredded plastic into the trash and set off to find the culprit. "Cash? I know you're in here, dog, and I know what you did!"

After ten minutes of swearing and sweating, I found him cowering behind the laundry hamper in Mark's closet. The red paw prints crisscrossed the upstairs hallway and the guest bedroom and bathroom, so he must have had quite a field day before I came home.

"You're toast." I shook my index finger at him. "Sit." For once, he obeyed.

I grabbed one of his front feet and sure enough, the fringes of fur between his paw pads were still wet with red liquid.

"You're in big trouble," I scolded. "First of all, you scared the crap out of me. Second of all, this is a mohair blend carpet. It's expensive to clean. Mark already doesn't like you, and when he sees this, he's going to . . ."

I trailed off as the implications sunk in. Mark hadn't been murdered and left to die in our pantry. Mark wasn't here at all.

So why hadn't he shown up at the courthouse this afternoon?

The phone on the nightstand rang, and I checked the caller ID before picking up.

"I'm sorry," he started, before I could say anything.

I sat down hard on the edge of the bed.

"Stella?"

My face felt like it had lost all muscle control. "I'm here."

"I know I should have met you this afternoon. I wanted to. But every time I think about going to the urologist on Monday . . . I just can't. I wish I could, but I can't."

"Why didn't you tell me?" My voice was raw. "I waited at the courthouse for hours."

He swallowed audibly. "I couldn't bear to disappoint you."

"I believed in you, Mark. I trusted you. And when you didn't show, I thought . . . I kept thinking you were hurt. Or dead. *Something.* Because for you to just leave me there . . ."

"This is hard for me, too." He did sound agonized.

"Well, why didn't you call me? Why couldn't you just say—"

"I hate that I can't give you what you need, Stella. I never want you to look at me the way you did on our wedding night."

"But you're torturing me." I flopped sideways onto the comforter. Cash nudged my knee with his warm, wet nose. "I feel like I'm being punished."

"I never meant for this to happen. I thought—"

"The whole time I was waiting this afternoon, I was in pain," I said. "Physical pain. I love you so much, but you just . . . you just . . ."

"I love you, too," he vowed.

"No, you don't."

"I do."

"Then why are you doing this to me?" I wiped my nose with the back of my hand.

The connection crackled.

"Mark?"

"I don't want this to be over."

I buried my face in the pillow for a moment, then said, "But it is over."

"Sweetheart, no."

"You lied to me. And you're still lying."

I waited for him to protest, to fight for me. But all he said was, "I'm sorry."

Cash, who had been nuzzling my face with great concern, hit the telephone keypad with his paw and disconnected the call. I curled up into a ball in the middle of the bed and waited for Mark to call me back. But the phone never rang.

25

ERIN

"Do you want me to stay with you until he's ready to go?" I asked Casey, glancing at the luminous digital clock by the nurses' station.

"No." Casey, still caked in dried mud, with bits of leaves and twigs clinging to her red fleece jacket, shifted on the Naugahyde-upholstered chair outside Nick's room. "You must be starving. Why don't you go back to the apartment and have dinner? I left salmon fillets marinating in the fridge this morning. Just squeeze some lemon on them and throw them in the oven at three fifty."

"Can't." I put on my jacket. "My friend Jonathan's in town for the weekend and I promised to meet him for dinner."

"Erin! Why didn't you tell me that before?"

"Because Nick's concussion is more important than my social life? I told you, Jonathan's like my brother. We're just going to go get burgers and bitch about work."

"What about David?" Casey asked.

"Well, he's not invited, obviously."

"No, I mean, what are you going to do about David?"

"I don't know," I admitted. "That's the other thing I have to talk to Jonathan about. I need a guy's perspective on the whole situation."

"Have you talked to David since you left the house?"

"Only briefly. He's still refusing to ask his mother to move out, and I'm still refusing to move back until he does, so we're at an impasse."

Casey shook her head. "Do you think you're really going to move back to Boston?"

I didn't have an answer for that yet, so I gave her a pointed look and asked, "Do you think you're really going to let Nick stay over with you tonight? He keeps asking."

Casey snorted. "Yeah, he's not above playing the invalid card. No shame."

"I can hear you, you know," Nick called from the exam room, where a haggard ER resident was concluding a final check for neurological damage. As Casey had reported, he'd lost his balance while attempting to kneel in the tree stand and had discharged his gun into the trees right before he'd landed directly on his head. Though he'd spent the ambulance ride to the ER fading in and out of consciousness, he'd been awake and alert for the last few hours. A head CT hadn't shown any evidence of a skull fracture or brain injury, and despite his doctor's recommendation that he remain overnight in the hospital for observation, Nick insisted on going home tonight.

As long as he got to go home with Casey.

"Stop eavesdropping," Casey called back to him. "No one likes a sneak."

"I'm not eavesdropping, I'm defending my manly honor."

"So what do you think?" Casey murmured. "Should I let him stay at the apartment or not?"

I gave her a look. "You're asking *me*? You must really be desperate."

"Not desperate," she corrected. "Just confused."

"That makes two of us."

"So what's your story?" Dr. Jonathan Witkowski, my longtime friend and one-time fellow intern, put down his glass of beer and commenced his interrogation across the wobbly table at the Blue Hills Tavern. From the moment we'd walked through the door, women had been ogling Jonathan—with his unruly black hair, classic features and fanatic devotion to the gym, he kind of looked like Clive Owen—but he'd given up flirting since he'd started dating Simone. "You move out to the sticks and everything goes to hell in a handbasket?"

I dipped a gloriously greasy French fry into a puddle of

ketchup. "Don't be a snob; it's not 'the sticks.' But otherwise, yeah, that pretty much sums it up."

"And you're *sure* you and David can't work this out?" he asked for the hundredth time. The peppy pop music blaring from the bar's speakers didn't match our somber tones, but dining options in Alden were pretty much limited to the White Birch or the Blue Hills Tavern, and I was in no mood for the White Birch crowd tonight. With my luck, I'd run into Renée.

I increased my pace of French fry consumption. Nothing like saturated fats to dull the pain. "I've done everything I can, but ultimately it's his call. And with the marriage license screwup, I feel like this is the time to make a change. No messy divorce, no ugly legal proceedings . . ."

"Except you own a house together," Jonathan pointed out.

"Except for that."

"And you love him."

"That, too," I conceded.

He narrowed his eyes. "You look exhausted—have you been sleeping?"

"Of course. Three solid hours a night."

"Just like residency."

I nodded. "But now, instead of racing around trying to save lives, I just lie in the dark and think about what could have been if only I hadn't agreed to move out here. And I'd said no when Renée offered to give us a down payment. And I'd been a better wife."

"Very productive." Jonathan kicked me under the table as I helped myself to a sip of his beer. "Well, the hospital would be glad to have you. As soon as you're ready to come back, just say the word. You could drive back with me tomorrow if you want. Simone's condo is ready and waiting."

I rested my chin on my hand, suddenly feeling the effects of the week's insomnia. "Hey, thanks for coming out this weekend. I really needed someone to talk to."

"No problem. I can't believe you and David are breaking up, though. He must be really—" Jonathan broke off and craned his neck to look at the door. "Oh man, here we go."

I whipped around and saw David march past the jukebox and the dartboard. His eyes blazed as he approached our table.

"What is he doing here?" David demanded.

I smiled weakly at our fellow diners, who had put down their burgers and were watching us intently. "Could you please lower your voice, David? You're making a—"

"I should have known! The minute we have turbulence, you go right back to him."

"Please don't start with that again," I said. "We're friends and that's all and you know it."

"Hey, Dave, how you doing?" Jonathan said mildly.

David ignored him and stared at my ring finger, which was now naked. "You didn't even wait a week to hook up with someone else?"

I shoved back my chair and slapped down my napkin. "I

am not going to sit here and listen to this." I made a beeline
for the ladies' room, but David stayed hot on my heels, and we
ended up locked in the closet-sized, wood-paneled bathroom
together.

"Why is he here?" David's face was flushed. "This is *our* town."

I started pacing the tiny room like a caged tiger. "Stop talking like that. Hate me if you must, but leave Jonathan out of
this."

David paused. "I don't hate you."

Someone knocked on the door. "Hello?" called a high, fem-
inine voice.

"In a minute!" I yelled, then resumed arguing. "What are
you really upset about?"

He looked incredulous. "Why do you think? I'm upset because my wife left me."

"Well, what do you want me to do?" I flung out my arms.

"How about not move to Boston, for starters?"

"I wouldn't be moving to Boston if you would get your
mother out of our house."

"Easier said than done."

"It's not, actually. She has plenty of money, plenty of
friends . . ."

"And only one son," he finished. "So don't ask me to cut
her out of my life."

"I'm *not;* all I'm asking is for you to cut her out of our
house! That's totally reasonable, David. Haven't you ever

thought about how much easier everything would be if she weren't constantly breathing down our necks?"

"I've thought about it," he said grimly. *Believe me,* I've thought about it."

"So?"

"So it's not that simple. Family's important."

"Yeah, and *I'm* your family!" I exploded.

"Family doesn't walk out the minute things get tough," he accused. "Family doesn't give impossible, split-second ultimatums."

"Ha! Your mother does all that and more."

"That's right, and I don't need you stepping up to do her job."

My ears started ringing. *"What?"*

"You got mad and stormed out and now you're pretending that our marriage never existed because you didn't get your way! You're trying to manipulate me, just like my—"

"Do not say it," I hissed. "Because if you do—"

Knock, knock, knock. "Excuse me. Could you please hurry up in there?"

"In a minute!" David and I screamed in unison.

I opened my mouth to enumerate the ways in which Renée and I were polar opposites, but David didn't give me a chance.

"Nothing I do makes you happy," he said. "You said you wanted to buy a house, you said Boston real estate prices were out of control—"

"Yeah, but I didn't want to move all the way out there!"

"Then why did you say yes when I asked you to move? Why did you say yes when my mother offered to help buy the house? You agreed to this, Erin. And now we're here, in the house you picked out, and all you can talk about is how much you hate it. So I give up. If moving back to Boston is going to make you happy, then go ahead."

The knocking on the door intensified to pounding. "I really have to pee!"

"Fine." I elbowed David aside, jerked open the door, and glared at the petite blonde waiting in the hallway. "We're done here."

While she waited for David to clear out, she regarded me with gentle reproach. "He has a point, you know. He did buy you that house to make you happy."

I put up my dukes. "Do I even know you?"

She slammed the door in my face. I heard the lock click.

David turned his back on me and stalked toward the bar, where I heard him ask the bartender, "Do you have any single-malt scotch?"

Jonathan had already paid our bill and gathered up our coats. "I figured it was time to go," he said. "Rumor has it you guys were brawling in the bathroom?"

I glared back over my shoulder toward the bar. "I made up my mind—I'm moving back to Boston. I'm packing tonight."

Jonathan's eyes widened. "Right now?"

"Once Renée gets word of this, she'll probably pile all my stuff on the front lawn and torch it. I better hurry. Do you think the U-Haul place is still open?"

I dropped Jonathan off at his hotel after we picked up the rental van—he'd offered to help me pack, but this was a one-woman job. I needed some time alone in the house I'd shared with David. To say good-bye to everything I thought I'd had with him.

After backing the U-Haul into the driveway (no easy feat, given my limited spatial skills), I grabbed a stack of disassembled cardboard boxes from the stack in the trailer and trudged up the front walk. The second I opened the front door, the living room lights blazed on and a clipped, arctic voice said, "Well, well, well. Look who's back."

Blinded by the sudden explosion of light, I dropped the boxes to rub my eyes. "What the . . . *Renée?*"

"That's right."

When my eyes adjusted, I saw her curled up like a cat in the tall blue wingback chair.

"I thought you were at bridge club tonight," I sputtered.

"Trudie Fischer's husband called from the Blue Hills Tavern. Are you here for your things?"

"Well . . . yeah."

"Good." She uncoiled herself from the chair and started across the room. "I've had everything packed and ready to go since you deserted my son."

"You went through my things? My private things?" *Of course* she had gone through my private things. Had I learned nothing?

"You broke David's heart." She tucked her brown bob back behind her ear. "I want you out."

"Oh no, you don't." I held up a hand. "Let's get one thing straight, lady. *I* didn't break David's heart. You did. You're the one who moved in here and pried this marriage apart with a crowbar."

"Nothing can tear apart a strong marriage."

"You sabotaged me from day one!" I ranted. "You tried to kill me! And maybe I could have gotten past that, but you went through my mail! You threw out my job offer from Boston!"

"I did no such thing." But her eyes gave her away.

"Save the martyr routine for David. I know what you did. The dog dragged the evidence out of the trash."

"The dog." She sniffed.

"That's right, Renée—the dog busted you."

She pointed imperiously toward the den, where I could see a tower of stacked cartons and suitcases. "Your boxes are ready and waiting."

"Well, you finally got rid of me. Congratulations." I grabbed two small boxes—books, I was guessing, from the weight of them—and staggered toward the front door.

"You never loved him enough." She said this almost to herself. "If you did, you would have stayed."

"You never loved him enough," I countered. "If you did, you would want him to be happy."

"He *is* happy."

"Keep telling yourself that." I dropped the boxes on the front stoop, then went back to the den for another armload.

She kept pace behind me, berating me in increasingly shrill tones. "I will not be spoken to like that in my own home, do you hear me?"

I laughed. "Here's the thing, Renée: this isn't your house. It's mine. Mine and David's."

"I gave you the down payment."

"How could I forget with you reminding me every five minutes?"

"You don't live here anymore. You're moving out."

"My name is on the title. Not yours. I'll speak to you any way I want. If you don't like it . . ." I gestured toward the door.

Her face puckered into an angry little move, but she stood her ground. "You were never good enough for him," she repeated. "Never."

"That's where you're wrong. I was perfect for him. And you couldn't stand it."

"But he picked me, didn't he?" She seized the cordless phone and commenced dialing.

"Who do you think you're calling?" I scoffed. "The police are not going to come and throw me out. Name on the title, remember?"

"I'm calling Mr. Reynolds. He'll help you move your furniture. The sooner you're out of here, the better."

"Finally, we agree on something."

"Hello, Henry?" She barked into the phone. "I need you to come over." She paused. "Yes, I'm back. Bridge broke up early tonight. How did I do?" She smiled at me, her eyes glinting. "I won, of course. I always win."

26

CASEY

Do you remember your name?" I asked Nick as soon as he woke up the next morning.

He rubbed his eyes, still groggy under the blankets I'd piled on the sofa last night. "Yeah."

"Do you remember *my* name?"

"Case, come on, don't treat me like a lobotomy patient."

"Well, I'm just making sure. When I found you in the woods yesterday, you were hallucinating and talking crazy."

"I was not." He propped himself up on his elbows, adorably indignant in his gauze bandage and Celtics shirt. I resisted-barely—the urge to reach out and ruffle his golden brush of hair.

"You thought I was Anna Delano," I reminded him.

"I did not!"

"Nick." I put my hands on my hips. "You kept calling me the prom queen."

He collapsed back against the pillows. "That— Okay, that—"

"Yes? I'm waiting."

"I did not think you were Anna Delano!"

"Uh-huh."

"I didn't! I was trying . . . I was referring to . . . ask Stella. She'll explain it better than I can."

"You want me to ask Stella why you confused me with Anna Delano in the woods yesterday? Here we go again with the crazy talk."

He got off the couch and strode toward the kitchen. "You just wait and see."

The sight of him in his boxers was making me remember things I'd rather forget. Like how much fun we'd had in the bed of our dilapidated honeymoon shack in the Adirondacks. And now, with Erin bunking at Stella's newly leased apartment for the next few days while Nick stayed here, there was no one to buffer the increasingly charged friction between us. I forced myself to turn away and occupy myself with sliding a pair of homemade scones into the toaster oven.

"How are you feeling? Erin said I could give you some Motrin if your head hurts."

"I'm fine." He found the carton of fresh organic orange

juice in the refrigerator and poured us each a glass. "I'm not an invalid."

"Well, you better get in touch with your parents. I called them last night and told them you were fine, but you know Alden—they'll hear some wild, distorted rumor about how you took a bullet to the brain and developed a split personality and amnesia."

He groaned. "Can't anyone in this town mind their own damn business?"

"In a word, no." I handed him the cordless phone. "Start dialing." The toaster dinged, and I pulled out the tray of freshly warmed pastry. "And have a scone. They're cranberry orange—your favorite."

"I'll call my parents in a second. But first I have to tell you something."

My knee-jerk reaction was to assume the worst. "Oh no. What now?"

"It's nothing bad . . ."

"You started dating again, didn't you?" I snatched up Maisy the cat as she strolled by and cuddled her against my chest.

He stared at me. "Why would I start dating someone else? I can't even handle the woman I have."

"Well, then, why do you sound so ominous? Just tell me, okay? And hurry up, because the suspense is killing me." I braced myself for the impending sucker punch.

One of his dimples appeared as the corner of his mouth tugged up. "Have you always been this paranoid?"

"Yes. Tell me."

"Fine. When I fell out of that tree, and I was lying on the ground, I didn't feel good."

"You had a concussion. That's understandable."

"No, not physically. I mean, I didn't feel good about my life. What happened with you and me . . . it's bad."

I focused all my attention on the cat. "That's true."

"So I was, lying there, and the world was spinning and I didn't know when anyone would find me and all I could think was, *Casey's going to be so disappointed.*"

"Because you fell out of a tree?"

"Because I went hunting with the guys. I know you hate hunting. Even though I didn't shoot anything, it was a dumb thing to do because, you know, I did what the guys thought I should do instead of what you wanted me to do."

"Peer pressure." I nodded solemnly. "It's a bitch."

"Don't make fun of me." He looked ready to shrivel up and die. "This is hard enough already."

"Okay, but Nick, who cares what the guys want you to do or what I want you to do? The real question is, what do *you* want to do?"

"That's what I was thinking about. Well, I was trying to think about it; I was pretty out of it for awhile there. But I figured this much out: life is short." He crossed his arms over his broad chest. "And I'm wasting it. I have to make some changes, Case. Big ones."

My gaze slid over to the phone. "Like not calling your parents ever again?"

"You're pushing," he said softly.

"Well, you're digging your heels in," I retorted, then sighed. "You're right. I'm sorry. Let's start over: what big changes do you have to make?"

"My job, for one thing. Why do I work in my dad's office? Seriously, I hate that place. I hate wearing a suit and tie, and I'll never be good enough for him. Ever since I quit law school, he's been a miserable bastard to me. I can't take it anymore."

"Good for you," I said.

Relief dawned in his eyes. "Really?"

"It's not really a secret that you aren't cut out for life in a law firm."

"Yeah, but all those years of expectations . . ." He chomped into a scone and gave me a pointed look. "I'm through getting pushed around."

I raised my eyebrows. "Are you implying that *I* push you around?"

He just chewed his scone and waited.

I started to lose my temper. "You're a grown man. If you didn't want to get engaged, you should have said something. So don't try to put that all on me, my friend, because—"

"You're right. If I didn't want to get married, I could have said no. But I didn't. And you know why I didn't?"

"Because you'd rather exact your revenge with years of psychological torture?"

"No. Because I wanted to marry you."

I squeezed Maisy a little too hard, and she yowled. "Then why did you show up at the church with no tux and try to talk me out of it?"

"I wasn't thinking straight."

"No kidding."

"I always wanted to marry you, Casey. Always. But the way we did it, I wasn't even part of the decision. You made up your mind for both of us, and that was that."

"But—"

"Hang on, I'm not done. I was a jackass about the wedding, and I was a jackass about Thanksgiving. And you deserve better. But I'm hoping you'll give me one more chance."

I made a valiant effort to maintain my ice queen façade. "You've had more than enough chances already."

"I know. But that was before I fell on my head."

"Don't do this to me, Nick. You keep promising me that you'll change, but . . . no." I held Maisy in front of me like a shield. "I'm sorry, but I can't."

"Let me move back in."

"No." I shrank back against the counter.

"I love you," he swore. "I'll always love you."

"You refused to go to the courthouse with me," I quavered.

"I'll go right now."

"Nick."

"I mean it, let's go." He headed for the bedroom. "Give me thirty seconds to put on some pants and I'm ready. Go warm up the truck."

"It's Saturday," I pointed out. "The courthouse is closed."

"Oh." He halted. "Crap. Let's go to Atlantic City, then. Or, I know, Vegas! I'll call the airlines and you pack your wedding dress."

"This is your concussion talking."

"Go ahead, mock me. But you're not getting rid of me. We are going to be together forever."

"So you're quitting your job and moving back in?" I hitched up my pajama pants. "And all will be bliss?"

"You're skeptical." He seemed to relish the challenge. "That's fine. I can live with that. Because I am going to win you back, baby."

"This isn't a game, Nick."

"I won't rush you. You take all the time you need. In the meantime, I'm going over to my folks' house. The three of us need to have a chat."

"You're not supposed to drive yet, remember? Doctor's orders."

"I'll call a cab."

"Don't be ridiculous. I can drive you."

"You have to go open the store."

"It's no big deal if I'm half an hour late. No one's pounding down my door to buy rawhides and dewormer at nine thirty on Saturday morning."

"Forget it—the days of you babying me are over. I'll take a cab." He strode out of the bedroom wearing jeans, sneakers, and a navy pullover that brought out the blue in his eyes.

"You don't have to do all this. I get the point."

"No, you don't. But you will." When he leaned over and kissed my cheek, I caught a whiff of his fresh, woodsy scent layered beneath the antiseptic hospital smells. "Have a good day at work, honey. I'll see you tonight. And don't worry about dinner; I'll take care of everything."

"So what do you think?" I asked Tanya later that afternoon. She'd dropped the kids off with our mother for the evening and had come over to chat. With a winter storm advisory in effect, the store was completely empty. "I'm an idiot for even letting him back in the apartment, right?"

She fiddled with the tarnished silver bracelet on her wrist. "You think he's going to disappoint you again."

"*Of course* he's going to disappoint me again." I tried to sound matter-of-fact about this. "Fool me once, shame on you, fool me twice, shame on me, right?"

She smiled, and for a moment, I glimpsed the incorrigible flirt she used to be. "You don't really believe that."

"Yes, I do!"

"Then why do you look so freaked out?"

I picked at the list of register codes taped to the counter. "Argh. You're right—I don't *want* to believe he's going to pull the rug out from under me again, but . . . people don't change over-night."

"Maybe he's matured," Tanya suggested.

"In the last twenty-four hours?"

"Maybe that fall knocked some sense into him." She laughed.

"Or maybe he's just taking advantage of the Casey Nestor Luxury Hotel," I said wryly. "A few breakfasts in bed, a few runs to the drugstore, maybe even a booty call or two, and then he'll be on his way. And I'll be so pissed with myself."

"You're having sex with him?"

"No, I made him sleep on the sofa last night, but he was walking around in boxers this morning, and I'm telling you, I almost tackled him to the ground. Damn pheromones."

I walked over to the front door and turned the Open sign over to Closed. "Come on, there's no point sitting around in here. Let's run up to my apartment and I'll give you the Lego sets I bought for the boys."

"I thought you said Nick was making you dinner tonight."

"Be serious. His idea of 'making dinner' is popping the top on a can of beer." I hit the light switch and dimmed the front display area. "I'm telling you, you're giving that boy way too much credit."

• • •

As I opened the door to the apartment, I smelled cooking grease. The entryway was dark, but the golden glow of candlelight beckoned from the kitchen.

"Nick?" I rounded the corner into the kitchen.

"Welcome to Thanksgiving, part two," Nick said grandly, stepping aside to reveal the table set with my antique china. "Dinner is served."

Words failed me as I took in the eclectic spread he'd put together—tater tots, canned cranberry sauce, stuffing from a box, defrosted vegetables, and the culinary centerpiece: an enormous, charred turkey.

Luckily, Tanya had the presence of mind to speak for both of us. "Wow. Did you fry that turkey?"

"Yes, ma'am. The tater tots, too." He looked so proud of himself. "Bought a deep fryer and went to town. I kind of cheated on the cranberries and the stuffing, but I did make an apple pie for dessert. With a graham cracker crust from scratch, even!"

Clearly, now was not the time to break it to him that apple pie didn't usually go with graham cracker crust.

He pulled out a chair for me. "Have a seat. Would you like red wine or white?"

Tanya headed back toward the door. "Have fun, Case. I'll call you tomorrow."

Nick looked chagrined. "You don't have to go. There's plenty to go around. I'll just grab another chair—"

"Actually, she does have to go. You guys can do the in-law bonding thing another time." I practically shoved Tanya out the door and whispered, "Don't even say 'I told you so.'"

"Bye," she called. "Have a nice evening. Don't do anything I wouldn't do."

"He's still sleeping on the sofa," I swore.

"Lie to yourself, but don't lie to me."

When I returned to the dining room, Nick was pouring me a glass of white wine with a dish towel draped over his arm like a snooty waiter. "Zees is a very fine vintage. Over seventy-six points in *Wine Spectator*."

I batted my eyelashes. "Ooh, la la."

"Zee finest Price Chopper had to offer."

"You really know how to spoil a girl."

"I'm learning." He sat down across from me and passed the tater tots. "I talked to my dad today. Told him I quit."

"How'd he take it?"

"Better than I expected, actually. There's an opening for a basketball coach at the high school, and I think I might apply." He watched my reaction closely. "What do you think?"

"I think it's a great idea." Maybe it was just those pheromones kicking into high gear again, but these were the best tater tots I'd ever tasted. "Everything looks delicious. I can't wait to taste the turkey."

"In a minute. First, a toast." He held his wineglass aloft and said, "Here's to starting over, one step at a time."

27

STELLA

"Ring the bell again," Erin instructed, stomping her feet on the welcome mat outside Casey's apartment. "Maybe she's in the shower."

"If she's in the shower, she's not going to hear us, no matter how many times we ring it," I said, but Erin just ignored me and jabbed the doorbell.

We huddled together on the stoop and listened for any signs of activity on the other side of the door.

"Maybe she's not home," I suggested.

Erin looked cranky. "She better be home. I talked to her yesterday afternoon and we agreed to leave at ten o'clock. It's"—she shoved back her coat sleeve to check her watch—"ten-oh-seven right now. She is officially late."

"Cut the girl some slack; it's Sunday morning."

"Ha. If I know Casey, she's probably already mopped the

floor, done two loads of laundry, and whipped up a homemade quiche Lorraine or some Welsh rarebit."

I shook my head. "You are in some mood today."

"Yeah, because I'm a marital refugee shuffled from couch to couch while my ex-mother-in-law takes over my house and burns me in effigy. Cut *me* some slack."

"Well, at least you didn't get dissed and dismissed at the courthouse by the man who promised to cherish you forever," I said. "Cut *me* some slack."

"We all need some slack," Erin declared. "That's why we're leaving the state. As soon as Casey gets her organic little posterior out here."

Before she could ring the bell again, Casey poked her disheveled head out. She looked like she'd just rolled out of bed—her reddish-brown hair was mussed and she had dark purple smudges under her eyes. "Hey, guys. Is it ten already?"

Erin looked ready to stroke out. "You're not even dressed yet?"

"Hey." I nudged her boot with mine. "We're going Christmas shopping; it's supposed to be fun, remember?"

"Yeah, but if it takes an hour to get there, and an hour back, then an hour for dinner, and we're planning to see a movie . . ."

"Hurry," I pleaded to Casey. "I can't take much more of this."

"Yeah, actually . . ." Casey stretched her arms over her head. "I don't think I'm gonna go."

"You have to go!" I jerked my head toward Erin. "Don't leave me alone with her today!"

"Sorry. Some stuff came up at the last minute, and you know how it is." She shrugged helplessly. "But you guys have a good time."

"Come on," I wheedled. "Can't you see we need retail therapy in the worst way?"

And then I noticed Casey's T-shirt. It was big. It was baggy. It had an NBA emblem on the front. "Is that Nick's shirt?" I asked.

She twisted the incriminating garment around her torso, trying to obscure the Celtics logo. "Uh . . ."

"You're sleeping in his shirt?" Erin asked in disbelief.

"No! I just put this on thirty seconds ago."

"And what were you wearing before that?" I prompted.

"Uh . . ."

"Honey? Who's at the door?" Nick ambled up behind Casey and peered over her shoulder. He also sported rumpled bed hair and wore only a pair of striped blue boxers. I couldn't help noticing he was one of those rare guys who actually looked better with fewer clothes on.

I looked at Casey, looked at Nick, and said, "You didn't."

"She did," Erin squealed.

"Can we talk about this later?" Casey asked. "I have a lot to do today."

"Yeah, I'll bet you do." Erin and I both cracked up.

"Oh, grow up." Casey folded her arms. "What is this, junior high?"

"No." Erin tried to suppress a laugh. "I'd say you need at least an R rating."

"Boinking in the Berkshires," I suggested. *"The Naughty Snowbunny and the Ski Patrol."*

"You're not funny," Casey said acidly.

"It's a little funny," Nick threw in. "Don't give me that look. I'm just saying—"

"Watch your head," Erin advised him. "Try not to bang it against anything hard."

I chimed in with my version of a cheesy porn sound track. "Bow chicka bow wow . . ."

Casey slammed the door.

Erin and I collapsed on each other, giggling.

"Well, I guess she and Nick are going to give it another try," I said when I caught my breath.

"Evidently." Erin rubbed her eyes. "You know, that really cheered me up."

"You're evil, but that's why I like you." I started back down the stairs toward the parking lot. "Now let's shop."

Our spirits improved even more when we drove past the large sign welcoming us to the Empire State.

"So long, Massachusetts!" Erin tapped the car horn. "Hopefully, our karma will improve in New York."

But before we even reached the thruway exit for Crossgates Mall, we were snarled in gridlock and inhaling noxious exhaust fumes.

"This is what we get for braving the stores two weekends before Christmas." Erin turned up the radio, which was playing a grand orchestral version of "Carol of the Bells." "But I have to send everything out this week if I want presents to make it to California by the twenty-fifth."

"At least you don't have to buy anything for Renée."

"Oh, I already did. A hideous little ceramic taco holder in the shape of a Chihuahua. Tackiest thing you've ever seen. I'll mail it to her after New Year's. Anonymously, of course."

"Leave it with me and I'll leave it on her doorstep in the middle of the night," I offered.

"You're a doll. Would you consider TPing the house while you're at it?"

"Sure, why not?"

"So what do you have to buy today? Are you almost done with your list?"

"Well, now that Taylor, Marissa, and Mark are no longer on it, my list is considerably shorter." I paused. "But I decided to sign up for one of those adopt-a-family programs, so I'll be stocking up on toys for a six-year-old boy and an eighteen-month-old girl. And I'm going to get my parents something. Even though they told me not to."

Erin nodded. "They want you to save your money for tuition?" Last night, we'd gone online to check out the prerequisites for the nursing program at Berkshire Community College. I'd have to take some science courses at night while working full-time at the preschool, but I estimated that I could finish the degree in two years if I stayed focused.

"Not exactly." I fiddled with the seat-belt strap. "They kind of disowned me."

Erin slammed on the brakes as the car ahead of us stopped short on the exit ramp. "For what?"

I stared up at the heavy gray clouds. "For letting Mark get away."

"What the hell do they think you're supposed to do? Drug him and lock him in the basement?"

"No, my mom thinks I should be happy with what I have and stop obsessing about a baby. She says there's a bunch of research proving that childless couples are happier in the long run, and I should hang on to Mark for dear life."

"But, even ignoring for a moment the fact that you guys can't agree on the baby issue, he *lied to you*. Multiple times. About big things like, *I can father children* and *I'll meet you at the courthouse to get married.*"

I sighed. "Well, my mom doesn't see it that way."

"She wants you to spend your life with a liar?"

"She wants me to spend my life the same way she did—with a wealthy guy to take care of me."

"And what does your dad say about all of this?" Erin asked.

"He's in prison," I said dully. "So not much."

"Right. Sorry."

"No, it's okay. His attorneys are appealing again, so there's a chance he could be out soon, but either way, they're bankrupt. Most of their snooty friends pretend not to know them. And they just want me to be protected from all that crap."

"But to stop speaking to you . . ."

"She'll get over it eventually." I cracked open the window for some fresh, cold air. "I hope."

We finally made it into the mall parking lot and found a spot right away as an SUV pulled out in front of us.

"See?" Erin clapped her hands. "Total karmic reversal. All right, let's get in there and focus. If we finish by five, we can still catch a movie, and I know there's a giant box of Sno-Caps with my name on it."

Everything went fine until we wandered into Baby Gap. I picked out socks, mittens, and corduroy overalls for my adopt-a-family toddler, but as I reached out to stroke a soft pink angora sweater, my face crumpled.

"Stella?" Erin stopped ooh-ing and ahh-ing over a miniature pair of red rain boots. "Are you all right?"

I nodded, mute with grief. My fist closed around the angora while tears streamed down my cheeks.

"Are you hurt? Are you sick? What the hell?"

"Babies." I gasped. "They've ruined my whole life and I don't even have any."

"Oh boy." She threw an arm around my shoulder and steered me into a corner. "Calm down. Deep breaths."

I grabbed the tissue she offered and blew my nose loudly. "My marriage didn't work because of a child that doesn't exist."

"Your marriage didn't work because the groom was a pussy," she said bluntly.

"I know I'm supposed to be ambitious. I'm supposed to want to be a lawyer, or a CEO, or a doctor like you, but I don't. I just want to be a mother. That's all I've ever wanted to be."

"There's nothing wrong with that," Erin soothed.

"I'm twenty-four, I've got my whole life ahead of me, and all I can think about is kids."

"And you'll have them. You've got plenty of time."

"When?" I wailed. "When am I going to be able to come in here and buy onesies with ducks on them for *my* baby?"

Erin made a face. "Ducks? Really?"

"I like ducks." I sniffled. "Kittens, pandas, little fuzzy bunnies . . . I love all that stuff."

"Okay, the pandas are kind of cute," Erin conceded. "But don't cry about it. Your time will come."

"I got my period this morning," I said. "I cried for twenty minutes."

"So that's why you took so long in the shower."

"Something's wrong with me. I'm a babyholic. The more I want to start a family, the more single I get. And now I'm back to square one."

"You're psychotic with hormones right now, but trust me when I say a million guys will be lining up to father your child as soon as you're ready to date again."

"But I need to find the *right* guy."

"You'll find him, I promise. When you least expect it."

I dabbed my eyes. "I hate when people say that."

"Hate away, but I know I'm right. When you least expect it, Stell. Wait and see."

28

CASEY

I can't believe you're really leaving," I said, as Erin topped off her glass of diet soda and offered me a refill. It had been a week since Stella's now infamous breakdown at Baby Gap, and Erin was preparing to leave for Boston. For good.

Erin placed the empty soda can on Stella's makeshift coffee table—an overturned shipping box from my store—and jingled the keys to the U-Haul parked outside. "I finished my last day at the office fifteen minutes ago and I am officially done with Alden, Massachusetts."

"How does it feel?" I asked.

She paused for a moment before answering. "Not so great. I thought I'd be triumphant and relieved, but—"

"But it's sad," Stella finished. "And you haven't heard from David?"

Erin shook her head. "Let's not talk about this right now. I want to leave on a good note."

Between Erin's packing, Stella's unpacking, and Cash's exuberant romps, Stella's new apartment looked like a Target after a cyclone. Books and magazines were piled high on every available flat surface, shoes and scarves were jumbled on the closet floors, and the kitchen counter was crowded with pots, pans, and cartons of dishes. Stella had managed to clear a small area for the sofa, Cash's fleece-lined bed, and a three-foot Christmas tree, which she and Erin had decorated with various earrings, necklaces, and hair clips. ("We did the best we could with what we had," Stella had explained when she caught me staring at it. "Neither one of us was in the mood to go shopping for ornaments and glittery stars.")

"I'm going to miss you guys," Erin said.

"We'll miss you, too," I said. "And if you decide to come back and try to work it out with David—"

She tried to look puzzled. "David who?"

"Give it up." I rolled my eyes.

"I'm over him," she blustered. "I mean it. He's not the man I thought he was."

"Neither was Mark," Stella said.

They both turned to me.

"Yeah, men totally suck," I agreed. "Hear, hear."

Erin smiled at Stella. "She says it, but she doesn't mean it."

"She's gone," Stella said. "Back to the dark side."

"I have not!" I protested. "Just because I'm reevaluating the situation with Nick—"

"And having sex with him," Erin added.

"And floating around on a little cotton candy cloud with puffy pink hearts where your eyeballs should be," Stella teased.

"—does not mean I've decided to get back together with him. I'm still thinking things over." I held up a hand to silence their jeers. "No, I mean it! Things have been great for the past week, but he's on his best behavior. All the sex has been fogging up our brains. It's only a matter of time before he starts backsliding into his old ways: stubbornness, absenteeism, monosyllabic answers to all my questions."

"Well, enjoy the brain-fogging sex while it lasts," Erin advised.

"Don't worry, I am. Speaking of which, I've got to get going. I'm meeting Mr. Brain Fog at seven, and I need to change."

"Someplace fancy?"

I flushed. "The White Birch."

Erin and Stella immediately launched into a chorus of *"Ooh . . ."*

"It's not serious!" I insisted. "It's just sex."

"Girl, if you're making an appearance at the White Birch on Friday night, you are officially an item."

"Yeah, you might as well put on his varsity letter jacket and wear his class ring on a chain around your neck."

"But I hate to leave while you're still here, Erin. I mean, who knows when I'll get to see you again?"

"I'm moving to Boston, I'm not dropping dead," Erin said. "It's only a two-hour drive. And I expect you both to come visit. We'll go bar hopping and troll for men. Bring your most inappropriate outfits."

"Aw, you guys." I got to my feet and held out my arms. "You're the best friends I could ever find out I'm not legally married with. Group hug."

Erin pretended to retch, but she joined in, and so did Stella.

"Safe trip." I gave Erin an extra squeeze. "Good luck. Don't forget us."

My stomach did a little samba in anticipation of seeing Nick, even though I should have known better. What if he couldn't keep any of the promises he'd made this week?

I found myself going back to my old marital mantra: *Do you want to be right or do you want to be happy?*

I wanted to be happy. Maybe, hopefully, just this once, I'd underestimated him.

The White Birch was packed with a dressy, Friday night date crowd, and Nick and I had to wait at the bar until a table opened up.

"I made reservations." He glowered. "I planned in advance."

"I know you did," I assured him. "It's not your fault the other diners are slow eaters."

He looked at his watch. "The hostess said they had an opening at seven sharp. It's seven ten and—hey! Those people got here after us! Why do *they* get to sit down?"

"Nick. Chill. We're having a nice time, remember? This is supposed to be fun."

"I don't want to keep you waiting." He drummed his fingers on the top of the bar.

I brushed back my hair and smiled. "I'm sitting here enjoying a glass of wine with a hot guy. What's the rush? If I wanted to freak out about falling ten minutes behind schedule, I'd go out with Erin."

He finally relaxed. "Did she ever forgive you for standing her up on Sunday?"

"Yeah, I made her some fudge and she saw reason. She's leaving tonight, you know. Probably on the road already. Going back to Boston to . . ." My train of thought derailed as I glimpsed a familiar face on the other side of the bar. "Hey! That's Renée."

Nick followed my gaze. "Renée?"

"Renée Schmidt. Erin's mother-in-law. Well, her former . . . oh, you know what I mean."

We stared at the willowy young brunette chatting with Renée.

"Who's the chick in the green dress?" Nick asked. "Is that her daughter?"

"David's an only child." I strained to get a better look at Renée's companion. "At least, I thought he was."

"They look exactly alike," Nick said. "Even their dresses look the same. What's up with that?"

The younger woman did bear a striking resemblance to David's mother. Same haircut, same ramrod posture, even the same shade of red lipstick.

"Maybe she figured out a way to go back in time and clone herself?" I suggested.

We got our answer two minutes later when David showed up, straightening his tie and stammering apologies about getting held up at the hospital. I couldn't see his face, but from the way Old Renée was cooing and shoving him toward Young Renée, it was clear she had orchestrated a date.

"I can't believe this," I fumed. "Erin hasn't even been gone two hours!"

"Bad form," Nick agreed, watching David shake Young Renée's limp, perfectly manicured hand.

"What a ho!"

Nick looked a little afraid of me. "Hey, maybe she doesn't know about Erin—"

"Not her—him!"

"Oh." He took a sip of his Jack and Coke. "Then yeah, pretty much."

"Who the hell does he think he is, going out and having a

good time while Erin cries herself to sleep every night? And with someone who looks just like his mother, talk about sick—"

"We shouldn't jump to conclusions. Maybe that's his cousin."

I sat back in my chair and fumed. "Ugh. Disgusting, the whole thing."

"Okay, just calm down—"

"I will not calm down! He lets Erin walk out of his life so his mom can be his pimp?"

Nick started to stroke my back soothingly. "It sucks, but it's really not our business. Let's just calm down and have a nice dinner."

"I'm going over there."

Nick clutched at the back of my blouse. "Do not go over there."

But it was too late. I weaved and dodged through the crowd like an offensive lineman on heels.

I was three steps away from David when he started yelling.

"For the last time, Mother, I do not want to date anyone! I'm married!"

I froze, along with everyone else in the front half of the restaurant.

Renée toyed with her pearl pendant. "Now, David, stop being ridiculous. Kaitlyn is a lovely girl, and I know you two will get along famously once you get to know her."

"I don't want to get to know her!" He turned to the shell-shocked brunette and murmured, "Sorry, nothing personal."

"Lower your voice," Renée admonished. "You're embarrassing me."

"I'm embarrassing *you?* The woman who springs a blind date on me with no warning?"

Kaitlyn tugged up the collar of her shirtdress and started edging toward the door, but Renée blocked her exit. "I'm not asking you to fall in love and propose tonight—although you could do a lot worse. Kaitlyn here is my protégée at the gardening club. She has a BA in horticulture, she's an excellent cook, and she likes to golf, isn't that right, dear?"

Kaitlyn smiled up at Renée with what looked like hero worship. "I've heard so much about you, David. You're very lucky to have a mother like Renée."

"Really?" David loosened his collar. "Did she tell you I'm married?"

"David, stop it this instant," Renée commanded. "You're not married. That woman left you high and dry, and I don't want to hear another word about her."

"Good night, Mom." David spun on his heel and headed for the coat check.

Renée dug her fingers into his arm.

"Let go of me," he bit out.

Her eyes widened at the steel in his tone, but she didn't back down. "Don't you talk to me that way. You're going to sit down and have a lovely dinner with us, and I don't want any more arguments."

I felt a pang of sympathy for Kaitlyn, who clearly would rather be facing down an amphitheater full of bloodthirsty lions.

"I didn't mean to cause any trouble." Kaitlyn—she really did look like Renée, the resemblance was eerie—cleared her throat. "I thought we were . . . I'm just gonna go." And this time, she managed to slip away to the hostess stand.

"Are you happy now?" Renée snapped at her son. "You've ruined what could have been a delightful evening."

"I didn't ruin anything," David said. "You couldn't leave well enough alone, could you? You always have to cross the line."

"I'm trying to make you happy. It's time you moved on. Erin was never right for you. She was uppity, opinionated, contrary—"

"Has it ever occurred to you that I *like* uppity, opinionated, contrary women?"

"You'd be much happier with someone like Kaitlyn."

"With someone like you, you mean. Whether you like it or not, Erin is my wife."

"Well, she's gone." Renée's smile was savage. "She gave up on you and went back to Boston. She didn't want to fight for you."

"She shouldn't *have* to fight for me." David's frustration was almost palpable. "I should have fought for her."

"She moved on," Renée crowed. "It's too late."

"Actually," I volunteered, "you only missed her by an hour."

David finally noticed me. "Where? . . ."

"She just left for Boston," I supplied. "She's staying at her friend's apartment. Simone, I think she said."

"Thanks." He bolted for the door.

Renée stumbled as she attempted to chase him down. "David, wait! You can't do this!"

He looked her straight in the eye. "I want my wife back. I want my whole life back. And I want you out of our house."

"You don't mean that! Where will I go?"

"You'll figure something out; you're very resourceful."

"But David, please, I'm your *mother*—"

He didn't give her a chance to finish, didn't even pick up his coat on the way out to the parking lot.

"I've got to call Erin!" I told Nick, whipping out my cell phone.

Nick sighed, all put-upon. "You're distracted."

"Uh, yeah. Biggest scandal of the season just went down ten feet away from us."

"But I wanted to talk about something important at dinner."

"We will; don't worry." I turned my back on him as Erin's voice mail clicked on. "Hey, it's me. Heads up; you'll never guess what just happened. Think Mothra versus Godzilla. Call me back!"

Ten minutes later, I was ready to resume my date but Nick, still waiting for a table, was doing a slow burn.

"This was supposed to be our night. I made all these big plans, and everything's gone to hell."

"Nothing's gone to hell." I glanced at the digital clock on my cell phone screen. "Do you think David is on the turnpike yet?"

"I don't want to talk about David." He raked his hands through his hair, his eyes wild. "We're supposed to be talking about us. You. Me. Who cares about Erin and David?"

"I'm sorry, honey. But Erin's my friend."

"I know. It's just . . . I had everything arranged, and we were supposed to be eating our entrées by now!"

"Who cares?" I exhorted. "It's just dinner."

He remained glum.

"Cheer up." I leaned over to kiss his cheek. "We're together, we're having fun—or we could be, if you'd stop acting so prickly. Tell you what, put on a happy face and we'll get an extra dessert after dinner. To go."

He perked right up. "Really? You want to do the dessert thing?"

I winked. "Sure."

"Hmm." He studied the specials menu, leering. "I'm thinking the cranberry tart. On the small of your back."

"Will you be deep-frying it first?" I whispered seductively.

"Just for that, I'm using a fork. A really pointy one."

I licked my lips. "Oh, baby. That's hot."

Just as we were launching into a really steamy PDA, a bow-tie-wearing server appeared at the bar. "Follow me, please. Your table is ready."

"Let's just get dessert to go," I urged Nick. "Who needs dinner?"

"You do," he said, capturing my hand in his. "You need the whole nine yards: dinner and dessert and everything after. Now stop asking questions. You'll ruin the surprise."

29

ERIN

By the time I let myself into Simone's tidy, white-walled condo, my temples were throbbing with a tension head-ache. The drive to Boston had given me too much time to think, and the van's staticky radio and jouncy suspension had left me achy and depressed. I needed half a bottle of ibuprofen, a bubble bath, and twelve hours of sleep, in that order. Unfortunately, Boston's real estate prices had rendered bathtubs an extravagant luxury, so I'd have to make do with a hot shower.

I turned on the faucet, twisted my hair up, and left my turtleneck, sweater and jeans in a heap on the green tile floor. After a few minutes of inhaling warm steam, I sank down to the shower's tile floor and curled up under the steady pulse of the water, hugging my knees to my chest.

There was no doubt in my mind that I belonged back here,

but from the moment I'd first sighted the city lights, I'd felt empty and alone. David and I had started in Boston. We'd thrived here, gathered strength from each other as we'd triumphed over what had seemed like impossible challenges: my board exams, his thesis defense. How could one petite senior citizen in a reindeer sweater destroy everything we'd had?

When I finally turned off the water, my cell phone was beeping—I had a message. The missed call log listed Casey's number, followed by David's. My tension headache made a roaring comeback.

Casey's message was garbled–all I could make out were the words "Mothra versus Godzilla"—and she didn't pick up when I called her back. David's voice mail said simply, "Call me on my cell the second you get this." Before I could even dial, my phone rang again. David. When I let it ring, he texted me: Code Blue. Our private equivalent of SOS. David had made many questionable decisions over the course of our relationship, but he had never once abused Code Blue. Something monumental must have gone down. I wrapped myself up in a bathrobe and dialed his number.

"Thank God you called me back," was how he greeted me when he picked up the phone.

"This better be important," was how I greeted him.

"It is. Meet me at our bar in half an hour."

I frowned. "What?"

"You know. The Cat and Canary. Corner of Boylston and—"

"I know where our bar is, David. But why are you in Boston?"

"Meet me in thirty minutes and I'll explain everything. And wear the black lace thong."

"I'm hanging up now," I warned.

"Okay, don't wear the black lace thong. Just be there."

He clicked off the line.

No way was I getting dressed and going back out into the subzero wind. No way.

Except . . . seriously. Why had he followed me to Boston? The curiosity was killing me.

Fine. I'd go to the bar, but I wouldn't get dressed up. No lipstick, no camouflage skirt, definitely no racy undies. If only I had a garish reindeer sweater. That would serve him right.

David had staked out a secluded booth in the back of the dark, noisy pub, which tonight was packed to the rafters with buzzed college kids and illicit cigarette smoke. The bartop where I'd gyrated with such abandon on the night we'd met was obscured by a wall of thirsty patrons. I made my way through the crowd at the pool table and slid into the seat across from David.

"I'm here," I announced, giving him what I hoped was a flinty stare. "What's up?"

"First, I'm sorry about the, you know, thing at the Blue Hills Tavern. I already called Jonathan to apologize."

I raised an eyebrow. "My *friend* Jonathan?"

"That's the one. Also, I want to show you something." He pulled a folded slip of paper out of his pocket and shoved it across the sticky, beer-stained table.

I unfolded the thin, bluish rectangle of carbon paper, which turned out to be a receipt he'd torn out of his checkbook. He'd written a check to Renée in the amount of . . . "Oh my God."

He sat up a little straighter. "Are you impressed?"

"That you gave your last remaining cent to your mother? *No.*"

He shook his head, impatient. "I didn't give her anything. I'm paying her back. For the down payment. This is all I have in the bank, but it'll have to tide her over until we sell the house."

"David." I stared at the sum scrawled on the receipt. "This is your entire emergency fund."

"Yeah, well. This is an emergency."

I looked up at him. "What happened?"

"Everything sucks since you left," he said. "That's what happened. I can't believe I let you go."

"You didn't *let* me do anything," I countered. "Trust me, I was getting out come hell or high water."

"Because I let things get out of hand. Moving to Alden, letting my mom move in, accepting that money from her, leaving the dog in the basement . . . I felt like we owed her something. But us, our marriage—that's worth a hell of a lot more than twenty thousand dollars."

I blinked. "And you're just realizing all this *now?*"

"No, I knew. But I . . . well, I let her play me." He lifted his chin. "She always said she wanted me to be happy. And I believed her."

"She does want you to be happy. The problem is, she thinks she knows what makes you happy better than you do. And I can't deal with it anymore. She always has to win, and that means I always have to lose."

"That's why we're selling the house. She's my mother, and I love her, but I won't give you up for her."

"You already did," I pointed out.

"Something happened tonight." He looked grim. "Something bad."

"Is that what Casey called about?"

"She tried to set me up with another woman. And I didn't like it. I *really* didn't like it."

We regarded each other for a long, silent moment. Finally, I asked, "What happened?"

"She ambushed me at the White Birch. She claimed she wanted to use that gift certificate and asked me to meet her for dinner. So I show up, and she's lying in wait with her latest disciple from her garden club."

"Shut up." I sat back. "She wouldn't. Even Renée wouldn't—"

"She did."

"That is—"

"I know. Things got kind of, uh, heated."

I arched an eyebrow. "And when you say heated . . ."

"I told her she had twenty-four hours to get out of our house. And it's going on the market on Monday. I left a message with our Realtor on the way out here."

"But we'll lose money," I protested. "After you factor in closing costs and commissions—"

"I don't care. I want my wife back."

I leaned forward. "I can't believe I'm saying this, but where's your mom supposed to go?"

"Already covered that. I called Henry Reynolds on the drive out here. He said he'd be delighted to offer up his guest room until she can move back into her house."

"But she can't stand Henry."

"If she doesn't like my solution, she can find one of her own. But I'm betting she'll have a miraculous change of heart about Henry."

I watched David carefully, searching for any sign of the conflicted, agonized guilt that had wrenched our relationship apart over the past few months. He looked tired, but utterly determined.

"I'm moving back to Boston," he informed me.

I had to laugh. "Oh, are you? And what if I decide that I don't want to go down this road with you again?"

"I'll wait you out. I'm very patient."

There he was—the forthright, take-charge man of action who'd managed to stop me in my tracks and charm the hell out of me, even though I'd broken his fingers. When we'd fallen in love, I'd never felt surer of anything in my life. And right now, despite my best efforts to remain bitter and detached, that certainty was settling back into my soul.

My husband had returned.

I shredded the edge of the check receipt with my thumbnail. "Christmas is coming up, you know."

"And?"

"I volunteered to be on call at the hospital this year. But soon enough, there'll be Easter and Fourth of July, and birthdays, and maybe someday we'll want to have kids . . ."

"What are you getting at?"

"Well, I'm glad you stood up to Renée. I am. But, for better or for worse, she's still your mother. What's the plan with that? Are we never going to see her again?"

He considered this for a moment. "It's your call. After what she did to you—"

"We can't hold a grudge forever. I don't want to cut her off like that." I rolled my eyes. "Don't get me wrong; we definitely need to set limits, but she does love you. A lot. Albeit in an all-consuming, desperate, scary kind of way."

"Erin." He shook his head. "The woman tried to kill you. Repeatedly."

"So we'll start small. Brief phone conversations. Very brief."

"You're forgiving her?" he asked, shocked. "Just like that?"

"I'm forgiving *you*," I said. "But that's the tricky thing about marriage: it's a package deal. Family comes with."

"If you say so."

"And we should send her something for Christmas." I grinned as I remembered the gift I'd picked out for her. "Something really special."

"Oh. That reminds me. She wanted me to give you this."

"I thought you said you yelled at her and kicked her out of the house?"

"I did. But while I was throwing stuff into my suitcase, she begged me to take this along." He lifted a red-and-green-wrapped box out of the brown paper bag beside him. "She said to tell you she's sorry and this is her peace offering."

"Here we go. Do I even want to know what's in there?"

We both eyed the box with mounting trepidation.

"Wait." He cocked his head. "Don't open it if you hear ticking."

I lowered my face and sniffed the shiny red bow. "I don't smell gunpowder. Or peanuts, for that matter."

We tore off the paper together, revealing a big white box sporting grease stains on one side. She'd bundled my gift into a used bakery container. Classic Renée. When I lifted the lid and rummaged through the crumpled tissue paper inside, I burst out laughing.

"What?" he demanded as I pulled out the green-and-yellow hunk of ceramic. "What is it?"

"It's a Chihuahua taco holder," I finally got out.

"You sure? It looks like a cat with massive spinal deformities."

"I'm sure. This is what I was going to give her for Christmas."

"And she's regifting already?"

"She must have found it when she packed up all my stuff."
I signaled the passing waitress for two beers. "Touché, Renée.
Touché."

He curled his lip at the misshapen Chihuahua. "We're
gonna have to move overseas to get rid of her. And change our
names."

"You know we're going to have to put this on display every
time she comes over."

"I see an unfortunate accident in this little dog's future,"
David predicted.

"Is that your way of asking me to get married again?"

"Are you saying yes?"

"Do we still get to go to Hawaii?"

"As long as we go alone."

"Done."

30

CASEY

"Do you think David's in Boston yet?" I asked as Nick and I left the White Birch. After a delectable four-star meal followed by a molten chocolate soufflé, we were stuffed but happy.

Nick consulted his watch. "He might be."

"I wonder what he's going to say to Erin?" I mused. "Do you think he'll beg for forgiveness or just kick down her door and kiss her like Clark Gable in *Gone With the Wind*, or what?"

"Casey. Am I boring you tonight?"

I unlocked the driver's-side door of my truck. "Of course not."

"Then stop thinking about Erin and David. Who cares

what's going on with them? The question is, what's going on with us?"

"We're having a great date night." I handed him the Styrofoam carton containing the cranberry tart. "And it's about to get even better."

"Not so fast." Nick buckled up in the passenger seat and turned to me with a mischievous glint in his eye. "We're taking a detour on the way home."

"But . . ." I gazed longingly at the Styrofoam box. "I wanna do the dessert thing."

"We will," he promised. "Later. Right now, I have a surprise for you. I'd drive, but . . ."

"No. The doctors said no night driving for at least another week."

"So play along and follow my directions. Trust me."

"This better be good, is all I have to say."

He directed me through the main street of downtown, past the country club and the golf course, until we reached the high school.

"Turn here." He pointed toward the school parking lot.

"Here?" I groaned. "This is the surprise? Nick, I hated this place when we were teenagers and I still hate it now."

"Trust me," he repeated.

As I steered the truck down the long, dark drive, my heart plummeted. A return to high school was *his* fantasy, not mine.

"Nick, I don't think this is a good idea."

"Stop here," he instructed as we rolled around the back, by the gymnasium doors.

"I don't want to."

"Casey, come on. Five minutes. Please."

"You can't make me go in there," I warned him. But I turned off the truck's ignition.

He sat back and sighed. "You're right. I can't make you do anything. But I'm asking you. As a favor. Five minutes."

I gazed out the window at the bare, black trees and the icy asphalt. "Give me one good reason."

"Because I love you," he said quietly. "And I promised I wouldn't screw this up again."

"Oh, all right." I jerked the door handle. "Five minutes. The clock starts now."

"Not so fast." He fished a long, gauzy scarf out of his pocket. "Put this on."

"You're blindfolding me? Are you going to stuff me in a locker, too?"

"Relax." He wrapped the thin material around my eyes and rested his warm, capable hands on my shoulders. "No need to panic."

"That's what the popular kids always say," I said. "Right before they pants you in the cafeteria."

"Let's go." He nudged me forward, his breath warm in my ear. "Hup, two three four."

We paused after a few yards, and I heard the telltale clink of the padlock against the metal gym doors. When he led me inside, I immediately recognized the chalky, sweaty smell of high school athletics.

"How did you get a key to this place?"

He shushed me, brushing his index finger over my lips. "Try to soak up the moment."

"I'm doing everything I can to *avoid* this moment. Seriously. How'd you get a key?"

"I applied for that basketball coaching job."

"Yeah. And?"

"And the old coach remembers me fondly. How could he deny his favorite point guard from the good old days?"

"Sad." I winced as the doors shut behind me with the resounding clank of a jail cell. "I feel nothing but pity for people who never get over high school."

"Unlike you, right?" he teased.

"What is that supposed to mean?" I yanked at the blindfold.

"Not yet." He tightened the blindfold and urged me forward. My wet heels skidded on the slick varnish, but he held me steady.

"Here's the thing," he said. "If I start coaching here, you're going to have to go to a game every once in a while."

"So?"

"You'll have to at least pretend that this place doesn't make you break out in hives."

"Fine. Give me a big thermos full of vodka before every game and we won't have a problem."

"That's one way to go," he admitted. "But I was thinking more along the lines of, well, here." He whisked the blindfold away.

A revolving, mirrored disco ball threw flecks of light across the hardwood floor and the fluffy rolls of cotton batting that were draped atop the first row of the bleachers. Green, white and red streamers hung from every rafter.

I started to smile in spite of myself. "Did you do all this yourself?"

Nick regarded the sagging, uneven loops of crepe paper with great pride. "Yep." He pointed at the mounds of cotton. "That's supposed to be snow. Christmasy-like."

"It's very Christmasy," I assured him.

"Good, because this is the winter formal."

"As in dance?"

"Exactly. Oh shit, I forgot." He loped over to the corner and turned on an ancient boom box resting by the bleachers. Smashing Pumpkins blasted out at brain-liquefying decibels.

"Son of a . . ." He turned down the volume and jabbed at the control console. "This was supposed to be my other nineties mix tape." When I offered my assistance, he waved me away. "Everything's under control. You go in the girls' locker room."

I wrinkled my nose. "Ew. Why?"

"Would you stop second-guessing everything I say and just go?"

As the voice of Billy Corgan continued to snarl about how, despite all his rage, he was still just a rat in a cage, I retreated to the relative peace of the locker room. The fluorescent lights flickered above the battered, puke-green lockers, the initial-carved wooden benches, and the prom dress.

At least it *had* been a prom dress, once upon a time. The tea-length skirt and pouffy sleeves were crafted of the shiniest taffeta I'd ever seen. Magenta. A pair of dyed-to-match pumps were lined up under the dress, along with a huge corsage of pink roses and baby's breath.

I had boycotted my senior prom the first time around. (In large part because no one had asked me.) But apparently, Nick had decided I deserved another chance.

So I stripped down to my bra and panties and wriggled into the garish, vintage dress. But I could only tug the zipper halfway up my rib cage—because somehow Nick had gotten the idea that I wore a size four. If only. At least the shoes fit perfectly.

"Casey?" Nick sounded impatient. "You ready yet?"

"Hang on." I took a moment to inspect myself in the mirrors above the rusty, dripping faucets and applied an extra coat of lipstick and mascara.

I clutched the corsage box and headed back out to the gym.

The frenetic angst of Smashing Pumpkins had been replaced by a mellow Chris Isaak song.

"You look beautiful," Nick said when I made my grand entrance, and I decided to believe him.

"You look pretty spiffy yourself."

He brushed off the tailored black jacket he'd changed into. "Look who brought a tux. And check it out—it actually fits this time."

"I'm impressed."

"Do you like that dress?" he asked. "I asked Tanya for advice, and she said you liked pink."

That would explain it. I had liked pink . . . in high school. Back when I'd worn a size four. "You did a great job," I beamed. "I love it."

He threw me a cagey look. "You hate it."

"I do not!"

"Liar." He started to laugh as he noticed the gaping zipper in the back. "You're going to throw it in the Dumpster as soon as we get home."

"Never. I'm going to keep this dress forever," I vowed. "To remember our winter formal."

"That reminds me." He handed me a plastic box containing a pink rose boutonniere to match my corsage. "We have to pin these on each other."

I felt oddly shy as I positioned the rose on his lapel. "Then do we do our spotlight dance?"

"Not yet."

"There's more?"

"Much more." He ducked behind the bleachers and emerged with a huge bouquet of pink roses. *Huge.* Think beauty pageant. Think Broadway curtain call. Think . . . "For the prom queen."

"Wow. Do I get a scepter and a tiara, too?"

"No, but you get to order the prom king around."

"Excellent." I waved my hand imperiously. "I order you to smooch me."

He obliged, sliding his hand over the exposed skin of my back.

"Somewhere, Anna Delano is writhing with envy," I teased.

"Forget Anna Delano. That's what I was trying to tell you that day in the woods—you're the only one I want."

I stroked his cheek. "And here I thought you were hallucinating."

"No," he growled. "I was trying to be sweet."

"You are sweet."

"Even though I can't pick out dresses and I can't make a turkey and I can't hang streamers worth crap, I'm trying."

"I know."

He suddenly drew back, then hit the floor so hard with one knee that I heard the thud over the music.

I flinched. "Honey, are you okay?"

He produced a small, red velvet box from his jacket pocket and thrust it toward me. "Here."

I snatched my hands away as if scorched. "Nick, what are you doing?"

"What I should have done the first time." He waved the box at me. "Open it."

My hands were trembling so much that I dropped the box twice. I ended up sitting next to him on the dusty gym floor, fumbling with the lid.

"Give me that; the suspense is freaking killing me." He flipped the top back to reveal a deep green emerald set in a white gold band.

I'd always wanted an emerald ring. Apparently, Tanya had divulged more than just my dress size.

"Okay, I know I was a tool before, but I love you so I have to ask: Casey, will you please marry me?"

I looked at the ring, then I looked at his hopeful face and the belated re-creation of all my teenage fantasies. "I want to say yes."

His whole body wilted. "But you're not saying yes."

My eyes welled with tears. "I'm scared. What if things go back to the way they were? What if we can't make it work?"

"We'll make it work."

"But what if we can't? I don't want to lose you again."

"You didn't lose me, you kicked me out," he clarified. "Look, I can sit here all night and promise you that you'll never have to do that again, but talk is cheap. I'd rather show you. Day after day, year after year, I'll be with you every step of the way."

"But how do I know for sure?" I whispered.

"You don't. You have to take a chance. But I swear I won't let you down again."

I nibbled my lower lip. "Well. I *do* like emeralds."

"Say yes."

I slipped the ring onto my finger.

"You're saying yes, right?"

I nodded vigorously. The dress slipped off one shoulder, revealing half of my bra. "But what will I do with my other engagement ring?"

He raised one eyebrow. "Did you ever pick it up off the floor after you threw it at me?"

"Tanya did."

"What a girl. You can wear it on your other hand. Or make it into a necklace. Or keep it in reserve for whenever you need something to throw at me." He got to his feet and extended a hand to help me up. "Come here."

"Now is it time for our spotlight dance?"

"No. Now it's time for the time-honored tradition of making out under the bleachers."

I feigned reluctance. "But I'll ruin my dress."

"Luckily, you hate it, anyway. Come on."

While the disco ball turned and the music of our lost adolescence played, we left our formal wear on the dance floor and chased each other under the bleachers.

My prom night wasn't perfect. It wasn't the glitzy, ribbon-trimmed fairy tale that the seventeen-year-old me had day-dreamed about. But it was more than the twenty-nine-year-old me had ever dared to hope for, and the perfect start to our new marriage.

31

STELLA

"Here, Cash!" My breath came out in bursts of white condensation against the darkening twilight sky. "Come on!"

Cash skidded to a stop by the far corner of the fenced dog park, then turned and raced toward me.

"Oof!" I braced for impact as the huge black dog slammed into my knees.

Together with our trusty tennis ball, Cash and I had spent most of the afternoon churning the snow-covered dog park into muddy slush. The weather had been so bad for the last few days that we'd been forced to skip our usual long walks, so today, Christmas Eve, I'd loaded him into the back of the Jeep I'd traded in my convertible for and driven down to the park.

Considering that I'd been planning to spend the holiday in Belize with Mark, I thought I was handling the night before

Christmas very well. Mark had given me the car and enough of what his lawyer deemed my share of the house to pay for most of my nursing school tuition, but I hadn't heard from him directly since he'd left me at the courthouse. My mother had lowered herself to speak to me again, but all she had to say was, "Why, Stella? *Why?* You were so close! If only you had learned to compromise!"

Casey had generously invited both me and the dog to her apartment for Christmas dinner tomorrow, and we'd accepted, even though I'd knew I'd feel awkward watching her and Nick grope each other eyes like a couple of high schoolers, which was basically all they did these days.

Alden was a very small town, and rumor had it that Mark had already started dating again. Since I'd moved out, he'd been seen brunching with Linda Lund, head of the hospital's charity fund-raising committee. She was older than me, with grown children already in college, and I could picture her sliding right into the space I'd vacated. Replacing the rugs Cash had ruined. Buying a new mattress to share with Mark. Winning over Taylor and Marissa with spa days and shopping trips to New York. Mark didn't like to be alone.

"Let's go." I clipped the red leather leash onto Cash's collar. He trotted over to the gate, sniffed the wind, and whined.

"I'm going, I'm going." I fumbled with the latch, clumsy in my mittens.

He pawed the ground and barked.

"Settle down," I commanded. "You just ran around for two hours. Aren't you tired yet?"

The second the gate swung open, Cash took off at top speed, ripping the leash out of my hand as he raced across the park toward the ice rink.

"Hey!" I lumbered after him, hampered by the knee-high snowdrifts that sucked in my boots like quicksand. "No! Bad dog!"

He streaked across the soccer field, a black blur against a background of pure white, on a collision course with the novice skaters wobbling on the public rink.

"No!" I yelled, falling farther behind. "Look out! Dog coming through!"

I knew I would never catch him. Cash would come back when he was good and ready, and not one minute sooner.

The dog yipped in surprise as he reached the slippery surface of ice. All four legs fell out from under him, and he spun toward the center of the rink, miraculously missing a pair of snowsuited toddlers clutching their mother's hands.

"It's okay!" I hollered. "He's gentle! Don't be scared! He's just . . . insane!"

The mother herded her children toward the bench at the far side of the rink and threw me a filthy look.

"Sorry!" I panted as I stumbled up to the edge of the ice. "I'll get him, okay? You don't have to—Augh! Cash, *no*!"

Cash had regained his footing and was galumphing toward

a little girl in a fleece-trimmed pink jacket and matching pink skates. His tail wagged frantically as she toppled to the ground.

Since I didn't hear any terrified shrieks of protest, I assumed the poor kid had either gone catatonic from fear or been knocked unconscious.

"Ohmigod, ohmigod, ohmigod!" I seized the dog's collar and yanked with all my might. When he lifted his head to give me a huge doggy grin, I heard it: delighted, high-pitched giggling.

"I've got you." I knelt down and wrapped my arms around the little girl, hauling her out of licking range. "I've got you."

"Daddy!" the little girl shrieked, directly into my ear. *"Dad-deee!"*

I scanned the ice for her father, hoping he wasn't the litigious type.

"Is this your dog?" demanded a tall, square-jawed man, jabbing his finger at Cash.

"Yes, he is, and I am so, so sorry. I know this looks bad, but I promise you, he loves kids. He just gets a little—"

"Where did you get him?" the man interrupted.

I shifted my hold on the little girl. "The pound. But he's had all his shots, and I swear to God—"

"When did you get him?"

I paused. "A few weeks ago, I guess."

"Which pound? Do you remember what day it was?"

I held out his daughter. "What does that have to do with anything?"

"Look, Daddy!" The little girl bounced in her father's arms. "It's Humphrey!"

"Actually, his name is Cash, sweetie. He's a very friendly dog; *too* friendly, in fact."

"Nope!" she crowed. "It's Humphrey. We founded him, Daddy. We founded him!"

"Hey, boy, come here." The man flashed a quick hand signal and Cash struggled to his feet and marched right over.

"Traitor," I hissed at him.

As the child threw her arms around Cash's neck, her father straightened up to address me. "This is incredible. Do you have any idea how long we've been looking for this dog?"

"There must be some mistake." I laughed weakly. "This is *my* dog. I adopted him from the county shelter; they said he was dumped there by some lowlife who didn't even bother to pay the twenty-dollar surrender fee."

"Humphrey!" Pigtails kissed Cash right on the mouth.

The man glanced at her, then motioned me aside. "Yeah. The lowlife? That would be my ex-wife. I had to go to London on business for a few weeks and my daughter couldn't bear to put Humphrey in a kennel, so my ex agreed to take care of him. When I came back, the dog was gone. She claimed he had run away." The little muscle in his jaw twitched. "She never was much of an animal lover, but I had no idea she was capable of—"

"Whoa. Let's just slow down a second." I grabbed Cash's leash and gripped it with both hands. "We're not even sure if this is really the dog you lost. Maybe he just looks like your dog. Shelters are chock-full of big, black, shaggy dogs; how do you know—"

He dropped to one knee and held up his palm. "Give me five, Humphrey."

Cash immediately jerked up his paw and made contact.

I crossed my arms. "Lots of dogs know how to shake. That doesn't prove anything."

The man spun around, turning his back to the dog and holding his hand low against his hip. "On the flip side."

Cash smacked paw into palm again.

I muttered an obscenity under my breath. The dog's tail was going a mile a minute, and both he and the little girl were making happy yelping sounds.

"After all I've done for you," I said to Cash. "This is how you repay me?"

The man pulled out his wallet and handed me his business card. "Thank you so much for saving him. This is a miracle."

I narrowed my eyes. "Not so fast. Legally, this dog belongs to me. I've got his license, his vaccination record, and a shredded leather couch to prove it. How do I know your ex-wife sob story holds water? How do I know you didn't dump him there yourself?"

He tapped his business card. "You can call my assistant. She'll verify that I was out of town on the dates the alleged dumping occurred."

I scanned the business card, which announced that he was a corporate consultant named Will Montrose.

"I can also provide vet records, his original rabies license registration, obedience school certificates, and multiple photos of the dog with members of my family."

"But . . . I got him microchipped," I floundered. "He's registered under my name. And besides, I love him."

"I can imagine." Will's voice softened. "We love him, too. Especially Isabel."

"I do love you, Humphrey!" Isabel squealed. "I missed you!"

Cash, aka Humphrey, aka Ungrateful Turncoat, had obviously missed Isabel, too. And the noble thing to do would be to relinquish him to his original preschool-age owner and her doting father. But . . .

"But I hung a stocking for him and everything," I said. "With his name embroidered on it. Cheesy, yes, but still. We were going to do Christmas morning together. Just the two of us."

That's when Will Montrose glanced at my left hand. He was subtle—I almost missed it—but suddenly I realized that he was kind of cute, in a dark, rugged, dog-napping kind of way.

"You got him a stocking?" His smile had a dimple on the right side.

"Yeah." I burrowed the bottom half of my face into my scarf. "I was going to put a bone and some organic T-R-E-A-T-S in there."

"So you two have bonded, huh?"

"Look, I know I sound incredibly selfish, not wanting to give a four-year-old her dog back." I kept an eye on the little girl, who was attempting to throw one leg over Cash's back while demanding a "pony ride," but Cash didn't seem to mind. In fact, he was loving the attention. "But I've never had a dog before. I kind of got attached."

"And he got attached to you." Will thought for a moment, then asked, "Are you new in town? I haven't seen you around."

"I moved out here from New York to get married and, well, that didn't really work out."

"Kids?" he asked.

I shook my head. "Just the four-legged kind."

"It's tough to be single again in a small town like this. I have primary custody of Izzy, so between that and work I don't get out much, but if you ever want to—"

"Daddy!" Izzy tugged her father's coat sleeve. "Humphrey wants to go home now."

I looked at Will. Will looked at me.

"Go ahead," I said slowly. "She's a little kid. Kids need their dogs."

"No, you bailed him out of the shelter." He shoved his hands into his coat pockets. "And you obviously love him."

"But so do you," I protested. "You taught him to shake on the flip side, for God's sake."

"There's only one solution. Joint custody."

"That's not gonna work," I scoffed.

"Sure it will. We can alternate weeks or—"

"Actually, I'm going to be starting night classes soon, so it'd be nice for him to have someplace to go while I'm at school." I was warming up to this idea.

"Absolutely. We can work something out. In the meantime, just give me your number . . ."

My flirting reflexes, dormant for the last year, snapped back into action. "I like how you just slid that in. Very smooth."

"What?" He tried to look innocent. "I need your number so we can negotiate terms."

"Tell you what. I'll give you my number if you let me keep the dog tonight." This guy was cute. And he liked kids. If I could just casually work the vasectomy question into the conversation, I'd be all set.

"How can I refuse? You bought him a stocking and everything. Izzy, honey, we're going to let this nice lady—"

"Stella," I supplied.

"Stella's going to take care of the dog tonight while you're at your mom's. And then tomorrow morning, when I come to drive you back to our house, we'll pick him up and he can open presents with you."

"And after presents, we watch the Grinch, right?" Izzy prompted.

"Right." Will turned to me. "Annual father-daughter tradition."

"And after the Grinch, we go to Thelma's, right?"

"Right," he told her. To me he said, "It's a greasy spoon diner by Pittsfield. The only place open on Christmas Day. Another annual tradition. I tried to do the whole turkey dinner one year, and the only one of us who could eat the result was the dog."

I laughed and recounted the tale of Cash's Thanksgiving dinner at my house.

"Classic Humphrey. Someday I'll have to tell you about what he did to our sofa."

"So what do you suggest we do about his name?" I asked Will as he sat down to unlace Izzy's skates.

"His name is Humphrey," Isabel informed me loftily.

"I don't know." I wrinkled my forehead. "The tag on his collar says Cash."

"Humphrey!" She giggled.

"Cash!" I pretended to pinch her toe.

"Ladies!" Will waded into the fray. "We'll settle this another day. Christmas is no time for a fistfight."

"We'll fight later," I whispered to Izzy. She kicked her feet while her father tried to cram them into pink boots.

"All right, *Cash* and I are heading home." I found a pen in my purse and scribbled my phone number on the back of a post office receipt. "Call me and I'll give you directions. See you tomorrow morning."

"Are you coming to Thelma's with us?" Izzy asked.

"Oh, sweetie, no, that's your special time with your dad."

"You could come," Will said quickly. "The more the merrier, right? But you probably have plans."

"Not really," I lied. Casey would understand. She knew all about the irresistible lure of stray dogs and hot guys.

"We get pie," Izzy offered as an enticement.

"Hmm." I mulled this over. "I do like pie."

"Then it's settled." Will gave Cash a farewell ear scratch. "See you tomorrow."

"Bye!" Izzy called as I tugged Cash toward the parking lot. "Hope you get lots of presents!"

"Me, too!" I called back, still checking out Izzy's dad. Who, if I wasn't mistaken, was still checking out me. Merry Christmas to all, and to all a good night.

"Nice work," I commended Cash as he hopped into the back of the Jeep. "If you had to have another owner, that was the one to have."

I climbed into the driver's seat, cranked up the heat, and turned on the radio. And then we drove off toward the snow-capped blue hills—just a girl, her dog, and the winding road stretching out ahead.

UP CLOSE AND PERSONAL
WITH THE AUTHOR

What inspired you to write this book?

Inspiration struck while I was enjoying a night out with a group of recently married girlfriends. These women are all smart, savvy, in their late twenties and early thirties, and they all had the same comment: "Marriage is just *different* from what I expected." Better in some ways, worse in some ways, but completely different from the expectations society had built up.

A lot of happy, long-married couples I know say that the first year is the toughest, especially if you didn't live with your partner beforehand. Most newlyweds aren't eager to talk about the day-to-day struggle—no one wants to admit they don't have the perfect relationship or that they're second-guessing their decision. The great thing about the friendship between the three brides in this book is that they're honest with one another about how much work it is to keep a marriage strong and how scary it is when you feel frustrated and lonely in a relationship that society tells us is supposed to satisfy our every emotional need.

**Why did you decide to set this book during the holiday
season?**

I see a lot of parallels between surviving the Christmas season and surviving the first year of marriage—there is usually a
ton of anxiety and drama roiling right under the surface, but
everyone pretends they're in a perpetual state of good cheer. We
put so much pressure on ourselves during the holidays! The
shopping, the parties, the family get-togethers, the financial
strain . . . and you're supposed to feel warm and fuzzy the
whole time. Talk about unrealistic expectations!

Stella's and Erin's relationship problems go from bad to
worse during Thanksgiving becasue they're forced to deal directly with their in-laws and the reality that their husbands are
deeply conflicted. Casey has to grapple with the fact that marrying the "perfect" guy from the "perfect" family doesn't magically grant her the "perfect" marriage. The disparity between
her hopes for a Martha Stewart Thanksgiving and the reality is,
well, it's enough to give anyone second thoughts!

**Which aspects of this book are autobiographical? Has
your mother-in-law ever tried to kill you?**

My poor mother-in-law! She's a wonderful woman, and no,
she's never tried to kill me, in or out of the kitchen. The char-
acter of Renée strutted into my consciousness one fine morning and refused to leave until she'd taken over half the book.
Bossy, bossy, bossy! Although Erin and Renée's story lines is in

no way autobiographical, I think it really resonates with readers because in-law "turf-wars" are so common in the early stages of marriage. Every family has a unique and unspoken set of rules, many of which make no sense to a newcomer. My own family has a long, proud tradition of wrapping paper fights on Christmas morning (think wadded-up gift wrap pitched at major-league speeds; my husband nearly lost an eye the first time he got caught in the cross fire) and annual "swamp wars" in the forest behind my grandparents' farmhouse. With camouflage gear and fireworks. Yeah. Don't ask.

The only true-to-life incident in this book involved Cash the dog.

Speaking of Cash the dog . . . Why did you decide to make one of your main characters canine?

Cash becomes a catalyst in all the girls marriages because he takes action in a way that the human characters can't. Erin is furious with her mother-in-law, but she is far too civilized to do what Cash does to Renée's bed. Stella may want to throw down with Taylor, but she could never get away with tackling her like Cash does. Dogs are traditionally loyal and persistent, and in my mind, Cash represents the warring loyalties that every bride has to struggle with—her desire to stay true to her independent spirit while still honoring her vows to join her life with her husband's.

The sad truth is that there are innumerable big, black dogs

languishing in animal shelters all over the country—they're typically the last to be adopted and the first to be euthanized. As the proud owner of three wonderful rescue dogs, I would urge anyone thinking of getting a pet for the holidays to check out local shelters and rescue sites like Petfinder.org. (Okay, total disclosure time: My dogs, although wonderful, are also kind of, ahem, high-spirited; the red pawprint scene at Stella's house was insprired by one very memorable evening with our lab mix, Friday. Thank God we have tile floors!)

What's the best piece of marriage advice you ever heard?

"Speak softly and carry a big stick." No, no, I'm kidding. From a philosophical perspective, the best advice I got was, "Marriage is not fifty-fifty; both people have to contribute one hundred percent." From a practical perspective, I am a big advocate of separate closets and his and her bathrooms.

Life is always a little sweeter with a book from Downtown Press!

 ENSLAVE ME SWEETLY
Gena Showalter

She has the heart of a killer…
and the body of an angel.

CARPOOL CONFIDENTIAL
Jessica Benson

You'll be amazed what you
can learn riding shotgun.

THE MAN SHE THOUGHT SHE KNEW
Shari Shattuck

What kind of secrets is
her lover keeping?
The deadly kind…

INVISIBLE LIVES
Anjali Banerjee

She can sense your heart's
desire. But what does *her*
heart desire?

LOOKING FOR MR. GOODBUNNY
Kathleen O'Reilly

Fixing other people's problems
is easy. It's fixing your own
that's hard.

SEX AND THE SOUTH BEACH CHICAS
Caridad Piñeiro

Shake things up with four
girls who know how to spice
things up…

WHY MOMS ARE WEIRD
Pamela Ribon

And you thought *your* family
was weird.

 **DOWNTOWN PRESS**
A Division of Simon & Schuster
A CBS COMPANY

 Naughty Girls

Available wherever books are sold
or at www.downtownpress.com.

15067-1

Whether you're a Good Girl or a Naughty Girl, Downtown Press has the books you love!

Look for these Good Girls...

The Ex-Wife's Survival Guide
DEBBY HOLT
Essential items: 1. Alcohol.
2. A sense of humor.
3. A sexy new love interest.

Suburbanistas
PAMELA REDMOND SATRAN
From A-list to Volvo in sixty seconds flat.

Un-Bridaled
EILEEN RENDAHL
She turned the walk down the aisle into the hundred-meter dash...in the other direction.

The Starter Wife
GIGI LEVANGIE GRAZER
She's done the starter home and the starter job...but she never thought she'd be a starter wife.

The New York Times bestseller!

I Did (But I Wouldn't Now)
CARA LOCKWOOD
Hindsight is a girl's best friend.

Everyone Worth Knowing
LAUREN WEISBERGER
The devil wore Prada— but the bouncer wears Dolce.

The New York Times bestseller!

And don't miss these Naughty Girls...

The Manolo Matrix
JULIE KENNER
If you thought finding the perfect pair of shoes was hard—try staying alive in them.

Enslave Me Sweetly
An Alien Huntress Novel
GENA SHOWALTER
She has the body of a killer... and the heart of a killer.

Great storytelling just got a new address.

DOWNTOWN PRESS
A Division of Simon & Schuster
A CBS COMPANY

Naughty Girls

Available wherever books are sold or at www.downtownpress.com.
15067-2